RAVEN'S CLAW

RAVEN'S CLIFF BOOK #2

RAVEN'S CLIFF
BOOK TWO

ELLE JAMES
KRIS NORRIS

TWISTED PAGE INC

Copyright © 2025 by Elle James & Kris Norris

All rights reserved.

No part of this book may be reproduced in any form or by any electronic or mechanical means, including information storage and retrieval systems, without written permission from the author, except for the use of brief quotations in a book review.

Without in any way limiting the author's [and publisher's] exclusive rights under copyright, any use of this publication to "train" generative artificial intelligence (AI) technologies to generate text is expressly prohibited. The author reserves all rights to license uses of this work for generative AI training and development of machine learning language models.

ISBN EBOOK: 978-1-62695-666-7

ISBN PRINT: 978-1-62695-667-4

To Elle,
Still fan-girling over our collaboration.

To all the readers who are as excited about this series as we are. We'd be lost without you.

AUTHORS' NOTE

Elle James is a *New York Times* and *USA Today* bestselling author known for her heart-pounding romantic suspense and thrilling adventure novels. **Kris Norris** is an acclaimed storyteller with a passion for weaving intense action and gripping emotion into every story. Together, these talented authors have combined their creative forces to launch the exciting new *Raven's Cliff* series.

Raven's Cliff Series
Elle James & Kris Norris
Raven's Watch (#1)
Raven's Claw (#2)
Raven's Nest (#3)
Raven's Curse (#4)

RAVEN'S CLAW

RAVEN'S CLIFF BOOK #2

New York Times & USA Today
Bestselling Author

ELLE JAMES
&
KRIS NORRIS

PROLOGUE

Operation Silent Veil
  Catskills Mountains — seven months ago

"Are you insane? We need to go!"

Ember glanced at the asset as he paced the room, eyes wide. Skin blanched white. A dead man walking if she was being honest. Because despite her skills, she had little confidence she'd be able to keep him breathing. Not with alarms already sounding inside the room — an increasing number of men converging on their location within the compound visible via a flickering camera feed.

She snagged his arm on his next pass, locking her gaze on his. "You need to calm down. You gave me the footage. You know the caliber of enemy we're about to make. If we're going to stab Scythe, and more importantly, Rook Donovan, in the back, we should be damn sure the intel's fully uploaded. Otherwise," she pointed at the dots on the security feed, "we might as well just wait for them to find us and save ourselves the gauntlet run out of here because either way, we'll be dead."

She pushed down the searing impulse to shoot the guy in the head and complete her mission as if she hadn't just discovered the past twenty years of her life had been a lie. That Rook was far from the man she'd thought he was.

He was the real monster hiding in the shadows.

Former tier-one operator and current Scythe handler, Rook Donovan was Scythe's senior Shadow Asset Acquisitions Specialist and head of their Asset Operational Division. He believed in control through precision. He didn't send an army. He sent ghosts — the kind who slit throats, erased fingerprints, and vanished before sunrise. There were only two acceptable outcomes to every mission — success or death.

With his record thoroughly scrubbed, Rook operated with complete anonymity. He was the man Scythe sent in to clean up any of the agency's messes before they became visible. And she'd just risen to the top of his termination list.

Her asset, Bart Conrad, inhaled, his gaze darting to those dots on the screen. The wet squad slowly closing in on them. "Oh, god. You don't think we're gonna make it out, do you? This is insurance." He shoved his hand through his unruly ginger locks.

"Where are you sending the intel? Some secure server that forwards it to a dozen newspapers if you don't put in some kind of code in the next twenty-four hours? Maybe to some of your other operatives? Are you even going to try to help me?"

Ember fisted her hands, pinning him to the far wall with nothing more than a stare. "If I was going to kill you, I would have put a bullet in your head instead of listening to you hyperventilate for the past ten minutes. But if we're going to have any chance at getting out of here in one piece, you'll need to do exactly *what* I say, *when* I say. So, stand there, shut up, and wait for my next set of instructions."

She turned when the computer pinged. "There. Now we can—"

The room went dark, the hum from the air exchanger in the far corner slowly winding down.

Bart gasped, the panicked sound excessively loud in the oppressive silence. "Shit! Did they cut the power?" He wheezed out a couple more raspy breaths, tapping on something in what she assumed was an effort to get the thing to pop back on. "How can they do that? I have backup generators. Batteries. An entire grid that's completely isolated."

Ember secured the decryption drive Conrad had made to decipher the intel, her comms unit nothing but dead weight in her ear. "They didn't cut the power. They hit it with an EM pulse."

"They have electromagnetic pulse weapons?"

"They have everything."

"That means they can breach the doors. Bypass all my magnetic seals and encrypted codes. Just waltz right in." More tapping, as if he thought hitting the damn unit harder would have a different outcome. "Christ, I never should have trusted you. I'm outta here."

Ember snapped her head toward him, his labored breathing the only means she had of tracking him in the utter darkness. "Don't move, and don't open that other door. It's likely rig—"

The explosion hit hard, lifting her off her feet and blasting her over a desk and into the far wall. Thick smoke curled through the room, distant shouts rising above the ringing in her ears. She blinked against the dust and debris, willing the room to stop spinning, when footsteps sounded off to her left.

Two scouts, searching the rubble. Laser sites mapping out their location as they scoured the room.

She pushed onto her hands and knees, staying below the top of the overturned desk beside her — judging their progression by the slight scuff of their boots. How the smoke swirled around them, making patterns in the air.

They stopped, those red beams skimming the top of the desk before she jumped up and over, kicking one in the chest as she caught the other in the throat. The first guy tumbled back, landing on something nasty because he started flailing — arms and legs shaking as if he was having a seizure — before stilling.

The other asshole managed to get his rifle braced in front, but she simply used it to smash his face, dumping him on his ass with a sweep of her feet. A boot to the head and neck, and he was out — head lolled to one side and foot twitching.

The rest of his squad must have heard the commotion because they fired a second later. Short controlled bursts punching through the smoke — cutting down everything in their path. Ember hit the ground, covering her head as wood splintered around her, raining down like bits of confetti. Sparks lit up the darkness, yellow muzzle fire flashing against the eerie gray.

More dots appeared amidst the smoke, fanning out across the room. The last man drew closer, AR-15 ghosting into view — laser site sweeping the far wall a good three feet above her. She counted it down then caught him in the knee, buckling his leg with a second kick to his ankle.

That got everyone moving.

Gathering together in the center to minimize any crossfire — keep her on the fringes.

She snagged a mag light and a couple frags off the guy writhing on the ground then tossed one of the grenades into the fray. She didn't know if it was smoke, incendiary or a light and sound show. Didn't care if it gave her a chance to make a break for the door.

The canister clicked along the floor, each tinny strike bolstered by the thick vapor. Someone shouted

— the dots scattered — but it exploded a heartbeat later, filling the room with light and sound. Damn near bringing down the roof as the entire bunker shook, more dust coming loose from the old wooden slats covering the ceiling.

The ear-piercing noise scattered what was left of her senses, tilting the room left and right as she flicked on the flashlight and stumbled toward the exit, climbing over what remained of the door. A few shots whizzed through the air next to her head, one of the men shouting her name.

Ember hit the tunnel half-running, half-tripping, the blast of cool air lifting some of the numbing haze. She took the second corridor on the right, then sprinted for the escape hatch at the far end — bouncing off the ladder when the signals didn't quite reach her limbs in time. She gave herself a shake, climbing the metal rungs before twisting the oversized wheel above her head.

It groaned in protest, finally releasing the thick lid with a rush of air. A foggy mist veiled the surrounding forest, a hint of moonlight shining from above.

She heaved herself up and out, crawling onto the wet grass as boots pounded the hallway beneath her. She rolled, then pulled that second pin — tossed the grenade through the opening. Ember covered her head, again, as it rattled down the rungs and clattered to the floor below.

Voices rose then retreated, a moment of uneasy

silence settling over the area before the canister exploded, flames shooting out the hatch.

She waited for the shaking to stop then pushed to her feet and took off. Not nearly as fast as before, but at least she was moving. Limping and falling her way to the tree line then beyond. She took what looked like a deer trail, scrambling through the underbrush until she'd put at least a mile between her and the compound. Not enough to be safe. but she needed to catch her breath — stem some of the bleeding.

Ember leaned against a moss-covered tree, doing her best to take stock. Blood soaked through her clothes, a scattering of shrapnel poking through the fabric. Her head still rattled from the combined explosions, all her exposed skin caked in soot and dirt.

Pain teased her senses, but she was too numb to register anything but the cold bite of reality.

She was burned.

Every identity.

Every resource.

Every lifeline — gone.

All that remained was the bitter taste of regret, and a series of dead-drop sites scattered across the country. Her only chance at retrieving the intel. Like the one near Raven's Cliff, Oregon, her uncle had mysteriously gifted her when he'd been killed during a Scythe mission. What he'd claimed might provide a form of salvation, and her last hope in a lifetime of lies.

She closed her eyes, letting it all sink in, when her comms buzzed — Rook's voice sounding through her head.

"Bravo, Ember."

She inhaled, hating the stab of pride that warmed her chest. The part of her that still wanted his approval. To belong, even if it meant selling her soul. She scoured the forest, half-expecting the man to step out from the shadows. But nothing moved other than the odd flutter of wings.

She tapped her earpiece, all the pieces falling into place. And she couldn't help but wonder if she'd really escaped, or if he'd simply lengthened her leash.

He chuckled, the sound hollow. Smug. "It's EMP proof, in case you were wondering."

She bowed her head, the truth cutting deep. "How long have you known?"

"That you had doubts?" He pushed out a long slow breath. "Since the day I saved you from that group home. Even at twelve years old, I always knew you were too smart, too unexpectedly moral, not to eventually question your place in the agency. I'd just hoped that after all this time — the years I put into beating every ounce of defiance out of you — it wouldn't come to this."

She grunted, blinking against the dots eating away her vision. "You didn't save me, Rook. You recruited me. I was just too young to see the difference. But I'm seeing everything clearly, now."

He sighed, as if her discovering his betrayal was

inconvenient. "Are you sure? I've been five steps ahead of you this entire time. Why do you think I sent you here? It was a test." He let out a weary groan. "Congratulations. You failed."

"Did I? Because this feels like a victory."

"I suppose that depends on your perspective. Like your asset. How do you know Mr. Conrad wasn't part of the ploy?"

"Because I know you. And if that intel wasn't half as damming as I think it is, we wouldn't be having this conversation. Which means... You're scared."

He laughed. Louder. Deeper. "You're exceptional, Ember. The best I've ever trained. But there's no way you can ever win this war. No future without me and Scythe in it." Another slow breath, this one colder than before. Any hint of compassion gone. "You've had your fun. Proven you've still got those morals buried beneath the muscle memory. Ones I intend to finally bleed out of you. But we can talk about that later."

"There's no later, Rook. No, *us*. There's just me."

"You know the score. No loose ends. If one ghost escapes, the whole house of cards collapses. Letting you go would set a precedent, and I can't afford to have anyone else think they can follow in your footsteps." He exhaled, the gruff sound bordering on a growl. "You're either with us, or you're dead."

"Then, you better hope the next group of men you send are better than the last."

"I won't just send a squad. I'll come for you,

myself. Because you didn't just betray the program — you betrayed me. And I can't let that go unanswered."

She straightened, pushing down the hurt and the pain. The absolute emptiness gathering in the pit of her stomach as she drew herself up. "Then, I guess this isn't goodbye."

A pause, as if he was still processing all the words. Coming to terms with the fact she'd defied him. Again. "Ember…"

"I'm the one giving the orders now. So, watch your back. I intend to stick a knife in it."

She tossed the earpiece on the ground, crushed it beneath her boot then struck off. There was a questionable diner not too far down the old state highway. She could hitch a ride. Regroup. Head west. Gather the intel.

One more target.

One last mission.

And she'd live by Rook's decree. She'd either burn him and Scythe to the ground or die trying.

CHAPTER ONE

"Seriously, Sinclair? I can't let you go down there. It's a one-way trip."

Kash Sinclair glanced at Raven Watch's newest recruit — Tucker Grant. Ex-Army medic, and the man Kash was trying hard not to throttle. The guy had been twitchy all day, stopping randomly to scour the tree line. Staring at the forest as if he expected something or someone to come barreling out. What Kash and his buddy Zain had done a thousand times in the field when they'd been hiking through hostile territory with roving bands of mercenaries on their asses.

Kash had brushed it off. New job. New crew. Extreme weather hampering their every move. Until Tucker had flat out yelled someone's name. Brook. Or Cook. Acting as if he knew some deep dark secret Kash wasn't privy to. He'd finally decided to send his canine partner, Nyx, to scout the perimeter — just in case — when they'd stumbled upon five missing kids. Miles off the search grid. Little hope of a chopper reaching them before it all went sideways,

Not that Tucker's assessment of the situation was wrong. The cliff was sheer and slick, with water pissing out of cracks and fissures. The narrow ledge where the boys were huddled was nothing more than a postage stamp — the adjoining trail now a heap of rocks at the edge of the surf.

Kash held the man's gaze. "Easy, buddy. We've got this. All I need you to do is hold down the fort and pull those kids over once I've got them tied on the rope so we can get them safely home."

Tucker looked at the crumbling ledge, a shiver working through him. "I want that, too, I'm not a monster. But you know as well as I do, we don't trade lives. No matter how much we want to." He shook his head, water spraying off the ends of his hair. "I can't do another Kabul. I just can't."

He'd been in Afghanistan?

Kash gave the man a light pat on the back. "I hear ya. But the chopper's a good thirty minutes out, and I don't think that ledge is gonna hold that long."

"Neither do I, but what the hell am I gonna tell your team if I can't get you back?" He leaned in. "Isn't there someone you want to live for? Someone special?"

Kash coughed. It killed him that the answer was no because he wanted one. Had the perfect girl in mind. One that haunted his dreams even when he wasn't sleeping. Jordan Archer — sweet on the surface, sharp underneath. Like she'd survived something no one else could see. He'd been manufacturing reasons to see her for the past few months — had drank more designer coffee from the trendy little café where she worked than he could stomach. He'd intended on asking her out to dinner a hundred times over, but she'd always had that look. As if she saw shadows in the forest, too. And he'd been too chicken to push.

He gathered his supplies, throwing the answer over his shoulder. "Not. Yet."

"Kash…"

"I get it. We're out here alone. There's a freaking cyclone bearing down on us. My buddy likely won't reach us in time. And if I thought there was another way — an option I could live with — that wouldn't make me want to punch my fist through the mirror every time I gazed at my own damn reflection, I'd take it. But there isn't. And I can't just stand here and watch them fall into the fucking ocean."

Kash looked at the ledge, the kids, the bloody chasm between them and success then grabbed Tucker by the shoulders. "So, I need you to pull it together and help me save these kids, because I can't do this without you, and I'd rather not die today."

Tucker pursed his lips, looking as if he was working through some complicated theorem before giving Kash a curt nod. "I've got your back."

Kash slapped him on the shoulder. "Hooyah."

Tucker rolled his eyes, anchoring the rope then giving Kash the thumb's up. "Before you go, what's her name?"

Kash looked back. "Who's name?"

"Your not-yet?"

He chuckled. "Jordan."

Tucker's left eye twitched, a hint of a smug smile curving one corner of his mouth before it faded. "The waitress at the diner downtown?"

Tucker knew who Jordan was? Had he even been in town long enough to venture out? Because Kash thought the guy had arrived late last night — had practically begged Atticus to let him do a trial run this morning. "You've been there?"

"It opens early. She's pretty."

"And smart and completely out of my league."

"She new, too? She doesn't move as if she's from around here."

She didn't *move* like a local? Had he heard the guy right?

"Fairly. You ready?"

Kash motioned for Nyx to stay, lined up the route then took off, jumping once he reached the end. The wind howled across the cliff face, the rain obscuring all but the ledge rising up toward him before he hit just shy of the lip, only his arms catching on the ragged edge.

He kicked at the slick rock, losing ground when bits of the edge started cracking — crumbling into the rolling waves. A massive breaker crashed beneath him, the icy spray soaking through the ends of his pants. He clawed at the surface, swinging his legs — trying anything to get some momentum. Give himself a fighting chance.

He must have cursed or shouted because Nyx yipped, then raced toward him, clearing the rift and sliding to a stop just shy of his hands. She turned, grabbed his hoodie, then pulled. Grunting and snarling, wiggling back and forth until he got a knee on the surface — slid the rest of the way on.

He gave the dog a scratch, heart high in his throat. Fingers numb from the strain. "Thanks, girl. I owe ya."

He wasn't sure how he'd get them both back over, but he'd worry about that later.

Kash gave the kids a once-over, keeping them crowded up against the cliff as he readied his side of the rope. Tremors rumbled through the ledge, a few rocks tumbling down the embankment then over the edge. Tucker twirled his finger, feet braced apart. Shoulders rigid. Whatever had been eating at him earlier had vanished, nothing but stone-cold control gazing back at Kash.

Kash gave the first kid a pep talk, then shoved him off, holding the rope taut as Tucker pulled from his end, slowly inching the kid toward the other side. A strong gust spiraled up the cliff, rocking the kid dangerously close to the jagged rocks before it passed, allowing Tucker to close the gap — lift him to safety.

One down.

Four more to go.

Nyx barked, keeping the boys contained as Tucker sent the carabiner and harness back over. The next trip went quicker, the boy arriving in half the time. Tucker had definitely silenced his demons, standing tall while Kash hooked up the third. He signaled for Tucker to start, frowning when the man whipped his head around, staring behind for a few moments before giving himself a shake, then tugging on the rope.

The kid inched across, starting and stopping several times along the way when Tucker had more of those episodes — always looking behind him as if there was someone far off in the distance before snapping back.

Kash cupped his hands, shouting as loud as he could to carry above the roaring storm. "Tucker!"

Nothing, just the guy's hands moving methodically along the line. Gaze fixed. Head barely moving.

Maybe he hadn't heard Kash over the crash of the waves. The screech of the wind as it kicked up around them. Tucker seemed to recover by the time they were down to the last rescue, the kid slipping along the rope in record time.

Kash waited for the other man to send back the gear. He'd hook Nyx up first — cart her over the same way then focus on getting himself clear.

It took longer than usual to get the kid out of the

harness and over to the edge of the tree line, the sun already low on the horizon. Kash wasn't sure how long they'd been working the ropes, but Foster had to be close. Likely pushing the chopper to the max in an effort to shave off even a minute of flight time.

Tucker finally waved his arm, readying his stance, when part of the cliff gave way above Kash. Rocks bounced down the side, sections of the ledge breaking off. A few cracks opened up, water shooting out — washing mud and gravel down the face. Kash grabbed Nyx's harness, heaved her onto his shoulders then lunged for a nearby boulder. Ducking and weaving —nearly falling off the side. He finally wrapped his fingers around the cold stone, keeping his body pressed against the rock until it all settled — the eerie echo fading along the shoreline.

Everything was gone. The ledge. The gear — eight of his nine lives. Only Tucker's rope remained, the end snapping in the wind. Kash repositioned Nyx, then slowly traversed the short distance. He slipped a few times, slicing some grooves down his arms, but he managed to reach the line — tie himself off.

Tucker watched from above. Distant. Almost uninterested. His voice strangely detached when he finally called down to Kash. "If you swing over to this side, it'll be easier for you to climb up."

Kash judged the distance. Maybe twenty feet. Nothing he hadn't done in the field. But he'd had Zain or Chase backing him up. Men he trusted. Who he'd bled for. Not some guy on the edge of a psychotic break. If Tucker lost it before Kash reached the other side...

"You ready?" Kash waited, squinting through the fog. "Tucker?"

"They're closing in on us. We're taking heavy fire." Tucker's voice raged above the howling wind. Choppy. Panicked. "I can't... I have to go. I'm sorry. I can't... They're all gonna die..."

"Who's gonna die? Tucker?"

Nothing.

No ghostly silhouette amidst the fog.

No sound.

"Come on, buddy. Just keep it together a bit longer. Beck's on his way. We'll catch a ride back. Laugh about this over a few beers." *Get you some fucking therapy.*

It wasn't as if they all couldn't use some. But Kash was lucky. He had his team. Had a chance at finally putting down roots — exchanging some of the bad memories for better ones. Making sure he didn't waste the second chance he'd been given.

Damn. He really should have asked Jordan out. Taken the chance while he'd still had time. Instead, he was hanging on the side of a cliff, rain pouring down around him, nothing but missed opportunities to cushion his fall.

"Tucker!"

The rope went slack, the end fluttering down the side then into the water.

"Crap." Kash scanned the rock. No large

handholds. No relief. Just smooth stone continuing fifty feet down.

Nyx whined, the rocks beneath his feet shifting.

"Easy girl. I've got this. No big deal. We're just gonna shimmy over…"

The whole cliffside went. Sloughing off. Crashing toward the water. Kash gave a firm shove, pushing away from the rockslide — juggling Nyx onto his chest a second before they hit.

The icy water curled in around them, holding them captive before ripping them apart. Nyx rolled with the next massive breaker, tumbling out of sight as the current dragged him along the rocky bottom before shooting him back up. He crested the surface amidst a shower of white foam, another incoming wave crashing over him.

He blinked back the salt and the spray, searching the white-capped surface as all that sand in his hourglass slowly slipped away. It couldn't end like this. Not after all they'd been through together. Nyx was more than just his partner. She was his best friend. The part of him that never broke. Never faltered.

Kash struck off, barely making any headway as one breaker after another took him under, repeatedly dragging him down before spitting him back up. Thunder sounded in the distance, the last of the light already fading into the growing darkness.

He gave one last push, pouring everything he had into cutting through the current, when Nyx bobbed to the surface, ears tucked back. Legs beating at the water. He dug deep — battling the pull, the fatigue, until he narrowed the distance. Grabbed her harness.

Nyx licked his face, eyes bright. Unconditional faith staring back at him.

He gave her a nod. "That's my girl. On my back."

Nyx clawed at his chest, finally shifting onto his shoulders. Steady. Strong. He kicked against the added weight, barely keeping his mouth above the surging tide as the irony hit him full force.

"I swear, Nyx. If I get us out of this..." He paused as he drew in a few choppy breaths. "And I don't go to jail for strangling Tucker, I'm gonna ask Jordan out. No more excuses. No more second guessing myself. I'm just gonna march into that café and kiss her." He bobbed beneath the force of the next wave, nearly losing Nyx, again, before pushing back up. "What do you think? That sound like a good plan?"

Nyx nudged his head, and he swore the mutt understood every word.

"I thought so."

He closed his eyes, picturing every moment of how that kiss would play out. How the next fifty years of his life could be if he just held on. Kept moving enough to stay afloat. Counter the roll of the ocean.

The rain picked up, clouds blowing in across the horizon when Foster's chopper ghosted out of the storm, screaming toward him ten feet off the deck. His buddy didn't even slow down, just shoved the aircraft into an aggressive flare before he was hovering over top, the downwash kicking up more spray.

The side doors opened, Chase hanging on the edge as the basket all but fell out of the helicopter. Kash snagged it once it hit the water, helping Nyx up and over the side. The dog slipped on the wet metal, nearly tumbling back into the surf before Kash gave her a firm shove — toppled her over the edge.

He grabbed the railing, heart pounding. His hands so numb he wasn't sure if they were even working. Chase yelled from above, looking as if he was a second away from jumping in when Nyx locked onto Kash's hood, pulling and grunting until he slipped over the rail and onto the base. He closed his eyes, coming to with Chase leaning over him, pushing a syringe into his arm.

His buddy huffed, shaking his head as he moved in close. "You jackass. I wasn't sure I was going to get you back."

Kash coughed, grabbing his ribs as pain shot through his torso. "Jesus, I close my eyes for five seconds and you're freaking out."

"You were out for ten minutes, dumbass."

Ten minutes?

Kash pressed his head into the seat cushion, every muscle seemingly cramping at once. "The kids?"

"Mac's got them."

Mackenzie Parker. Ex-Coast Guard pilot, and the love of Foster's life. They'd been living together a few months now, and Kash suspected it was only a matter of time before they either got hitched or pregnant. The kind of future Kash could have if he held true to his promise and grew a set.

"What about…"

Chase sighed. "*He's* with her, too."

Kash nodded, looking around the chopper. "How's my girl?"

Chase thumbed at the cockpit. "The minx called shotgun while I was working on you. I swear that dog's half-human." He smiled. "She's fine. Might have a bit of a limp for a few days, but she's better than you, all things considered."

His buddy sighed, shifting on his seat for a few moments before shaking his head. "We need to talk about Tucker."

Kash grunted. "Does he still think he's back in Afghanistan?"

"Zain managed to calm him down — snap him back but… Shit, Kash. If I'd thought, for one second…"

"Not your fault. Not really his, either. We've all been there. But he needs to deal with whatever's riding his ass before he goes back into the field."

"Atticus already has some kind of intervention planned." Chase snorted. "Old coot speak for a few beers and a good pep talk. But it's a start. If you're okay with that."

Kash shrugged. "All good, brother, because I've already got plans."

A mission, really, and far more pressing than worrying about nearly dying. Every one of them had nearly died a dozen times. It was still living that mattered. And he wasn't going to wait for the universe to hit him over the head, again. Because life was too short to wonder if a woman like Jordan might say yes.

CHAPTER TWO

Jordan Archer stared out at the stormy night, counting the headlights as they punched through the heavy cloud layer, lighting up the café's windows before fading into the darkness. Rain puddled on the slick sidewalks, the heavy downpour keeping all but the diehard patrons from venturing out.

It had been seven months since she'd limped out of compound, bloody and broken, Ember a fading memory in her rearview, and she still searched for shadows in the darkness. For a glimpse of a familiar face or a car that didn't quite belong. A suggestion of the men hunting her.

She'd gotten lucky. The long-haul truck she'd flagged down had been heading west, and she'd made it all the way to the Raven's Cliff — a fog-covered dot on the Oregon coast with no cameras, spotty reception and a population eager to look the other way. She'd only intended on staying a couple months

— just long enough to lick her wounds. Regroup. Maybe source out that salvation her uncle had hinted about.

Until Kash Sinclair had breezed into the overly hip diner and turned her life inside out. Had her breaking ranks — settling into a routine that was bound to eventually bite her in the ass. And all so she could spend those precious thirty minutes a day with him and his furry sidekick, Nyx. Share a cup of coffee across the counter while he talked about nothing and everything. Likely, not what her uncle had considered salvation.

Not that she cared because that time with Kash was the only part of her life that made her feel human.

He hadn't even asked her out — hadn't tried to take their connection further than the easy friendship they'd developed over the past few months. But she'd be lying if she didn't admit she wanted more.

Wanted him.

Which was crazy. While she'd had her share of sexual encounters over the past thirty-two years, they'd never been more than that. A mutual release that hadn't lasted longer than it took to get the job done. She'd never gotten emotionally involved. Never shared, and she sure as hell had never risked her safety — her sanity — over a roll between the sheets.

Knowing she'd risk everything for a chance to be with Kash hit hard. Confused her on a level she didn't quite understand. Sure, the man was ruggedly handsome, with a sarcastic wit that immediately put her at ease. But it went beyond his stunningly good looks and easy charm.

It was the essence of who he was. Or maybe it was what he represented. Strength. Intelligence. And above all else, safety.

An odd concept for someone who'd spent her entire life meting out justice. Being the ghost in the night others feared. But ever since she'd learned the truth — that Rook and Scythe had used her for their own personal vendettas designed to further some hidden agenda — she'd been floundering. Like a boat left adrift to fight the rising tide.

Kash was stable. A calming voice in a hurricane-force storm. One she was slowly becoming addicted to.

He was interested. She knew that much. His tone. The subtle glances. How he found a reason to drop by, even if he wasn't working. And no one needed that much coffee. But she hadn't exactly given off the kind of vibes that suggested she'd be open to more, and he seemed content biding his time. Waiting for some kind of sign that she wouldn't simply brush him off.

A fact that scared her down to her soul. She should have run, already. Another town. Another name. Whatever it took to stay ahead of Rook until she figured out how to access the intel without him and his death squad showing up on her doorstep like every other dead-drop site she'd tried to access and failed. But the more time she spent around Kash, the more she'd started to believe that maybe he was strong enough to know the truth. That he was one of the few men who could stand against Rook and walk away still breathing.

Kash hadn't gone into depth about what he'd done in the service. But she knew a black ops soldier when she saw one. Just like the rest of his teammates. Foster Beckett and Chase Remington had been Air Force — a pilot and a medic respectively. Though, if Beckett hadn't been part of Flight Concepts she'd eat her damn apron. The man exuded that kind of quiet confidence. And Chase had definitely been more than the average stitch and run type. Pararescue, she guessed. The guy they sent in when special operations went south.

Then, there was Zain Everett. Calm. Calculated, with a hyper-awareness that was off the charts. The guy screamed Army Ranger turned SAR specialist. Likely a sniper. Which meant Kash had been a Ranger, too. And it was obvious they were more like brothers than teammates. To say she envied their relationship was an understatement.

Which was part of the reason she hadn't pressed for more. Kash had a way of bypassing her barriers. Getting her to lower her guard without anything more than a smile. And she knew, if she ever acted on the thoughts bouncing around inside her head, she'd confess far more than just her feelings.

She'd bare her soul.

Jordan sighed. She'd definitely lost her mind. Or maybe she'd just been lost for so long she couldn't fight the pull anymore. Needed one last good memory before she faced the cold reality that Rook had been right, and she didn't have a future beyond Scythe.

A clap of thunder startled her from her thoughts, and she cursed under her breath as she made her way back to the counter. She needed to get a grip. Find a way to untangle herself from the dreams inside her head. Being with Kash wasn't realistic. Not because she thought he'd turn her down, but because of the kind of man he was. Honorable. Steadfast. And she knew that if they crossed that line, he'd become more than just her lover. He'd become her champion. And she couldn't risk his life just so she could have a chance at one.

The door creaked open behind her, a rush of cold, winter air swirling in with the rain. She turned, and her heart stopped. He stood in the doorway, one arm braced against the frame. Looking as if he'd fall on his face if he tried to stand on his own. His skin was tinged blue, his hair dripping water down his face. He scanned the small room, his gaze locking on hers.

She swallowed, wondering if the chef had turned up the heat. Left all the burners on high. Something to explain the burst of warmth beneath her skin that didn't involve Kash Sinclair.

His teammates brushed past him, heading for their usual table in the far back corner. Oddly subdued as they ambled past. Nyx limped along with them, glancing back at her handler before continuing behind Zain.

Kash waited until they'd settled at the table then took a step, teetering a bit until he found his balance. Her chest squeezed tight, all her reasons for not asking him for more fading beneath the weight of his gaze.

She wanted him. Wanted to run her fingers through his shaggy mass of brown hair. Stare up into his brilliant green eyes. Run her hands over every inch of smooth skin as he moved inside her.

But more than anything, she just wanted to feel.

Everything.

With him.

Jordan wasn't sure if she said his name or if Kash was on some kind of mission because he took a breath then started walking. Quickly closing the distance between them in firm, measured strides. He didn't say a word, just reached out, slid his cold fingers through her hair, tilted back her head and kissed her.

Had any man ever tasted this good? Like those words from that country song her boss played on repeat — *fast cars and freedom*. How she envisioned her life could have been if she'd gotten a different roll of the dice.

She must have gasped because Kash tangled his tongue with hers a heartbeat later, deepening the kiss as she wove her hands through his hair — pulled him closer. Savoring the muffled groan that rumbled through his chest and into hers until he finally eased back, their breath mixing. His mouth still dangerously close.

Jordan blinked, staring up into all that stunning green. Trying to calculate how to get him to kiss her like that again. If she should just tiptoe up — dive in.

He brushed his thumb across her lips, looking as if he might dip down, again — shatter any lingering doubts — when he smiled. "Have dinner with me."

She coughed. Why he was talking about food when all she wanted him to do was pin her to the wall — thrust inside?

Kash chuckled, giving her a ghost of a kiss before letting his forehead rest on hers. "Is the way you're looking at me your version of yes?"

She froze, everything rushing back. The door. The café. His entire team watching from the sidelines. She swallowed, impressed when she didn't end up spitting some of it across his face. "Don't you think you should have asked me that before you kissed me?"

He shrugged, a hint of his boyish charm tugging at his mouth. "I needed to hedge the answer in my favor. Because I know your gut instinct is to say no."

That cooled some of the heat. Had her inner voice chiming in. "Kash, I…"

The café door opened, again, another swirl of damp air breezing past them. The hairs on her neck prickled, something about the way the pair of boots scuffed the floor drawing her attention. She managed to drag her focus away from Kash — glance over his shoulder.

A guy. Late thirties. Looking as if he'd been standing in the rain all day, shouting at the wind. His gaze bounced around the room before landing on her and Kash, all the white in his eyes glowing in the overhead lights. He took a few faltering steps, then picked up speed, each footfall more deliberate. She caught a flash of metal and leather — fingers clenched around a grip.

Jordan zeroed in and moved before the bastard cleared his holster. Pushing past Kash and stepping into the attack. She slid one hand along the barrel — ejected the chambered round back at the perp. He jerked his head to the right and opened up his left side.

Precision strikes to his throat and groin — a couple firm kicks to the inside of his knee — and he reeled back. Breath wheezing out. His gun clattering to a table as he clutched his neck. Jordan fisted his jacket, then kicked off that table and vaulted over his back, grabbing his piece as she slammed his head onto the smooth surface.

He spat out some blood, gasping when she twisted all that fabric around his throat — cut off most of his air before leaning in. Her breath hot against his neck. Her voice low.

"Who the hell sent you? Rook? Does he know I'm here, or are you one of his advanced drones?"

He tugged at his collar, sucking in raspy little gasps. "They're... coming." He laughed, the sound like metal grinding over stone. "We're all gonna die."

She tightened her hold, trying to make sense of his gibberish, when the door creaked.

She turned, keeping one elbow jammed between the asshole's shoulder blades as she targeted the front of the room. Bright headlights cut through the fog beyond the open door, a black Hummer slowing down as it crept past before turning at the next corner.

Sheriff Greer Hudson and her deputy Bodie Page stood in the entrance. Guns drawn. Feet braced apart. They glanced at her, then over to Kash's teammates gathered behind her. Looking as if they weren't sure whether to start shooting or start talking.

Jordan focused on Bodie. No hint of fear, just his gaze rock steady on her — his muscles primed for a fight. He'd seen battle. The way he moved — how he took in an entire room in one glance. Like Kash and his teammates. Definitely ex-military. Ranger or maybe a SEAL. He was the threat. And she'd deal with him, first, if it came down to it.

Kash inhaled, then stepped between her and them, holding up his hands. She shifted her focus enough to keep Greer and Bodie in her peripheral vision as she met Kash's gaze.

He gave her a guarded smile, nodding at the weapon. "Easy, sweetheart. Tucker's not what you think. Now, give me the gun, and let Greer and Bodie finish this, okay?"

Give him the gun? Was he nuts?

What if this was all a distraction, and Rook suddenly burst through the door, guns blazing? Or half a dozen highly trained assholes crashed through the windows, throwing flash bangs and smoke grenades? What if the guy nearly choking from the way she had his jacket clenched in her fist miraculously recovered and launched another attack?

Kash shifted to her left, closing off more of her view. "Jordan. We're all friends, here. But I need the gun."

She held firm, the tension in the room at the breaking point. Everyone poised on the edge, waiting for a reason to start firing. A breath. A misstep. Maybe a cup clattering to the floor. Kash waved his fingers, holding his ground as she weighed her options. Knowing she only had one if there was any hope in defusing the situation before it couldn't be stopped.

She took a breath, slowly easing up as she let the gun rotate around her finger. Kash inched forward, exaggerating his movements. Giving her plenty of time to anticipate his hand reaching up — gently taking the piece. She raised her palms next to her shoulders, still working on how she'd counter an attack if Greer or Bodie changed their minds, as she took two calculated steps back.

That set her off. Had her pulse thundering in her

head. Every nerve twitching. This was wrong. Backing away. Giving up the gun while there were still threats in play. She'd never stood down. Never surrendered. Willingly giving up that control...

It hit her hard. Had snippets from that last mission looping through her head. The smoke. The explosions. The blood soaking her clothes. How she'd all but passed out once she'd found some roadside bathroom to clean up in. If that kind trucker hadn't taken pity on her, she never would have made it out of the state alive. Would have been unconscious on that grimy floor when Rook eventually showed up.

Either she'd made a noise, or the color had drained from her face because Kash stepped in close and tugged her against his chest. He didn't talk, just slid his hands across her neck and waist, surrounding her with all that muscled strength. She fisted his hoodie, her chest heaving. Every instinct begging her to run. To fight her way through the masses then hop on her bike and never look back.

Finally acknowledge that she'd only ever be Ember — Scythe operative and the woman destined to fade away.

Kash held firm, waiting until she'd finally released her death grip before dropping a kiss on the top of her head. He grabbed her chin with his thumb and forefinger, holding still until she met his gaze. "You okay?"

She pushed down the riotous roil of her stomach, allowing her head tilt back. "Considering how I just neutralized a guy in front of a dozen witnesses? I've been better."

He chuckled. "Spoken like a true warrior. And it's not as if we all didn't think you were capable of it, it's just… damn."

"Damn about sums it up."

He nodded toward the counter. "Come on. Let's get you a coffee. Give you a chance to rein in some of that adrenaline."

"Trust me. I'm in complete control."

"Then, you can drink because you look like a damn ghost."

"You're the one who's blue. Do I want to know why you smell like the ocean?"

It was subtle. Just a hint of salty brine on his skin — what she suspected hadn't washed off in the shower. But it was there.

Kash sighed, thanking Zain when he darted behind the counter and grabbed the coffee pot. "Long story."

She grunted. Every sense still on overdrive. Every muscle still primed for a fight. "Doubt I'm going anywhere. And I could use the distraction."

Kash gave her a once-over. Looking as if he knew exactly how raw she was. How little it would take to set her off. "Let's just say our newest recruit wasn't quite up to the task. Tapped out while I was hanging on the side of a cliff with Nyx over my shoulders — a series of poor decisions dragging us down. Then the cliff gave way, and—"

"Wait. Him?" She nodded at the creep. "He's with Raven's Watch? Since when?"

"This morning. It was a trial run." Kash tilted his head to the side. "He said he's been in here before. Claimed he knew who you were. Do you recognize him?"

She studied the guy's face — reran the last few months' worth of people she'd put into memory. "No."

Which meant he'd either been shadowing her without her realizing it or he was lying. Neither of which sat well with her. "How long has he been in town?"

"I thought he'd gotten in last night, but he never confirmed that. Does it matter?"

"Everything matters." Especially if he was an advanced scout — working his way through every blip of a town along the Oregon coast. "Is he the reason Nyx is limping?"

"If I say yes, are you gonna lose it?"

"No, but I might want that gun back?" She huffed. "On second thought, I'll just use my hands."

"Easy there, *Agent Romanoff*. Might be best if we let Greer handle the situation for now. Get this a few levels down from DEFCON ONE."

Jordan frowned. "Agent who?"

"You don't get out much, do you?" He handed her the coffee mug Zain placed on the counter. "Drink."

She took a sip, allowing the hot liquid to ease the

fluttering feeling in her gut. The one that wasn't quite ready to stand down. "Thanks."

Zain waved it off. "No, thank you." He laughed. "I'm so winning the pool."

"Pool?"

Kash looked as if he wanted to smack his buddy up the side of his head. "And they say I'm socially awkward." Kash pursed his lips when Greer ambled over, arms crossed. Eyes wary. He gave Jordan's hand a squeeze then moved back, allowing Greer to take his spot.

Jordan eyed the other woman, working out how much of the truth she'd have to weave into her story to satisfy all of Greer's unspoken questions without completely burning her identity. "Sorry about not backing down sooner, but with that guy walking in here and pulling a gun…"

Greer nodded, leaning against the counter. "I get it. You thought he might have more friends backing him up." She arched a brow. "You learn that move at the Y, too?"

Jordan bit back a smile. The other woman definitely had a great memory if she recalled a single comment from a few months ago. Though, Jordan had just taken down a couple bikers twice her size.

Not that she expected anything less from a former government agent. FBI or maybe NSA. Something serious, but not so strict Greer walked around as if she had a giant stick up her ass. But the lady had skills, and Jordan needed to respect that. Give Greer that hint of truth without signing her own death warrant.

Jordan sighed. "I think we both know I've never stepped foot in a Y."

"Ya think?" Greer scanned the diner, her gaze always falling back to the guy handcuffed in the chair. "Riddle me this. If, hypothetically speaking, I ran your name through a federal database, would I have a U.S. Deputy Marshal knocking down my door the next day?"

Jordan didn't answer, just met the woman's expectant gaze. While it wasn't exactly the truth, Rook knocking on Greer's door had far graver consequences.

"Well, shit." Greer crossed her arms. "Are you a danger to my town, Jordan?"

"I'd like to think not."

"Not exactly the benchmark I was hoping for."

"I'm not looking to hurt anyone, if that's what you're asking."

"But you could. Based on that Krav Maga move you just pulled without breaking a sweat. I suppose Kash's team might give you a run for your money. Bodie, too. But then, you've already figured out who the threats are, haven't you?" Greer muttered a few curse words at Jordan's silence. "That's what I thought. Hang tight. I need to talk to Bodie about Tucker Grant."

Greer pushed off the counter then turned to face

Jordan. "He's the guy you took down in all of two seconds, by the way."

Kash moved in beside Jordan, nudging her shoulder. "Greer's good people. She won't do anything that might put you at risk." He shrugged. "In case you were wondering."

"You sure about that? Because she looks like she wants to use me for target practice."

"Greer's had a rough few months. She's still cleaning up Sheriff Thompson's drug running mess, and she can't seem to find anyone she trusts to sign up. Other than Bodie. But she doesn't spook easily."

"Is that your account or Chase's?"

"It's a general consensus." He nodded when Greer reappeared. "Everything all right?"

Greer scoffed. "Let's see... Atticus keeps ringing my cell because he's already heard there's been an altercation at the diner, and he knows you're all here grabbing coffee. I've got *Black Widow* taking out military guys like it's just a regular Friday night. And I have an Army medic in a full-blown PTSD flashback because he thinks he's back in the Stan. So, you tell me."

Kash pursed his lips, shaking his head as he kicked at the floor. "That's on us. We thought we'd talked him down — gotten him through this episode." Kash held up one hand. "I swear he was fully coherent when he left the hangar. Said he was heading to Seattle for a few days — was going to visit an old teammate. Get his head on straight. If we'd thought he was still a danger..."

"Yeah, well I just checked on that old teammate. Turns out his new address is a headstone at Medical Lake."

Kash let his head tip back, a rare moment of vulnerability bleeding through the sarcasm and strength. He'd obviously lost teammates, the truth evident in the lines around his mouth. How he looked over at his buddies before visibly shoving everything down. "I..."

Greer gave Kash a pat on the shoulder. "Not blaming you or your crew. You did your best. But it does put me in a difficult position."

"What are you gonna do?"

Greer snorted. "The man pulled a Glock in the middle of a café. Legally, I'm obligated to take him back to the station, throw half a dozen weapons charges his way, and let him rot in a cell until the judge comes back from his dirty weekend in Portland."

"And not legally speaking?"

"I guess that depends." Greer raked her hand through her hair, glancing over her shoulder for a moment. "Bodie's got an in with a rehab house for vets that specializes in Tucker's particular issues. They're willing to take him in, tonight, and keep his ass there until he's feeling more like himself. Assuming he's willing to go. But that means I have to look the other way, and neither you, nor Ms. Archer, can press charges."

Kash nodded. "We're all just one bad day away from screaming at the shadows. The man needs help, not a cell."

Greer arched a brow, looking at Jordan. "And you?"

Jordan held up her hands. "I'm not looking to put my name on a report."

Greer snorted. "Right. I'll see what I can do. I'm gonna need everyone to come to the station and give a formal statement. Jordan, you can drop by after your shift. With all the other accounts, I can probably stick yours way in the back where it might get lost or filed incorrectly. But I still need to take it."

"I'll be over as soon as I'm done."

"I'll hold you to that." Greer walked off, talking to Bodie before they helped Tucker up then escorted him out the door.

Kash nudged her shoulder. "So, are you okay to make your way to my place? Say, seven? Or should I wait at Greer's office and give you a lift?"

Jordan stared at him. Had she said yes before everything had gone sideways? "You still want to have dinner? After all this?"

"The guys will likely try to blackmail us into joining them at Beck's. But they can be disappointed."

Her stomach clenched, those gorgeous eyes and

full lips looking expectantly at her. Only now, she knew exactly how he tasted. "Kash, I..."

"How about I make you a deal? I won't ask any probing questions, and you won't have to lie. Okay?"

She glanced at the table where the entire evening had unraveled. Chances were, she'd have to run. Especially if Greer dug too deep. Why not give herself one unforgettable night? "I might be a bit later than seven, if Greer's chatty."

"I'll tell her to keep it brief." He reached up and brushed his thumb across her lips, again. "Seven, Jordan."

She nodded, following him to the door. He jumped into one of the trucks, Nyx landing on his lap a second later. He gave the canine a scratch, smiling as Chase backed up then pulled onto the street, their taillights fading around the far corner.

Dinner.

She only hoped it didn't dissolve into a war zone. Ruin her chance at making one last pure memory. Because come morning, she was done hiding. She'd told Rook she'd bring the fight to him, and it was time she started hunting.

CHAPTER THREE

Jordan straddled her dirt bike and stared at the expansive house stretching across the property. A series of lights brightened the darkness, the warm yellow glow chasing away the worst of the shadows. Fog rolled across the grounds, clinging to the tress like ghostly apparitions waiting to strike as rain puddled in the driveway.

She swallowed, the inklings of doubt shivering down her spine — manifesting as goosebumps across her skin. Twenty years under the iron rule of Rook and Scythe. Covert missions to places even Kash and his teammates likely hadn't ventured — the threat too chaotic, too raw to be worth the fight — and for the first time in her life, she was scared.

She didn't do nice. Didn't attend gatherings or make small talk. Not unless it was part of her cover. And since Rook abhorred any form of joint operation — any chance of the world catching even a suggestion of Scythe's existence — she'd lived her private life like she had her missions. Alone. Always searching the shadows. Ready to bolt on a moment's notice.

She could adapt. Like working at the Lighthouse Café. It was a role. A way of gathering intel without exposing herself more than necessary. People talked. She listened. Nothing more, nothing less. So, agreeing to dinner, knowing full well it would likely involve the rest of Kash's team in some capacity...

It was foreign. Like her feelings for Kash. An anomaly that had her so far outside her usual orbit, she was surprised she hadn't crashed.

The front door opened, a daunting figure stepping out onto the covered porch. She couldn't tell if it was Kash or one of his teammates — the man's silhouette barely visible through the driving rain. But he waved her in, standing tall as if he was ready to chase after her if she changed her mind.

She turned off the engine then made a dash for the porch, jogging up the steps then into the house. The door slammed shut behind her, Foster staring at her as if he hadn't quite believed she'd venture inside.

She sighed. "You're not Kash."

"Glad you can tell us apart." He frowned, giving her a thorough once-over. "When I saw the single headlight, I'd assumed the other was burnt out. But... Did you seriously drive here on the rusty piece of shit I've seen parked outside the diner?"

Jordan crossed her arms over her chest, hating the

shiver that shook through her as a deep chill settled in her bones. "She might not look like much, but the engine's sound."

"Great. So, it'll still be purring when a flash flood washes you off the road." He shifted on his feet, rolling his right shoulder as he shook out his hand. "Why didn't you tell us that was all you had? We would have tossed it in the flatbed and given you a lift."

"This isn't the first time I've driven in the rain, Beckett."

"But it could have been your last." He raked his fingers through his long hair, then held out his hand. "Give me your jacket. There's a guest room up the stairs at the end of the hall on the right. You can shower or dry off. Whatever you want. I'll call Kash and get him back over here with some dry clothes. I believe he's putting out a small fire in his kitchen. Something about burning the lasagna."

Jordan scanned the room. "I can just go over—"

"You're soaked, your lips are blue, and despite your best efforts, you're shivering." He moved his hand closer. "I promise I won't rifle through your pockets or anything else you might be worried about."

"I'm not worried."

"After the way you handled Tucker, that makes one of us." He pointed to the staircase, this time. "Go. I'll put your stuff in the washer once you come back down. Everything should be clean before you leave."

Jordan stared at his hand, mentally sizing him up, but he didn't appear as if he had ulterior motives. Wasn't looking to grab her wrist or try to tackle her to the floor. In fact, he seemed genuinely worried that she could have gotten hurt on the ride over.

The thought sent another shiver down her spine. This was why accepting Kash's invitation had been a bad idea. She'd been an agent too long to shift gears, now. Acclimate into the world without the sum of her missions coloring her views. Seeing everyone as a threat she'd eventually have to deal with.

Except where Foster looked as if he'd do battle with her. No explanations. No doubts. And she wasn't sure if she was impressed or terrified.

Foster shifted on his feet, glancing at the puddle slowly forming beneath her boots then back to her. She gave him a small smile then slipped out of her gear — handing him her keys and a white bag along with the clothes.

Foster grinned, turning the bag over a few times. "Supplies for later?"

She scoffed. "It's bacon for Nyx, wiseass. She had a bad day, too."

"But it's looking up. For Kash, as well."

Jordan rolled her eyes then headed for the stairs, making her way to the bedroom, then into the bathroom. It didn't take long for the water to heat, steam softly billowing into the air. She grabbed a clean towel, hung it on one of the hooks next to the glass door, then stripped and stepped inside, letting the warm water ease the day's tension.

Maybe she'd been wrong. Maybe Kash and his buddies could help her. Give her a chance at bringing down Rook without dying in the process. They'd volunteer. That much was obvious. But it meant coming clean — letting them see behind the curtain. And she wasn't sure if she was strong enough to face their reaction. Thinking she might be an agent was one thing. Seeing it spelled out in blood and bodies…

Five minutes.

That's how long she'd give herself to gather her composure. Get her head on straight. Decide how much of the truth she'd share — just like with Greer. They already suspected she'd worked for some kind of agency, either CIA or worse. She could use that to her advantage. Because if the first two minutes of the evening were any indication of how the rest would play out, she was in for one hell of a night.

Kash stopped outside the bathroom door, some sweats, socks and a hoodie piled in his arms. Somewhere between kissing her in the café and setting the lasagna on fire, he'd forgotten about the dirt bike. Too busy reliving the soft play of her lips — how she'd slid her fingers into his hair and pulled him closer — to make all the necessary connections.

Thankfully, his oversight hadn't ended with her trapped in a river or dangling from the side of a cliff. Which meant, he still had time to salvage the night. Show her that he was worth the risk.

He frowned. There had been something in her eyes when she'd agreed to dinner that had been gnawing at him. A look that had put his protective instincts on high alert. As if she'd come to a decision, but not the one on the table. Something deeper. Darker. And Kash bet his ass it had to do with whatever agency she'd been part of.

The way she'd taken down Tucker had confirmed everything he'd been thinking. That her past was filled with redacted files and above top-secret clearance. Missions that didn't exist in places few ventured. The only question was whether she was running or hunting. Burned or biding her time.

She didn't act like a hunter. The hyper-vigilance. The distance. It struck him more as someone trying to blend in. Who wanted to vanish into normalcy. Which explained why she'd taken the job at the Lighthouse Café. Just another face behind the counter. Close enough to the pulse of the town she stayed current on the local gossip without drawing attention to herself.

That had changed tonight.

And that's what scared him.

That this wasn't the beginning of forever, but the start of goodbye.

Kash pushed aside the thoughts. He needed to clear his mind, or she'd pick up on the tension. She hadn't bolted yet. And if he played his cards right, he might be able to steer her onto another path — one that involved him and his buddies rallying around her. For now, she needed to believe he was still in the dark.

He took a breath, pushed his shoulders back, then knocked on the door. "Jordan?"

The handle jiggled before the door opened amidst a curtain of steam. It took a moment for the room to clear, her terry-clad silhouette taking shape within the mist.

"Damn."

There was no other way to describe her. Smooth pale skin. Strong firm muscles. Her long brown hair curling around her face, making her baby-blue eyes seem twice as bright.

She arched a brow, looking too damn sexy as she smiled, slowly moving over to the doorway. "Damn?"

He coughed. He hadn't realized he'd said the word out loud. "I..." He chuckled. "That seems to be my go-to where you're concerned, today. And I meant it exactly how it sounded."

"I guess there are worse things you could say." She nodded at the clothes. "Are those for me?"

He held them out, drinking in the floral scent of her skin mixed with a hint of coconut in her hair. "They'll be big, but..."

"Big sounds pretty perfect." She glanced behind her. "I have to admit, I didn't expect Foster to have soaps and shampoo that didn't smell like pine trees and bad decisions."

"Pretty sure that's Mac's influence. While I haven't been deployed with Beck for several months, I can assure you he's never smelled as incredible as you do after a shower." He motioned to the pile of clothes stacked on the counter. "Can I take those down and get them in the washer?"

She bit at her bottom lip, looking as if no one had ever offered to help her, before. "You don't have to do that."

"It's the least I can do after forgetting you only had that bike." He leaned against the frame, getting dangerously close. "Though in my defense, I can't really be held responsible for anything after that kiss."

A hint of pink burned up her cheeks. "And here your buddies claimed you were awkward."

"Glad to know they've got my back."

Her smile fell a bit. "More than you know."

Had he imagined the pang of sadness in her voice? "I'll get these loaded then meet you downstairs."

He forced himself to turn — head down the hall. He made his way to the laundry, tossing everything in then starting the cycle. Jordan was already descending the stairs when he made his way back to the sitting room.

Foster walked in from the kitchen, a couple beers in his hands. "I realize you probably have other plans, but you're both welcome to stay. We've got enough food to feed an army."

Kash stilled. He didn't want Jordan to feel trapped, especially if his hunch was right and she was already on the verge of running. Her gaze darted to the door then back to the hallway leading to the kitchen as laughter erupted in the other room, the scent of fresh bread wafting through the air.

Kash nudged her. "Jordan..."

She reached over and gave his hand a squeeze before looking at Foster. "Are you sure? Because I've seen you all eat."

Foster placed his hand on his chest. "Ouch. And I promise we got extra just for Zain."

"I heard that." Zain's voice carried to them from the other room.

"I damn well hope so. I practically yelled it." Foster offered them both a beer. "Anyway, you can join us, or you can grab a plate and run, seeing as *chef Ramsay* here burned his masterpiece. Your choice."

He didn't wait for either of them to reply, heading back into the other room.

Kash tugged Jordan closer. "We don't have to stay. I can grab some food and—"

She placed her finger across his lips, silencing him. "It's fine." She removed her hand as she took a step before she stopped and looked back at him. "No one's going to try and kill me though, right? Because that might get awkward."

His mouth gaped open, a slight ringing in his ears as he stared at her. Wondering if she'd really just admitted she was an operative.

She laughed. "God, your face. I'm kidding."

Kash held firm when she went to move. "Are you?"

She simply stared at him.

He closed the distance. "C'mon, before Zain proves Foster wrong."

Kash led her into the other room, holding her chair before sitting next to her. There was a round of greetings, then everyone settled into an easy conversation. And Kash had to admit, his brothers kept it light. Nothing about her past — how she'd vaulted over Tucker like a damn gymnast. Safe topics. The weather. The café. Some of their adventures with Raven's Watch. Anything, but what really mattered.

They'd been sitting there for about an hour when Jordan sighed, shaking her head as she gazed around the room.

She pushed back in her chair, resting her hands on the top of the table. "While I realize Kash probably threatened you with some form of horrific punishment if you said anything remotely controversial, the obvious tension is starting to take a toll."

The room fell silent, everyone staring at her. Mouths pinched tight. Eyes narrowed. Even Nyx stopped panting, pushing onto her haunches at Kash's side.

Jordan dabbed the corners of her mouth with a napkin, studying them all in turn before sighing. "How about I clear the air a bit." She took a breath, looking at Foster and Mac. "I'm not a sleeper agent." She moved on to Zain. "I've never worked for the CIA." Finally, Chase. "And I'm not part of the mafia."

Her confession lingered in the air, like an echo still playing in the distance. She'd been serious. The even tone. The steady eye contact. Kash wasn't sure if this was progress — if she was starting to align with his way of thinking even if he hadn't voiced it, yet — or if she was upping her schedule. Giving them just enough of the truth, they wouldn't question it when she vanished.

Foster leaned forward, his forearms braced on the table. "But you did... Work for an agency."

He hadn't framed it as a question. Just a simple statement. No judgement. No hidden implications.

Jordan gave Kash a quick side-eye, resting one arm over the back of her chair. "I did... Until seven months ago."

Chase nodded. "Did something change?"

"We had a... difference of opinion." She shrugged. "And we parted on less-than-ideal terms."

"What kind of terms are we talking? Bad blood and a shitty job reference, or a tactical squad showing up on your doorstep?"

Jordan slipped Kash another glance. "Nothing I can't handle."

Zain narrowed his gaze, giving the room a quick sweep before inching forward. "So, more of the second. Makes me wonder if you thought Tucker was coming for you."

Jordan didn't blink. "You seem fairly certain he wasn't."

"Atticus vets potential crew fairly rigorously. And I'd expect your former agency to send someone worthy of you breaking a sweat. Not a guy you took down in all of five seconds."

"Different skill sets for different outcomes." She folded her hands on the table, again, but not before Kash noticed the slight tremble. "Hypothetically speaking, of course."

Zain obviously noticed too because he sat a bit straighter. "Are you suggesting they'd send someone you could neutralize in your sleep just to get you to show your hand?"

She stared directly back at Zain, pulling in a few easy breaths, before shifting on her seat. "I just wanted to clear the air."

"Well, that's a yes. And now I'm thinking I want to rethink my pool strategy. Side with Kash."

Her breath caught, the corners of her mouth tightening. As if she'd realized she'd given them a bit too much.

Kash pushed back his chair, then stood. "And that's our cue to head back to my place." He leaned in. "I promise I can make a killer cup of coffee without setting the room on fire."

Jordan clambered to her feet a second later, her palm sliding over his. His buddies all stood, hands digging into their pockets.

Foster moved around to their side. Close, but not to the point Kash thought she'd see him as a threat. "I'll make sure your clothes are stacked by the back door, so they're ready whenever you need them. And for the record... Just because we're not still wearing the uniforms, doesn't mean we've stopped stepping up. We all spent twenty years eliminating threats. Nothing's changed."

Jordan glanced down, staring at her feet, or maybe the floor. She inched closer to Kash before looking up. "I'll keep that in mind. Thanks for dinner. It was... pleasantly uneventful."

"I meant what I said, Jordan. We don't scare easily, and we don't back down. All you have to do is talk to us."

"And with that we definitely need to leave." Kash gripped her hand a bit tighter. "Thanks for the dinner save, Beck."

He turned, whistled to Nyx, then headed for the back door. They made a dash down the path, avoiding the larger puddles until they reached his house. He barely slowed, shoving open the door and waving her inside before closing it behind them — tapping on a box next to the entrance. Arming the insanely sophisticated security system Zain had installed in all the homes after the shitstorm with Striker a few months back.

A few soft lights burned overhead, the warm glow casting lazy shadows on the floor. Jordan kicked off her boots, smiling as she picked her way over to the living room, giving the open area a good once-over. Nyx trailed behind her, stopping when Jordan gave her a quick scratch behind the ears before curling up on one of her beds.

Kash leaned against a wooden beam, watching Jordan assess the room, pausing on anything he assumed presented a threat, or maybe an impromptu weapon, before moving on. "Well?"

She glanced at him over her shoulder. "Exactly the way I'd envisioned, other than the hint of smoke."

"It definitely wasn't the first dinner I've ruined." He ambled over to the edge of the counter. "So, how'd we do?"

Her brow furrowed, adorable lines creasing the bridge of her nose. "With regards to what?"

"Our reaction to the suggestion of your previous employment. Was it a pass or fail?"

To her credit, she didn't react. Just stood there, staring at him before pushing out a slow breath. "I guess it depends on whose side you're looking at. Because I'm starting to think I failed mine by either saying too much..." She tilted her head to the side. "Or too little."

Kash closed the distance. "To be fair, too much is never enough for guys like us."

She coughed, stepping back until she leaned against the wall. "Right. Guys like you."

He moved with her, bracing one arm above her head, the other off to one side. "I know what I promised..."

She snagged her bottom lip, staring up at him with those big blue eyes. "Kash..."

"I'm not going to push. I just need you to know that if you really are in trouble, I can help. My team can help."

"It's not as if I haven't considered it, but... You don't want this kind of trouble at your door."

"A threat's a threat." He lifted his hand and toyed with one bouncy curl. "And you heard Foster. We've all spent twenty years eliminating those."

"Not like this." She palmed his cheek, brushing her thumb along his jaw. "Not like him. And if I ask for your help..." She closed her eyes for a moment, her shoulders drooping in apparent defeat. "It won't end well."

"Maybe." He cupped her chin. "Or maybe we're exactly what you need."

She sighed. "Have I read this wrong? Or do you want to make love to me, as much as I need you to?"

He leaned in, stopping a breath away. Drinking in her floral-scented skin and how her breathing sped up until her chest heaved against his — her other hand fisting his shirt. He shifted a bit closer, staying poised on the edge. All that anticipation on the brink of spontaneously combusting. He hadn't missed her choice of words. The way her hand shook ever so slightly as it rested against his chest. Or how her eyes held just a hint of something behind the blue depths.

He wouldn't label it yet, but it gave him a glimmer of hope.

She groaned. "Kash..."

That did him in. The low, sexy tone of her voice. The shadowed look. How she ate at his mouth the second he kissed her.

Two seconds in, and she had her hands in his hair, one leg wrapped around his calf. Practically riding his thigh as he stepped into her, crushing her against the wall, every damn inch touching.

Her head fell back as he nipped his way down her neck, sucking at her pulse point. Every touch drawing a strangled moan. She arched against his hand when he cupped her breast, trying to work out how to get them naked without releasing her.

She must have had a solution because his shirt flew over his head a heartbeat later, that oversized hoodie he'd lent her quickly joining it. He took a moment to drink her in. Appreciate the creamy expanse of pale, soft skin. The stunning curve of her breasts and how they fit perfectly in his hands.

She yanked him down for another round, smoothing her hands along his chest, up his arms then across his back. Kneading his muscles before finally landing in his hair, again. Tugging on the strands, taking him to the brink with nothing but the suggestion of more.

He wasn't sure how long they'd been standing there, the storm still raging outside, his body strung so tight he'd likely burst the second she touched him before she eased back — lowered her hand and squeezed him through his denim. He rested his forehead on hers, dragging in a series of ragged breaths.

Jordan tiptoed up — nipped at his ear. "Kash..."

He pulled back. Not much. Just enough to meet her gaze. "Before I hike you up on my shoulder and carry you into the bedroom, I need to ask you one last thing."

She hummed, eyes heavy lidded. Only a hint of blue around the outside. "Pretty sure the answer's yes."

"Good. Because I need you to look me in the eyes and tell me that this isn't just a one-off. That forever's on the table."

She blinked, brows furrowed as if she hadn't understood the question or was trying to translate some of the words into a different language before she stilled. Breath held. That hand shaking against his chest. "I..."

"I'm not asking for promises. While we've known each other for months, I know this is new. That your past makes things... complicated. But after everything's that's happened..."

Losing Sean that fateful night. Having Rhett still stuck in a coma. Nearly drowning in the damn ocean today. It was as if his heart had cracked, and everything he felt for Jordan was pouring out, threatening to drag him under just like the waves had.

She stared up at him, lips slightly parted, nostrils flaring before she placed her hands on his face — inched him closer. "If there was any chance I could make forever an option, I'd want to spend it with you."

CHAPTER FOUR

Jordan had lost her mind.

That was the only explanation for why she was standing in Kash's living room, half-naked, staring up at him and telling him she wanted a future, too. That whatever forever looked like, she'd choose to spend it with him.

Not that wanting to be with him was crazy. The man was sexy and smart, with more honor than anyone she'd ever met. And the way he kissed…

She was surprised they hadn't started another fire. Set off all the smoke alarms in the place because she was definitely burning up. But knowing it was only a matter of time before Rook found her — that she'd be lucky if forever lasted beyond tonight…

That was certifiable.

And had she really asked him to make love to her?

She'd never used that term. Never thought about

sex as anything other than physical. But this was different.

He was different.

Kash narrowed his gaze, looking as if he'd followed her internal monologue — knew exactly how far she'd fallen. He leaned down — claimed her mouth. Only, it felt different, now. More intimate. As if he'd found that one loose thread and started pulling, unraveling her defenses until all that remained was the part of her Scythe hadn't taken.

He dropped his mouth to her neck, licking and sucking as he tugged at the cord holding up those oversized sweats. A yank and a pull and they dropped — pooled around her ankles. His jeans and boxers hit the floor a second later, leaving them standing there with nothing between them but the weight of their expectations. What felt like the start of the rest of her life.

She reached down — took him in her hand. Wanting to feel all that power flow into her. His breath caught, one arm lifting to brace against the wall. As if he wasn't quite sure he'd survive what she'd hinted at without some kind of anchor.

She went to her knees. She didn't just want to taste him. She wanted to devour him. Know that he trusted her. Was willing to make himself vulnerable. Even if just for tonight.

Kash fisted her hair. Whether to pull her back to her feet or give him a better view she wasn't sure. She paused for one agonizing heartbeat, then moved along his length — took him deep then slowly drew back. He made some sort of primitive guttural sound. Not quite pain, but not quite pleasure. More like a heady mixture of both. The kind that suggested he was already gone.

That had her smiling around his length. Moving faster, deeper. Whatever it took to push him over. Have him shooting down her throat in record time.

He lasted several minutes before he started moving with her. Doing his best to meter his thrusts but failing. His hand in her hair flexing then releasing. As if he couldn't decide whether to hold her still or pull her away. She'd gotten him to the brink when he grunted, then stopped. His breath practically growling out of his chest.

She looked up, and she was lost. The way he stared at her, as if she held far more than just his body in her hands. That he was as wrecked as she was.

He tugged, and she stood, eating at his mouth, all but climbing him in an effort to get closer. He wrapped his arms around her, lifted, then spun. She didn't know where his bedroom was, but anything more than a foot away was too far.

He seemed to agree because he took a step then all but fell across an oversized ottoman. What looked as if it doubled as a padded coffee table. They didn't quite fit, her ass riding one edge as her head fell off the other. But it was perfect. Just enough room he could pound into her without having to bridge any of her weight.

He loomed over her, his massive shoulders eclipsing all but a hint of the wooden ceiling above them. That soft lighting accentuating the streaks of gold in his hair. He settled between her thighs, clenching his jaw as if simply staring at her tested his control. Pushed him farther than if she'd finished him still on her knees.

She threaded her fingers in his hair, dragged him down. Needing all that weight grounding her. "Kash..."

"Condom."

The word rasped between them. Not quite a question, but not really a statement.

She met his gaze — said the only thought that formed in her head. "Implant."

Not that she'd ever trusted it before. There'd been no place in her life for doubt. Both Scythe and Rook had made that brutally clear. That she belonged to them, and any complications would be met with extreme consequences. But here, now, she didn't want any part of her past intruding on the present. Didn't want anything between them.

He froze, as if he wasn't sure he'd heard her reply. Then, he moved. Slid one hand under her ass, then thrust inside. She wasn't sure if it was his size, the force or just the sheer magnitude of the moment that stole her breath — tipped her head back. The muscles in her neck straining as she tried to suck in some air.

Kash shoved his other hand under her head, held it up as he claimed her mouth. Kissing and moaning as he set up a punishing rhythm. Every stroke pushing her higher. Binding them together in a way she feared she'd never undo. That future he'd wanted on the table.

She clung to him, clawing at his back as she wrapped her legs around his hips. Anything to get him closer. Have more of his skin touching hers.

Kash was obviously on board, using that one hand to lift her hips more fully against his. Change the angle a bit. Somehow allow him to go even deeper.

She bit at his shoulder, needing something to stop her from screaming his name. Begging him for more. For the life he'd painted with those few words.

"Damn. Jordan. I can't…"

His voice was raw. Desperate. And the mere sound of it crushed the last of her defenses. Had her chanting his name. Arching into every thrust.

He shifted his hips — hit that sweet spot.

Everything exploded.

Her head. Her heart.

Shattering outward until there was nothing left but his body strung tight above her. His mouth latched on her shoulder.

He managed a few more jerking strokes, then he collapsed on top of her. Chest heaving. His breath rasping in her ear.

She clung to him, body shaking. Lungs barely working. Nothing left of the walls she'd spent a lifetime building. She'd never reacted like this — given so much of herself — and she wasn't sure whether to scream or cry. Maybe see if he was up for another round because once had barely eased the need still burning beneath her skin.

Kash pushed onto his elbows, any tension from earlier no longer straining his muscles. He smiled, then dipped down for a soul-searing kiss. It was soft. Coaxing. And her heart damn near burst, pounding against her ribs as if trying to break free — to join his.

He shifted so he could brush one hand along her cheek. "Damn..."

She laughed, praying her voice didn't crack when she tried to speak. "At least, you're consistent."

"I'd say it was amazing or mind-blowing, but those don't even come close." He glanced at their position, shaking his head as his shoulders drooped. "Unlike my choice of venue. But the bed seemed too far away."

"You don't hear me complaining, do you?" She ran her hand along his shoulder then down his chest. "But if you'd like to try, again..."

His eyes rounded, then he moved. Practically fell off the side of the ottoman before scrambling to his feet, scooping her off the top. He headed for the back, took the hallway near the far-right wall and continued all the way to the end. She wasn't sure what the other doors hid — bedrooms or bathrooms. Maybe some kind of battle-ready weapons arsenal. Didn't care when he stopped in the middle of the master and gently placed her on her feet.

He cupped her jaw — kissed her.

It was just as intense as before. Maybe more so now that they'd gotten a taste of how it could be. An explosive mix of lust and something she wouldn't label. Something far more dangerous than the men she knew lurked in the shadows, waiting. Maybe not here, but the threat lingered in the background like a hum she couldn't turn off.

Kash tilted his head to the side, frowning. "Are you okay? Because some of the color just drained from your face."

She smiled, pushing the riotous thoughts aside. There was time to worry about Rook later. To agonize over the decisions she knew would eventually break her. But not here — not now. This was her time. Her one chance at being human. And she wasn't going to waste a second of it. "Probably still chilled from the ride."

His lips pursed, and she knew he didn't believe her. But he didn't push. Instead, he took her hand — led her into the adjoining bathroom. "Sounds like another quick shower might help."

Kash had the water warming and two towels on the counter a few heartbeats later. She leaned against the counter, savoring the play of his muscles beneath his skin. How the thick bands created dips and shadows along his chest and abdomen.

He turned. Smiled. "Trust me, the view's much better from where I'm standing."

"I find that hard to believe because... damn."

He laughed, the sound light and easy. "Teasing me already."

He closed the scant distance between them, running his hand along her skin. He looked down, sighing at the obvious scattering of scars across her body, the ones from the compound still pink.

She placed her hand over his, waiting until he raised his gaze to hers. "Those are my past."

He traced along some of the more prominent ones. "I'm more worried, they'll become your future."

"It'd be nice if they didn't."

"I'm going to hold you to that." He tugged her toward him. "C'mon. I owe you a shower then another shot at getting this right."

Getting it right? She wasn't sure what he thought he'd done wrong, but she wasn't going to argue if it meant he'd love her like that a second time.

Damn. She'd used that word, again, even if it had only been in her mind.

Kash guided her into the shower, blocking most of the spray as he backed her against the wall — kissed her as if he'd already forgotten the way she tasted. She hadn't forgotten anything. Not a second. A kiss. How he'd made her feel safe for the first time in her life. Even before she'd ended up at that group home, she'd never had any sense of security. Had been an afterthought most days. So, lying there on that stupid ottoman with him staring down at her, what looked dangerously like the inklings of love gazing back...

It had changed something inside her. Filled a hole or maybe healed a wound she hadn't realized was still festering. The kind that infected every other aspect of her life.

Until now.

Jordan kept him close when he would have stepped away, resting her head on his chest. Allowing herself to just be. To drink in the pure scent of his skin. Savor the strong weight of his arms wrapped around her. And for a moment, that future he'd talked about seemed almost real.

Kash held her tight, drawing easy patterns on her back until she exhaled a long slow breath. Then, he smoothed a bar of soap across her skin, doing the bare minimum before shutting everything down — stepping out.

He had them both fairly dry and heading back to the bed before her head caught up as he placed her in the middle of the mattress, fanning out her hair before claiming her mouth. Taking her to the brink from the kiss, alone — the way he smiled once he'd straightened before moving lower.

She closed her eyes, pushing her head into the sheets as he kissed his way down her body, licking and sucking every inch until she practically vibrated. At some point, her hands landed in his hair, all that thick mass wrapped around her fingers a moment later, the damp strands adding another layer of sensation.

Was this normal?

The way her heart couldn't decide whether to speed up or stop dead. How her skin burned beneath every swirl of his hands. Or the sobering realization that the more he loved her, the more she needed him.

Because she'd spent twenty years preparing for any possible scenario…

Except him.

Kash hummed against her skin, drawing a strangled moan from deep inside her. The same guttural plea he'd made when she'd been touching him. He took that as some kind of sign, dipping lower, then swiping his tongue along the length of her.

"Christ." The word tore free. Raw. A testament to how far he'd pushed her.

He repeated the motion, teasing her with a bit of penetration. Nearly sending her over as all the heat billowed up through her core. She moaned his name, arching into the next pass — all but grinding herself on him. He placed one massive forearm across her hips, holding her still, drawing a growl, this time.

He eased up, snapping her back from the precipice a moment before she soared off. "Someone's got their claws out."

Jordan managed to pry her eyelids open and push onto one elbow. "I swear to god, I'll use every skill at my disposal if you don't freaking finish this."

He merely arched a brow. "I thought women were all about foreplay?"

"Well, this woman's about to kick your ass if you leave her hanging like this."

A smile tugged at the corner of his mouth. "Has anyone ever told you that patience isn't your strong suit?"

"A few, but they didn't live long enough to regret it."

That smile he'd held back flourished. "Damn, I'm crazy about you. Fine. Relax. I'll give you what you need."

She fell back on the bed, promising to get revenge as soon as she could string together a thought that didn't start and end with his name. That didn't feel like the beginning of forever.

Kash held true to his promise, lowering his head and taking her back to that edge a second later. Licking and sucking and something that had her fingers fisting in his hair — her eyes rolling. She fought against the surge of heat, everything closing in around her. Cutting off her ability to breathe before her muscles clenched tight, holding her captive as she teetered on the brink…

She broke.

Died.

Shattered into a million pieces.

All that heat exploding outwards until she laid there in a numbing haze, her heart thundering in her chest. Her pulse pounding so hard it felt like one long beat.

She came back to her senses as Kash moved over her, thrusting inside as he ate at her mouth. Setting her off again before she'd even recovered.

He didn't stop, pumping his hips, shaking the bed as he slid his hand behind her head — fisted her hair. The firm tug had her crying his name, her fingers digging into his shoulders, her heels notched around the small of his back. He picked up the pace, changing the angle, hitting that spot like he had before.

Dead.

She had to be dead because nothing but heaven could feel this good as her release shot through her, stealing her breath as she clung to him, every nerve firing at once.

Kash gave a few more forceful thrusts before his head tipped back, and he emptied inside her. Hips jerking. The muscles in his neck cording.

He collapsed a second, hour, maybe week later, crushing her into the bed. Sliding everything into place with the warm caress of his breath against her skin. The firm weight of his body on hers.

She shifted just enough she could draw in a bit of air before wrapping her arms around his back. Holding him close.

Kash nuzzled her neck, kissing the curve of her shoulder before rolling enough to look down at her. His hair a tousled mass of brown locks, his skin flushed a healthy pink as he smiled, drawing his finger along her jaw. "Christ."

She smiled, wondering if she'd float away as soon as he moved. "Is that a step up from damn?"

"More than a step. That..." He leaned down — claimed her mouth in a kiss so soft, she couldn't breathe past the lump in her throat. "You okay?"

"Perfect."

"Damn straight. Hang tight for a second."

He rolled off the bed, striding into the bathroom. Water splashed in the background, shutting off a minute later. He returned, a cloth in one hand before he settled on the bed next to her — cleaned away the proof that she'd definitely lost her mind.

He tossed the cloth back toward the bathroom, indifferent when it landed on the tile floor. Then, he trailed his fingers along her hip, smiling when she inhaled. "So, naked or tee?"

The words bounced around in her head, but she'd sworn he'd spoken another language. "What?"

"For sleeping. You strike me as the kind of person who wants the minimum on in case you have to take out a wet squad in the middle of the night."

She blinked. *Sleep? As in together? All night in the same bed?* Which, honestly, she hadn't really thought through — what happened after they'd had sex. Which was another issue because it hadn't been just sex. Not with how her heart pounded. How she already wanted him, again. Like a drug that just kept her coming back for more.

Kash frowned at her silence. "You have slept over at a guy's house before, right?"

This was why she wasn't fit for regular life. Nothing about her past was remotely normal. "Will you freak out if I say, no?"

He coughed, eyes wide as he waved between them. "But this wasn't…"

"Wasn't, what?" She groaned. "The first time I've had sex? I'm thirty-two."

"I realize that, but…"

Great. Now she'd completely embarrassed herself. "Yes, I've had sex. Nothing in the last… It's been a long long time and it's never been…" She huffed. "You're… different. Special, I guess."

She pushed her head back, laying her arm across her eyes. "Do me a favor, and just shoot me, now."

The mattress shifted, then he kissed his way up her ribs, pausing at her breast before gently nudging her arm aside. "I'd say you're special, too, but you're so much more than that."

He held up one of his shirts, helping her slip it on before climbing under the sheets, then motioning her to join him. She settled in next to him, not quite sure whether to roll into him or just stay on her back, when he gathered her in his arms, resting her head on his chest.

Talk about *damn*…

She placed her hand over his heart, counting each strong beat, when the door creaked as Nyx bounded in, leaping onto the bed then jumping over to them.

She licked and yipped, tail swishing as she stood over them, looking as if she was trying to figure out the best way to squeeze between them.

"Nyx—"

"It's fine." Jordan gave the pooch a scratch, smiling when the canine finally circled, then curled up at the foot of the bed. "I assume she usually sleeps with you?"

"She does, but—"

"No buts. Besides, it's kind of nice knowing she's there keeping watch."

"Nothing can get within fifty feet of this place without her knowing. Promise. Which reminds me... Will you do me a favor?"

She glanced up at him.

He looked her in the eyes. "If all those voices in your head get too much and you bolt, take my truck. The keys are in a bowl by the door. I can grab it later at the café. And the alarm code's one, one, seven, three. So, you don't have the rest of my team racing over thinking we're being infiltrated when it sends out a blanket nine-one-one."

"You want me to take your truck if I bolt?"

"The roads are shit, so yeah."

She was so screwed.

"I won't leave. I might have to do a perimeter check." She sighed. "To quiet those voices."

"I can live with that. And take Nyx if you do."

"I'm not a handler let alone hers."

"That's okay. She's very adaptable. And it's not

like it's a mission or anything. She can do a lap around the house without needing me at her side or losing her shit."

"Do you tell that to all the women who've stayed over?"

He just smiled. "Haven't had any besides you, here. Sleep. I've got plans for breakfast."

Jordan relaxed against him, letting the quiet whisper of his breath soothe her to sleep. She'd worry about how to leave in the morning. But for now, she'd bleed out every second of being in Kash's arms because she knew, the moment she let herself believe she had a chance at a future, the past would come for her.

CHAPTER FIVE

You're either with us, or you're dead.

Jordan opened her eyes, Rook's voice lingering in the air. She bolted upright, searching the shadows, planning how she'd dive across the bed — use whatever was on Kash's nightstand as a weapon. Hell, the guy was ex-special forces. He probably had a gun or three shoved into the drawer.

Silence filled the room, nothing but bad memories staring back at her from the darkness. She waited, muscles primed, senses alert, until the uneasiness passed. Nyx lifted her head, tilting it left and right — clearly confused as to why Jordan sat there, ready to pounce.

Jordan glanced at Kash when he stirred, rolling toward her and laying his arm across her waist before drifting back to sleep. She studied his face, noting the way his mouth twitched in his sleep. Or how peaceful he looked cuddled up to her.

Her chest tightened, that lump from earlier nearly choking her, and she found herself slipping out of the bed — heading for the main living area. She snagged the sweats and socks off the floor where Kash had left them in a heap along with his clothes, tugging on everything. He must have had the lights on a timer because the room was dark, just the distant glow from Beckett's place brightening the shadows through the windows.

She walked over to the bookshelves on the far wall, smiling at the collection of photos. Mostly him and his teammates, uniforms caked in dirt. Looking as if they'd faced hell and won. Which, they probably had, based on the various locations. Most she recognized, others... Yeah, she'd been to those kinds of places, too. The ones not easily found on a map. That came with kill orders and a lifetime's worth of ugly memories.

She lifted one near the end, running her finger across the faces. She picked out Foster, Chase and Zain instantly, wondering who the other two men were standing shoulder-to-shoulder with Kash. Grinning like they'd won the lottery. It looked fairly recent, the lines on their faces still the same.

Ghosts, she assumed. Like her.

She placed it back on the shelf then made her way over to the kitchen, grabbing a medium-sized knife from the drawer. She tested out the weight, getting a sense of where she'd have to hold it if she had to toss it at an asset, before making her way back to the door. She'd already donned her boots and jacket when claws clicked across the floor. Nyx stopped a few feet away, gaze focused. Looking up at Jordan, then at the door. Making it clear Jordan wasn't getting outside without the dog tagging along.

Jordan chuckled to herself as she tapped the code into the unit next to the entrance, waiting until it blinked twice before turning the handle and easing the wooden slab open.

Cold, damp air spilled through the doorway as thick clouds covered the sky. It wasn't actively raining, though she knew that could change in a heartbeat. Nyx followed her out, staying close as Jordan closed the door, giving her eyes a few minutes to adjust before moving over to the edge of the house. Tall trees swayed in the wind, the black silhouettes like monoliths against the sky. She scanned the tree line, narrowing in on a dense section over toward one of the other buildings — either Chase's or Zain's homes she assumed — the hairs along her neck prickling.

She waited, staying in the shadows, careful not to let her breath give her away, when an obviously male figure darted between two trees. Large. Fast. Carrying something over his right shoulder. She caught a glimpse of him a few seconds later, creeping along the edge of the brush, stopping every so often to scan the property.

Scope. Handheld. Either night vision or infrared.

Maybe both. Which meant, she'd have to stay out of his sight line.

She smiled at the thought, darting down the side of Kash's place then into the woods beyond. It wasn't as open as she'd hoped, with bramble and ferns crowding most of the available space. She picked a route that wouldn't out her position, then headed for the other side of the yard.

Nyx stayed on her six, sniffing the air whenever the wind kicked up. Jordan waited to see if the dog would react, but Nyx carried on, unfazed by whoever was out there.

Jordan continued until she reached a small break in the foliage. Not quite a clearing, but large enough she'd catch any movement on the other side of the trail. She hunkered down, Nyx shouldering up beside her. Jordan waited, attention centered on the trees beyond that gap, listening for any hint of movement. An owl called in the distance, the odd cricket chirping in the underbrush.

Her internal clock ticked inside her head, warning her that the guy was taking too long to reach the junction. That she needed to double back — rethink her strategy — when a shadow crossed the path.

She jumped up and moved a second later, mimicking the guy's movements — keeping Nyx at her back. The guy picked up speed, leaping over logs and brush, darting through the forest like a damn wood nymph. Completely silent. Even the air seemed to move around him without giving away his presence, the fog seemingly opening up then closing.

She pushed harder, mud splattering up her legs, water from the evergreens soaking through her pants. Nyx kept pace, the wind now blowing from the wrong direction to carry the guy's scent across their path. Jordan just prayed the canine wouldn't take off and attack the guy on sight. Not just because she had no idea how she'd call off the dog, but because she didn't want to show her hand — allow whoever was out there to know she'd made them. If this was one of Rook's scouts, Jordan needed to lure the bastard away before he tried more lethal methods while on Foster's property.

Before she put the only people she'd gotten remotely close to at risk.

The guy kept moving, doubling back — taking her on a freaking tour of the property. She worked hard to keep up, aware that if there had been more of a defined path, he would have pulled ahead.

That got her thinking, examining this from a different perspective. The way he moved. The silhouette. Why Nyx hadn't sprinted ahead.

Jordan pulled up beside a large white pine, holding her position as the wind whistled through the branches. Water dripped somewhere off to her right, a heavy feeling building between her shoulder blades. She glanced at Nyx, noting the way the dog tilted her head, tongue lolling out. She snorted, staring behind them for a few moments before sitting and looking up at Jordan.

Jordan shook her head, turning so she could lean against the trunk. "Did you spot me after I'd started tailing you, or as soon as I stepped out of Kash's place?"

Zain chuckled, moving into the opening off to her left. He had a rifle slung over one shoulder, a vest with a collection of gear strapped around his torso. A laser scope hung around his neck, an obvious holster clipped onto his pants.

He gave Nyx a scratch when the dog trotted over to him, leaning into his legs for a few moments before returning to Jordan's side. "Pretty much as soon as you stepped out. But damn, you're good."

"And you're fast. You would have lost me in a flat out run."

"I hope so. I've got several inches and probably eighty pounds of muscle on you. Though, the way you're carrying that knife, I might not have made it too far. You actually know how to throw those?"

She flipped it a couple times. No sense lying when she'd just put on another show. Given him even more reasons to shift his line of thinking, like he'd said at the table. "It's wise to have options."

"What kind of distance are we talking?"

"About thirty feet. Maybe a bit more if the gods are smiling on me."

Zain whistled. "You that talented with a rifle, too?"

"I can hold my own, but I'm not a sniper." She arched a brow. "Not like you."

"Kash tell you that?"

"He didn't need to." She waved the length of him. "The attention to detail. The situational awareness. You're more focused, more serious than the others. Not overtly, but in the way you carry yourself. You always want to have that coveted position at the table in the café that affords you the best sight lines, and the fact your teammates don't fight you for it means they respect your skill set, especially when it comes to security. Like the setup in Kash's place. Way upscaled for somewhere this far out of town. And Foster has the same one." She took a breath. "That all screams overwatch."

Zain simply nodded.

She motioned to the scope. "Just night vision or IR, too?"

"What do you think?"

"I think you don't do anything half-assed."

He studied her for a moment, doing a quick scan of the area. Muscles still primed. Gaze scrutinizing any place that could hide a target. And Jordan knew he'd be shoving her to the ground if he sensed so much as a hint of danger, despite knowing she was trained. That she could handle herself. Which meant, she'd been right, and Kash's team would rally around her without question if she was strong enough to let them in.

He relaxed slightly, his attention back on her. "So, were you looking for trouble, or leaving it behind?"

"Just needed some air. Then, I saw you dart past, which I'm guessing you planned." She tilted her head. "A test, not unlike the one I gave at dinner. Which seems fair. So, did I pass?"

"Undecided."

Which she assumed was guy speak for it depending on whether she hurt his friend. How she answered his original question.

Jordan pushed off the tree and closed the distance. "If I'd been making a run for it, I wouldn't have let Nyx tag along."

Zain glanced at the dog, then back at her. "She gave me away, didn't she?"

"More that she didn't react."

He nodded, shifting on his feet, a sudden awkwardness slowly bleeding out the available oxygen. He opened his mouth, closed it, then stared at her.

She held up her hands, wondering how to push past him without making the situation worse. "I should get back…"

Zain moved aside, letting her pass before he grunted. "Kash is crazy about you."

She froze, those five words weighing her down until she thought she'd crumble beneath the strain.

He took a step toward her. "Has been for months. I guess it took that plunge in the ocean to finally get him to realize that time is always limited."

She attempted to swallow, coughing when it didn't quite go down right. "Zain…"

"Just hear him out before you run."

She looked at him over her shoulder. "I'm just trying to keep everyone safe."

"What's good being safe if you've got no one to share it with?"

"It's not that simple."

"The hell it isn't." He held up one hand. "I get it. You're got secrets that come with termination orders and wet squads. The kind of shitstorm that levels everything it touches. And when the first inklings of that pressure system arrives at your doorstep, you pack your bags and head for clearer skies. But sooner or later, that rain's gonna catch up. Wouldn't you rather have half a dozen more umbrellas surrounding you to weather it when it does?"

"Of course, I would. But if this storm finds me…" She shivered, trying not to picture the fallout. "The rivers'll run red. And I can't be the reason he…"

She wouldn't say it. Wouldn't put it out into the universe for Rook to pick up on and manifest into reality. The odds were already stacked against her. She couldn't afford to tempt Fate, too.

She thumbed toward Kash's place. "I really should get back."

Zain kicked at the mud, muttering something under his breath as he shook his head. "I'll walk with you."

"That's not necessary."

He simply waved at a slightly nicer trail, then followed behind, moving in beside her once they made it back to the long driveway. He didn't talk, just kept walking, constantly sweeping the area.

Jordan gave him a nudge. "Seriously. I'm fine, and I've got Nyx with me."

Zain brushed it off as if she'd told him she didn't need to breathe. "My mother would crawl out of her grave and haunt my ass if I didn't see you safely back to Kash's. It was one of her rules. Always walk a lady to her door and make sure she goes inside." He smiled. "Even if she *is* lethal."

Jordan smiled. "That's…"

"Weird? Sexist? Tragically old fashioned?"

"Sweet, actually. That your mom loved you enough to impart her wisdom."

His brow furrowed. "That kinda sounds like yours didn't."

She slowed as they neared Kash's door. "My parents only had several years to impart anything. And they were too tweaked out on whatever they were dealing to remember to feed me most days, let alone give me any worldly advice. After the accident…" She shrugged. It seemed so long ago, she often forgot she'd had a life before Scythe and Rook. "Not much changed, actually. There were too many kids with too much baggage for that group home to feel like anything other than a weigh station. So, yeah, I think it was sweet."

She stopped just shy of the covered area

stretching the length of Kash's home. "We're here, safe and sound. Thanks for the tracking lesson. Looks like I need to brush up a bit before our next session."

"Sheesh, you two spend all of ten minutes together, and you're already talking shop." Kash moved out of the shadows, cup in one hand, a travel mug in the other. "It's like you just can't help yourselves."

Jordan jumped. She'd been so focused on Zain, she hadn't noticed Kash lurking in the dark. Which suggested she really was slipping, especially when she should be on high alert.

Zain shrugged. "Occupational hazard."

Kash shook his head. "That's lame, brother." He held out the travel mug. "Figured you'd need a hit before you head off. Assuming you're done with the war games for the night."

"Just because I didn't find any trouble doesn't mean it's not out there, brewing."

"Which implies it's not ready, so you can afford to get a few hours of sleep."

Zain didn't reply just tipped the mug at them then headed off. He crossed the open lawn, disappearing into the building off to their right.

Jordan moved in beside Kash. "First, I don't realize you're actually awake when I slip out of the bed, then I don't see you in the dark. Are you trying to make me question my skill set?"

"Your skill set's fine. I'm simply attempting to prove that you're safer as part of a team than the lone wolf mentality you seem to think is your only option." He nodded at the knife. "I hope that's one of mine because if it's not, I'm not sure I want to know where you were hiding it."

"I got it from the drawer next to the dishwasher. And have you stopped to consider that I'm trying to keep you safe? That I don't want to be the reason you get hurt?"

"I've considered it. I just don't accept it." He waved to the door. "Coffee?"

CHAPTER SIX

Kash waited until Jordan slipped through the doorway before scanning the grounds one last time, checking the tree line twice before shaking off the goosebumps prickling down his spine. He glanced at Nyx. She seemed fixated on a section of the forest at the outer edge of the property — where an old, heavily overgrown two-track met the fence. It wasn't four-by-four worthy without a hefty lift and a couple backup trucks for the eventual tow out, but a dirt bike might be able to eek its way down the winding path.

He gave Nyx a couple more seconds to decide if the area warranted further action, but the dog finally snorted then trotted inside, most of her earlier limp gone.

The alarm chirped as he armed it before making his way to the kitchen. Jordan appeared around the corner dressed only in his over-sized hoodie and a pair of socks, her feet silent against the well-worn wooden floors. She stopped across the island from him, claiming one of the bar stools then sliding him the knife.

He picked it up, testing the weight, wondering if she'd chosen it for tossing or slicing. "Nice choice." He placed it back in the drawer, giving her an arch of his brow. "Anything else hiding beneath the hoodie?"

She grinned. "I might let you find out... after some coffee."

He poured the fresh brew into a mug then slid if over to her, holding up a sugar bowl and some creamer. "I believe you take *three* sugars..."

"Don't judge, just enable."

"And there's salted caramel or hazelnut—"

"You had me with salted caramel."

She added the sugar and creamer, blowing on the top before taking a cautious sip. "God, this should be illegal. Like a deadly sin kind of thing, it's so damn good. Why would you ever buy coffee when you can drink this every day?"

He took a swig of his then leaned in, admiring the flecks of darker blue in her eyes. "To see you."

She smiled at him across the mug, and his damn heart gave a hard thud. He rubbed his chest, wondering if she'd heard it or if he was simply going insane. The only theory that explained the non-stop clench of his stomach, as if he was falling but never hitting the ground. Or the way he wanted to make her a dozen more cups of coffee just to keep that smile on her face. Have her look up at him, all blue-eyes and ruby-red lips, the way she was right now. As if he'd quieted some of those voices in her head.

He gave her a moment to savor the drink, then took a breath — blew it slowly out. "See anything interesting outside?"

She paused, studying him for a few seconds, as if she wasn't quite sure if he was making small talk or suspected there was someone lurking in the shadows. That heavy feeling he'd felt before coming inside.

"Just Zain." She leaned back in the chair, still sipping the coffee. "Damn, the guy's fast. Leaps over brush and logs like a gazelle on steroids. You can barely tell he busted his right knee recently."

"How do you know about his knee?" Kash knew Zain rarely talked about it. Not when it was a result of that fateful mission. All the baggage none of them were ready to unpack. Except maybe Foster. Though, that was all Mac's influence.

Jordan scrunched up her nose. "He hides it well, and it's not nearly as noticeable as when you all first came into the diner, but it's stiff. Anyone who looks hard enough would notice."

Kash chuckled. "I'm not sure anyone looks at people and situations the way you do, sweetheart."

Her lips quirked at the endearment, and he had to mentally force himself not to round the island and take her in his arms. Give her another reason to smile.

She placed the mug on the counter, giving him a

thorough once-over. "Does he always scout the perimeter? Or did I get his sniper-senses going at dinner?"

She knew he was a sniper, too? Which, of course she did. Even Kash agreed Zain didn't hide that side of him all that well. He was too wired — too focused on having their backs to ever truly stand down. And that bled through his warm smile and easy banter.

"It wasn't you. Or at least, not just you."

Kash gave in the urge to circle around to her side, needing just a hint of contact to ease the jumpy feeling in his gut. The one that wanted this to be a foreshadow of the foreseeable future — her, there with him. But he could tell by how she kept fisting one hand then releasing it, she wasn't ready to hear that. For him to show her exactly how far he'd already fallen.

She turned to face him, grinning when he wedged his thighs between hers, her breath catching for a moment before her chest rose a bit quicker. "So, he searches the woods every night?"

"Pretty much. We had some trouble a few months ago, and things got ugly before we finally dealt with it. Between that and our last mission…" Kash sighed. "Despite what he claims — how he tries to smile it away — he's having a hard time letting go."

"You're talking about Jack Voss, better known as Striker. Gun for hire and a giant dick. I'm glad you boys took him off the playing field. The jerk was a nightmare, always tweaked out on something. Tended to shoot anyone who disagreed with him, regardless of which side they were on. I hope they tossed him in a pit and lost the ladder."

Was his mouth hanging open? Drool dribbling down the side? Had he fallen and hit his head because he was pretty damn sure she'd just shared personal information without blinking an eye.

"Okay, you can't say shit like that and complain when I ask you how the hell you know about him and what went down. I know Greer had to release a public statement but... Striker wasn't part of that."

Jordan closed her eyes, looking as if she was counting to ten or searching for some kind of biblical intervention before she grunted then met his gaze. "You really must have blown my mind because I don't make mistakes like that — just let intel spill out. But since I did... All I can say is that I ran across guys like him. Usually in places that didn't produce any witnesses if someone got shot in the street in broad daylight. I wasn't part of that world, and I can assure you, he *never* saw me or knew I existed, but..."

But she'd been exactly what Kash had thought she was. Shadow Ops. Likely part of a military branch that didn't technically exist. Just an innocuous name on a file that went unquestioned.

He nodded, inching closer. "I'm trying really hard not to cross that line — give you a reason to run when I know you already have plenty. But I need you to hear me when I say... It doesn't have to be that way. You. Running. You have options."

He held up his hand when she inhaled, eyes suddenly wide. Her breath held as if she'd forgotten how to breathe. "I know. It's complicated. I just…"

How could he say he needed her to trust him? To give him a chance to pull her back from the fray? Have her six against whatever forces were shadowing her? They'd only scratched the surface of whatever was building between them. What he swore was far more than lust or loneliness. What he saw when Foster looked at Mac. It was crazy, and yet…

He couldn't imagine not having her in his life. That all those hours they'd spent talking over coffee, no matter how benign it had seemed, had been the start of this. Them. Together. And he couldn't go back. Not without losing the part of himself he'd reassembled after that last mission. All the blood and stitches he'd used to move forward. He wasn't sure if he'd truly dealt with that night. The guilt. The loss. But with Jordan… He could give it a try. Learn to make peace with the ghosts. All she had to do was let him in.

Jordan stared up at him, her usual bravado slipping away, leaving a version of her that wasn't looking for all the exit points. Wasn't sizing up the rest of his knives or calculating how many seconds it would take to launch over the counter, grab the coffee pot and cold-cock him in the side of the head with it.

It was honest. Vulnerable. And he had her in his arms, his mouth crushed to hers before he had time to consider the consequences. If she'd toss him on his ass or jump in.

Thankfully, she chose the latter, spearing her fingers through his hair, using the stool to wrap her legs around his waist — lever into his arms. He thought about simply shucking his pants and taking her on the damn counter. But that seemed dangerously close to the kind of encounters he suspected had been her norm. Fast. Hard. With no strings to worry about once it was over.

He'd already screwed up and skated that line by loving her on the ottoman. True, she'd been all-in, but he wanted her to know this wasn't just two people grinding against each other. A means of release. Not that he believed a quick shag on the counter, or against the wall, or in the shower equaled how he felt. But until he knew she believed that too, he'd go the extra mile. Do it right, with soft sheets and her gaze locked on his.

When she had no other option but to feel.

He slid his arms under her ass, grunting when he met only soft skin. Some of that resolve slipping away with the flex of her muscles as she writhed in his embrace, pressing against him as if she wanted to crawl inside.

She broke the kiss, glancing over her shoulder before raising a brow. "Counter's fine."

He clenched his jaw, focusing on something other than the raspy tone of her voice. The image that surfaced from her suggesting what had already been playing inside his head.

He managed a step, then another, meeting her wide eyes as he headed for the bedroom. "Next time because I need..."

You. All of you.

Had he said it? Thought it?

He wasn't sure. Tried not to overthink it if he had let it slip free as he got them to the bed in record time. He eased her onto her feet just long enough to strip them both down before he had her snugged against him, bracing her weight as he took them both back onto the bed. She cupped his face with her hands, holding him suspended above her, watching him as he settled between her legs and slowly inched inside.

This was what he needed.

All those walls she hid behind noticeably absent. Nothing between them but the promise of a future.

He didn't move, just stayed there, fully seated, waiting for a sign that she was ready for more. Her hands shook, a single tear pooling in her eye then slipping down her cheek.

He went to his elbows and kissed away the dampness before taking her lips — softly tasting her mouth. A strangled sob sounded between them, her breath shuddering around him in hurried gasps.

He smiled down at her, nuzzling her nose as he eased back then slid forward, reclaiming every lost inch. She inhaled, her head tilting away as her teeth snagged her bottom lip.

He kissed the slight hurt, thrusting, again. "Eyes on me, sweetheart."

She squeezed them harder together then pried them apart. "Kash..."

"No looking away." He pulled back, paused, then slid forward. "No telling yourself I'm not completely invested." Another retreat followed by another thrust. "That this is just another hit and run." He moved a bit faster this time, biting back the fire burning along his spine. "I don't care who you were, Jordan." One more slow stroke. "But I damn sure want to be part of who you become."

He let go.

Holding her gaze while he upped his pace. Fast, then faster. Harder. Until the bed shook, his body quivering. He wasn't sure how long he could hold out, every nerve on edge, threatening to explode.

Jordan clenched her jaw, her chest heaving against his. Her focus pinned on his face. She slid her fingers up his jaw and into his hair, anchoring them together. Daring him to break the connection.

Not a chance.

Instead, he upped the ante, using one hand to tilt her hips — graze over that one spot...

"Yes!"

The word bounced off the walls as she threw her head back, clawing at his scalp before she stiffened — body strung tight. Clamping around him so hard it was all he could do to keep moving. Take her the rest of the way over. She held her breath, back arched. Her mouth opened in a soundless scream.

Then she ground against him, a deep pink flushing her skin, as she shook in his arms. Eyes closed. His name a prayer on her lips.

That did him in. Sent him over. All but destroyed him as he emptied into her, muscles straining. His skin so hot he was surprised the sheets didn't go up in flames. He closed his eyes, sucking in air, praying he didn't crush her as his strength gave out and he collapsed.

Forever.

That's what this felt like.

Her body wrapped around his. Her breath hot against his damp skin. And he swore he'd do whatever it took to get her to see them the same way.

Kash wasn't sure how long he'd been lying there, his head next to hers — completely spent — before he regained enough of his senses to think beyond dragging air in then pushing it out. He shifted, cursed, hoping he hadn't actually crushed her when her fingertips dug into his shoulders, urging him back down.

She kissed his jaw, holding his gaze when he managed to focus enough to look her in the eyes. "Don't go. Not, yet. I…"

He smiled, settling over her with just enough of his weight braced on his elbows she could breathe without it being some kind of Olympic event. "I'm not going anywhere. So, close your eyes. I'll clean us both up once I can feel my feet. And I promise I'll hold you the rest of the night. Okay?"

A few more tears slipped free as she nodded, closing her eyes as he dipped down for a soft kiss. He rested his forehead on hers, listening to her breathe. Lingering in the moment. He wasn't sure what they'd be in the morning, but he'd give this everything he had.

It took a while before either of them seemed willing to move. Jordan huffed, looking like she really would dump him on his ass before he coaxed her with a kiss. She wrapped her arms around his neck, resting her head on his shoulder as he carried her across the room to the ensuite. He didn't rush, running the soap over every inch of skin, doing his best to map out all her scars.

The fact there were too many to keep track of cleared some of the residual haze. Had him wondering if she'd gotten them all during her missions or if some were the result of a questionable childhood. The snippets of her past he'd heard her tell Zain.

None of it had sat well with him, but Kash got the sense that her real story began after her parents had either died or been labeled unfit. That group home she'd landed in once the courts had shuffled her into the system.

To her credit, she didn't seem fazed by the way his fingers danced across her skin, following each line or puckered indentation. What were obvious knife and bullet wounds. She simply watched him as if she was trying to puzzle him out.

He managed to get them both clean without running out of warm water, then took her back and helped her into his shirt. He raised his arm, and she burrowed against him, drifting off a second later. Like someone had thrown a switch.

He relaxed, listening to her snuffle, smiling when Nyx jumped onto the bed and reclaimed her spot. At least, she'd waited until he and Jordan were done before joining them. Though, he got the feeling Jordan would have laughed it off if Nyx had interrupted them. Important, since he was hoping they'd all be eventually sharing the same space.

He closed his eyes, pulling her closer, fading into that blissful haze, when someone knocked on his door. Loud. Insistent. He blinked against the wash of gray filtering through the window as Jordan bolted up beside him, reaching under the pillow before grunting.

"Damn."

Her voice sounded low. Gravelly.

He pushed onto his elbows, arching a brow. "Really? You keep a weapon under the pillow?"

Jordan huffed. "The real question is, why don't you?"

"There's a Sig in the nightstand if that'll make you feel better, but I don't think we'll need it. It's obviously one of the guys or Nyx would be losing her shit."

He tossed off the covers and swung his legs over the edge, stumbling to his feet. Everything ached, though that probably had more to do with falling off the cliff than making love to Jordan half the night.

Jordan tossed a pillow at his head, hitching out one hip. "Are you going to answer the door with that caveman grin on your face? Because I'll definitely grab the Sig if that's the case."

"Shouldn't you be more insulted if I wasn't this happy?"

"There's happy, and then there's you smiling like some nerdy teenager who's just lost his virginity to the prom queen in the back of a flatbed."

"Personal experience?"

"Do you think I was ever a prom queen?"

"Damn it, Kash, I know you're awake." Zain's voice echoed through the converted barn.

Kash blew out a rough breath. "I swear, one day…" He pointed to the closet. "There're more sweats in there. Take whatever works. We'll grab your clothes after I strangle my brother."

Kash walked over to the doorway, pausing to watch Jordan shuffle across the floor, his shirt hugging the bottom of her ass. The woman was just too sexy for his well-being.

He turned, then headed for the front room, drawing in a deep breath before opening the door.

"Someone better be in jail or dying. And if it's the first, they can wait."

Zain huffed, crossing his arms over his chest. "It's damn near eight. Since when do you sleep past six?"

"Since I had a damn good reason to stay in bed. What couldn't wait?"

Zain looked past him, and Kash turned, inhaling as Jordan walked toward them, hips swaying. Her long brown hair pulled up into a ponytail, the ends swishing over her shoulders as she moved. And it wasn't hard to see the operative in her. Imagine her taking out a bar full of tangos with whatever was handy on the tables.

Zain slapped him in the chest. "You might want to close your mouth before Jordan slaps that stupid look off your face."

Kash glared at his buddy. "Why are you here?"

The hint of humor faded as he glanced at Jordan when she stopped next to Kash, then over to him. "Someone vandalized your truck."

"They did what, now?"

Zain leaned against the doorframe. "All four tires. Slashed."

Jordan scoffed. "We went by Kash's Chevy at four."

"I know. Which means they were either waiting for us to go inside or planned to strike just before dawn. Neither scenario sits well with me."

"Crap."

"I agree." Zain gave Kash a pointed look. "And you say I'm paranoid."

"Because you are." Kash pulled back — took a calming breath.

"Obviously, not quite enough, or I would have been standing behind the asshole when he tried to cut that first tire."

"Zain. I get that it was your job to protect us. That you spent ten years watching our every move through a scope from a nest a mile away. Keeping our path clear. Holding the line until everyone else was safe. Then another ten, running point — identifying any threat before it bit us in the ass. That it's hardwired into your damn DNA. But you can't work all day, then run maneuvers at night. Like it or not, buddy, even you need to sleep."

"Tell that to the guy who breached our perimeter."

Kash sighed. Arguing with Zain about security was like trying to get Foster to fly without his hair on fire. "You've got cameras everywhere. Have you checked the feed?"

Zain merely stared at him.

Kash scrubbed a hand down his face. He was way too tired for this shit, and he'd already lost his chance at impressing Jordan with breakfast in bed, followed by what he'd hoped would be one hell of a good morning. "Of course, you have. And?"

"I'm downloading all the footage to the tablet in Foster's kitchen. We should head over."

Kash snagged his arm. "Look. If you really think we need more security, we can hire the guys Bodie has helping him out with his security company while he's backing up Greer. Have them do a few rounds every night."

"There's no way in hell I'm letting anyone else handle yours, Foster's or Chase's security."

"They're not anyone. They're former military."

"Yeah, well Stein and Adams were part of our damn crew for six months — were apparently the best agents the fucking CIA had crapped out of the Farm in the last ten years — and look what trusting them got us. Sean in a pine box, and Rhett..." Zain swallowed, looking as if he might puke it back up. "We all know where that's heading. His brain just hasn't caught up with that fact, yet. So, sue me if I take all this a bit personally."

He turned, took a few steps toward the door, then stopped. "Don't take too long, or I'll send Chase over."

Kash leaned against the wall as Jordan grabbed her boots and slipped them on, accepting the vest he handed her. "Hey. Are you okay?"

She stopped short of tugging up the zipper. "Fine."

"Jordan..."

She closed the distance, drawing one finger across his chest. "Not exactly how I pictured the morning playing out, but..."

"Me, either. I'd planned on making you breakfast

in bed. Coming up with some creative uses for the can of whipped cream I have in the fridge."

Her breath caught, her pupils dilating before she leaned in — kissed him.

It was deep, and hungry, and he half wanted to hike her up on his shoulder and carry her back to bed. Let his buddies deal with his truck and the footage. But there was something in the way she brushed her thumb over his mouth once she'd eased back — that same look from the café when she'd agreed to have dinner with him — that got those voices chattering in his head. His protective instincts on alert.

She stepped back, looking everywhere but at him. "We should go." She turned and headed out the door, glancing at him over her shoulder. "And in case you hadn't figured it out already, last night was…" She closed her eyes for a moment. "Unforgettable. Just like you."

CHAPTER SEVEN

This was a mess.

She was a mess.

All because she'd allowed herself to have a glimmer of hope — believe, even for just a second, that maybe she could have a future with Kash. That, with his team backing her up, she could access the intel, topple Scythe and Rook, and somehow walk away unscathed.

Four slashed tires.

Coincidence? Some vendetta against Kash? Rook toying with her, just to make her sweat? To draw out the inevitable ending. Shred the last bits of her soul that she'd salvaged when she'd limped out of that compound.

Kash caught up to her, slipping his hand over hers. He didn't ask her any uncomfortable questions, just gave her hand a squeeze as they stopped at the back door. "You good?"

She tiptoed up — kissed him. Not long and hot and deep like she wanted. Like back at the house. What might have been her last chance to fully taste his mouth. This was soft. More of a brush of her lips across his. And it hit her just as hard. Had her stomach clenching, her head spinning. She thought about trying, again, when Nyx nudged them, tail wagging. Tongue hanging out.

Kash sighed, tsking at Nyx. "Traitor. You just want in because you know they probably have bacon."

Kash opened the door, letting Nyx dart inside. He took Jordan's hand — looked her dead in the eyes. "If this turns out to be your brand of trouble, promise me you'll talk to me before you take off."

Her throat closed, her chest tightening. "Let's hope it's not."

It wasn't the answer he'd obviously been hoping for, but it was the best she could give him without lying to his face. After everything they'd shared — the way he'd held her as if she might fly apart — she couldn't do that to him. Maybe if they'd only had that one round on the ottoman — what was closer to her usual hit and run — she could have smiled and rattled off an easy *yes*. But when she'd told him she was fine with a quickie on the counter, and he'd insisted on taking her to bed. Holding her close. Watching her reaction as he moved inside her, daring her to deny that somewhere between him waltzing into the café and her dumping Tucker on his ass, she'd fallen for him. Broken the ultimate rule. That killed any chance she had of making this a clean getaway.

Foster cut off mid-sentence, smiling at Kash as they walked into the kitchen. "I was just about to send Chase over to bust down the door. Coffee?" He grabbed two mugs off the counter, handing them over. "Not as good as Kash's, but it's hot, and you two look like you could use the kick."

Jordan held the mug between her hands, taking in the gathering of people. "Does anyone need to get any ribbing or chest pounding out of the way before we go over the footage? Maybe exchange some cash for whoever won this pool?"

Chase laughed. "I did, and we've already settled, but thanks. Though, we all know you were really just worried about Nyx."

She smiled. At least his buddies weren't overly concerned, yet. Weren't slipping on tactical vests or nailing plywood over the windows. Bracing for the storm she might have brought to their doorstep. Instead, they just waved her and Kash over.

Zain ran his fingers through his hair, looking less than impressed. "The footage isn't great, but judge for yourself."

He hit the button, and the screen popped on, the driveway flickering to life in eerie shades of gray. Kash's truck loomed in the distance, just visible amidst the thick fog. Nothing happened for the first few minutes, the truck fading in and out as the mist rolled across the ground.

There.

Back end.

Creeping up the side. A figure. More mist than man. A shoulder, then a leg. Crouching down. She caught a flash of something hanging down his neck for the split second his head took shape, a few square items protruding from his chest area, then it was gone. Nothing but the grainy feed showing the truck slowly sinking a bit as the air bled out.

Kash scrubbed his hand down his face. "That's it?"

Zain fisted one hand but didn't slam it down. "I've been more worried about people infiltrating the house than taking a shot at one of our trucks."

"No argument there, brother." Kash gave her a quick side-eye, and she knew he'd noticed it, too. "Can you zoom in on the guy when his head's somewhat visible?"

Zain sighed. "Already have, though I'm glad you spotted it, too."

Damn. That meant it had been a comms unit.

Who needed to coordinate with a team to slash some tires?

Foster crossed his arms. "We were thinking the same thing."

Jordan stilled. Had she spoken that thought out loud? She glanced around at Kash's buddies, groaning inwardly. And she'd thought she was off her game last night.

Foster leaned against the counter. "You look a little pale, Jordan. Everything okay?"

She swallowed, impressed when she didn't puke. "I need to change."

Mac scooped her clothes from yesterday off a nearby chair, then handed them over, leaving her set of keys still lying on the surface. "There's a bathroom just down the hall."

"Thanks." Jordan left the keys as she headed for the bathroom, stopping when Kash hooked her elbow. "I just need a few minutes, okay?"

He held firm, studying her face — probably looking for any sign she was lying to him — before nodding. He released his grip, his gaze following her as she walked down the hall then slipped into the washroom.

The lock clicked over, though it wouldn't keep anyone out for more than a few seconds. The amount of time she'd give herself to grieve the loss before she boxed it away. Did her best to bury Jordan with it — bring Ember back to life.

While she hadn't recognized the silhouette, it screamed Rook. The kind of guy he would send to mess with her head. A warning, she supposed, of how far he'd take it if she didn't surrender.

That he'd kill Kash and his teammates without a moment's pause. That's why the creep had slashed all the tires. It represented Kash's team. That they'd all pay the price if Rook found her there.

And despite how much she wanted to stay — to ask them for help — she knew she'd never survive if she got them killed. That the part of her she'd kept hidden — that she'd given to Kash — would die with them.

After a couple sobbing breaths, she changed in record time. Pushed down all the thoughts of Kash and the future until they were nothing more than a hint of a suggestion. Something she could examine later — agonize over.

He'd be pissed. She knew it.

But at least he'd be alive.

While that might not be enough for him, it meant the world to her.

It took a full minute to bypass the window alarm and slip out — drop to the ground a few feet below. She hit two since she'd locked the door behind her as she reached the corner of the house. What she figured was their limit for how long it took to change — maybe splash some cold water on her face.

A quick sweep, then she raced toward her bike, all the while avoiding any direct sight lines from the windows. She popped the spare key out from under the cowling, then straddled the bike.

The front door opened. Kash and his buddies busting ass across the porch and down the path. She kicked the pedal, giving the motor some gas. It sputtered, then caught, revving loudly as she spun the rear tire then peeled out, shooting mud out the back. Her name sounded behind her, but she knew, if she so much as glanced over her shoulder, she'd stop. Cave to Kash's way of thinking. And as much as she wanted his help, she knew exactly how it would end.

* * *

"Jordan!"

Kash slid to a halt, mud splashing across the bottom of his jeans as the bike's taillight vanished around the far bend — where the driveway met the main road. He doubted she'd stay on the old highway for long. Not if she suspected someone was shadowing her.

Nyx gave chase, flying down the gravel road, ears straight back. Looking like a damn missile shooting across the ground. He whistled her back, aware there wasn't a chance of her keeping up. And he couldn't risk her getting hurt. Not when he suspected this was far from over.

He should have reacted faster. He knew Jordan would try to run. But he'd thought it would take more than two minutes for her to bypass Zain's system and make it out to her bike. Especially with her keys still sitting on the counter from when she'd given them to Foster the night before.

She'd done that on purpose. A red herring of sorts. Knowing he'd assume he could catch up before she'd had enough time to hotwire the bike.

And he'd bought it.

Chase came racing across the path, cell in hand. He stopped next to them, shaking his head as he gazed at where Jordan had disappeared. "You're not gonna like this. Greer just called. Seems someone broke into the sheriff's station last night. Made it look like a routine smash and grab. But when she checked, the only thing missing was her report from the café." Chase stared directly at Kash. "Including all of Jordan's info."

Kash's stomach clenched. "Do we honestly think Jordan gave Greer her real address?"

Chase paled. "Greer already knew from when Jordan took down those bikers who'd tried to steal that purse. Maybe Jordan thought lying about it would only make her look more suspicious. If she's half as good at reading people as we think she is, she's pegged Greer as an ex-federal agent. Regardless, Jordan's renting some old prospector cabin several miles from here. Completely isolated."

"So, whoever took that report…"

"Knows where she lives. I bet my ass she's heading there now to grab whatever she can't leave behind before she vanishes."

Kash stared up the driveway. "Not on my watch."

Zain clapped him on the back. "I'll drive. Chase, send us the address."

Kash headed to Zain's truck, letting Nyx jump in the back of the cab before sliding in the front. His cell pinged, Jordan's address flashing across the screen.

Zain took a look, then roared out, mud spraying across the road as he hit the corner, barely slowed, then turned right and picked up speed. The truck rocked down the highway, everything passing in a gray blur.

Zain looked over after a minute or two, hitting Kash in the arm before focusing on the road. "Tell me everything you know about her."

Kash grunted, resisting the urge to punch his fist through the dash. "Anything I know that you don't, isn't something I'm going to share."

"Not about her that way, dumbass. The woman's rock solid. But she lets her guard down around you. I'd be surprised if she hasn't let something slip after…"

"She said she knew Striker — had come across him and others like him in the field. That whoever was hunting her wasn't like any other threat we'd faced. That it wouldn't end well."

"In other words, nothing we didn't already suspect."

Kash let his head fall back against the seat rest. "I knew she'd run."

"We all knew she was going to run, buddy."

"This was different. The way she kissed me before we joined everyone." He gave Zain a quick glance. "It was goodbye."

Zain sighed. "This isn't about you, Kash."

"Really? Because it feels pretty damn personal. She knows we'd have her back." He tapped his chest.

"That *I'd* have her back. No questions. No hesitation. Obviously, that didn't matter."

"She ran because she doesn't want to have your blood on her hands. Because she's afraid that whoever that asshole was who slashed your tires is part of whatever Shadow Ops agency is gunning for her." Zain snorted. "Yeah, you were right. Don't gloat. And honestly, I can't blame her."

Zain glared when Kash gave him a swat. "I didn't say I agreed, jackass. But she's obviously never had anyone stand up for her before. Never had anyone care. Her little trip down memory lane last night is proof of that. And that's a hard habit to break, brother."

Zain pulled over at the end of a long, winding gravel driveway, switching maps — getting an aerial view. "Looks like there's a building about three hundred meters down. Nothing else showing for a good mile in any direction."

"I'll hoof it in from here." Kash slipped out. "Do me a favor and keep Nyx with you."

The dog whined, jumping into the front seat.

"I know you want to come along, but the three of us won't fit on the bike." He gave her a scratch. "Besides, I need to know at least one of my girls is safe."

Zain chuckled. "Does Jordan know about your possessive side?"

"Shut up."

"I'll wait until you confirm you haven't missed

her. Then, we're all heading into town — see if Bodie can source some intel." Zain thumbed toward the flatbed. "Take my vest and whatever else you think you'll need. In fact, take it all. And assume her place is rigged, and there's a fucking wet squad waiting in the living room."

"So, basically the same as dropping by your place unannounced."

Zain rolled his eyes as Kash headed to the back, grabbing enough supplies he could counter some serious resistance, then returned to the passenger door.

He slipped a wireless headset over one ear then started down the driveway. He kept to the edge, veering into the woods once he was clear of the main road. The thick underbrush clawed at his pants, but he managed to battle his way around the perimeter before stopping at the rear entrance.

An eerie silence settled over the cabin, even the birds oddly quiet. Kash inched closer. Nothing. No movement from inside. No tracks leading in or out of either door. No tire marks carved into the mud.

She could have parked the bike and hiked in. Maybe used a window.

A hum.

Barely there. More of a vibration than an actual sound. Drifting on the wind before cutting out. A couple birds took flight off to his left, squawking as they headed north. He waited, crouched behind some bushes, ready to dive out shooting if a bunch of tactical assholes showed up, guns blazing. A hushed rustle of evergreen branches, then Jordan slinked out of the forest, pausing, scanning the cabin, then moving another foot. She searched the mud, just like he'd done, crouching to trace some sort of outline before making her way to the rear steps.

She checked the doorframe. He wasn't sure if she'd coated the top with powder or left a sliver of paper in the jam, but she seemed willing to risk entering. She cracked the door open. Stopped. Ran her fingers along the edges — probably checking for wires. Another three-sixty scan of her surroundings, then she disappeared inside.

Kash fired off a text to Zain, giving Jordan a minute to recheck the area from the windows then crept out. Staying low. Carefully placing each footfall to avoid making even a hint of noise. He pressed his back against the side of the house, listening at the door.

Still nothing.

He grabbed the handle. Turned.

She was on him the second he slipped through. Kick to the ribs. Another to the shoulder. He dodged the elbow to his head, blocking her next two strikes before she was up on his shoulders. Spinning like a damn top. Taking them both to the floor as she shifted her weight — knocked him off balance. He hit hard, pain scattering dots across his vision as she rolled off — scrambled to her feet.

He managed to snag her leg — tumble her onto

her back before he straddled her hips. Blocking more of those strikes — the way she tried to thrust him up and over her left side — as he wrestled both her hands into one of his. Pinned them above her head as he loomed in close. She looked ready to head butt him, when their gazes locked.

She froze. "Kash?"

He didn't let up, putting more of his weight on her as he dipped in low, his mouth a breath away from hers. "We need to talk."

CHAPTER EIGHT

Shit, shit, shit.

This couldn't be happening.

He couldn't be here.

Jordan stared up at Kash, chest heaving. Every nerve strung tight. He didn't budge, holding her captive, staring at her as if he wasn't sure if he wanted to lean down and kiss her or help her up and tear her a new one.

She swallowed, coughing as it struggled past the lump in her throat. The one still mourning his loss. He released a weary breath then shifted, gaining his feet then offering her his hand. She practically flew off the floor, hitting his chest before he grabbed her shoulders — steadied her.

She glanced around the room, expecting some of Rook's men to crash through the walls, but it was just the two of them. Standing there. Each waiting for the other to break the oppressive silence.

Her training caught up with her, and she gave Kash a shove. "What the hell are you doing here? Were you followed? How do you even know where I live?"

Kash grabbed her shoulders, again, checking the room before looming in close. "What do you think I'm doing? Stopping you from going off half-cocked on some suicide mission, because God forbid, you let anyone help you."

"What if the place had been rigged? Or there'd been some of Rook's men waiting in the damn living room? What if I'd shot you, myself, before I realized it was you?"

"Not my first rodeo, sweetheart. I've actually entered enemy strongholds before, though you seem to keep ignoring my twenty years in the service." He leaned in impossibly closer. "Ten of those as a Ranger. And you're far too savvy *not* to recognize me."

"I haven't ignored them. You and your teammates impress the hell out of me. But this isn't the kind of battle you're accustomed to."

"You don't know that."

"Yeah, I do. Because I've spent my entire adult life running Rook's missions. Paying the price of his disappointment. There were no pats on the back. No jobs well done. You either succeeded or had the failure 'trained' out of you. This isn't the brotherhood you have." She tamped down the roil of her stomach. "It's a tactical cult. And those who don't believe…"

She did her best to distance herself. "That's why I

left you behind. So you didn't end up stuffed into a black bag with nothing more than a damn toe tag to show for all that honor."

"Don't you think I should get a say in what I think is worth dying for?"

"Not this time. I can't..."

She took a step back. She'd left him once. She wouldn't be able to leave him again if he stayed that close. Kept looking at her as if she'd already hurt him. "Go. Please. While there's still a chance I can redirect his focus."

"Not until we talk."

"Christ. You just don't know when to cut your losses." She turned, scouring the room. "Talking will have to wait until I check the cabin."

Kash scoffed, looking too sexy standing there with a tactical vest accentuating his wide shoulders and narrow waist. "Pretty sure if there was a tango hiding in your shower, he would have come out while we were rolling around on the floor." He arched a brow. "Is that how you approach every fight?"

She gave him a quick glance, carefully picking her way around the room. "I'm not built like a tank. My only real advantage is agility. I get in close and keep them off-balance. And I'm not looking for *tangos*."

"You have way more advantages than that." He moved in behind her, shadowing her every move while guarding her six. "Fine, I'll ask. What *are* you looking for?"

"Proof he's been here."

"So, you did recognize the guy on the video."

"No. I saw what you did, but..." She stopped searching for a moment. "As I see it, there're only two possibilities. Either your team didn't round up all of Striker's men, and they're messing with you, or I'm burned. It'd be nice to know which way it's leaning."

"But, either way, you're gone."

"Kash..." Jordan drew in a shuddering breath before pushing it out. "Are you going to help or just stand there, growling."

"I'm not growling." He crossed his arms over his chest. "What should I look for?"

"Nothing overt. It'll be behind a photo or inside a drawer. A message. But check everything before you open it." She motioned to the back of the room. "I'll take the bedroom. You take the bathroom."

"So, you can ditch me, again?"

Jordan stopped — faced him. "I didn't leave because I don't care. I left because I do. Because I wanted to save you. So, I wouldn't put your brothers at risk. But now that you're here, I'd never leave you behind."

"Are you sure about that?"

"Pretty damn sure I wouldn't abandon the man I—"

She caught herself, but it didn't matter. The way he inhaled, his eyes widening, he'd known what she was going to say.

She pushed out a rough breath. "I'm giving you my trust, Kash. You should know what that means."

She turned, making her way into the bedroom. Ignoring the heavy weight of Kash's stare until she'd moved out of his sight line. The floorboards creaked in the bathroom. Proof he was searching the other room.

She focused on the small space — what seemed so sterile compared to Kash's. Nothing appeared out of place. The pillows, the sheets — exactly the way she'd left them. Even the socks she'd tossed on the floor hadn't moved. Of course, Rook wouldn't send anyone to mess with her who wasn't capable of the task. Assuming he hadn't ventured inside, himself.

I'll come for you myself.

His words played in her head as she combed through every book, every drawer, every possible spot he could have left a warning. She was in the process of slowly inching up the mattress when Kash appeared at the doorway.

"Jordan. You need to see this."

Her stomach fell. The pinched lips, the narrowed eyes. He didn't like whatever he'd found.

She drew herself up then walked over to him, following him into the bathroom. He went over to a small mirror on the edge of the counter, then flipped it, stepping back so she could read the word on the frame.

Ember.

Nothing earth shattering or covert. Just her code name printed in bright red. Not lipstick unless Rook had brought some. Blood maybe. Likely hers, from one of the bags the Scythe doctors had bagged for emergencies.

She let the truth sink in, then grabbed Kash's arm. "I'm burned."

She darted into the bedroom, prying up a board in the closet, then removing a small metallic box. She put her thumb on the print reader, tapped in her code then waited for the voice prompt.

"Access authority Archer five seven two six."

It popped open, and she palmed the decryption drive as Kash stood inside the doorway.

"What's Ember?"

"It's not a what, it's a who."

"And?" He scoffed when she didn't answer. "You? Your code name's Ember?"

"We can talk about this later?"

"What's on the drive?"

She froze, then held it up. "A decryption algorithm that opens the kind of intel people kill for."

"Is that why they're after you?"

"Mostly. And it's definitely the reason I chanced coming back here." She held it between her thumb and forefinger, then offered it to him. "You should hold onto it. Just in case."

He stared at her hand, then slowly reached up and grabbed the drive. He didn't say anything, but he got the message. She was entrusting him with the one item she needed to have any chance at a life. "I'll call my team. Get them to meet—"

"Not here. For all we know, Rook's got a damn

parabolic mic outside. Or a predator drone overhead. Maybe a satellite feed zeroed in on this cabin. We take the bike, get as far away as possible, and if we're still breathing, we'll go from there."

"Jordan..."

He jerked his head around, shoved her against the far wall then grabbed the door — slammed it against the asshole trying to creep through. The guy bounced off the frame, giving Kash another chance to coldcock him with the door before he hit the ground. A few kicks and a hard cross, and he was down.

That had Jordan racing out of the bedroom — heading for the main door. Two men dressed in black tactical gear busted through while she was a few feet back, AR-15s notched in their shoulders. She shifted her next stride, kicked off the wall then caught the guy on the right with a massive left hook, the force from the leap spinning him into the wall. A twist and a jump, and she was on the other guy's shoulders, just like she'd done with Kash.

Two hard claps to his ears and a tilt, and they hit the ground, all her weight crashing the back of his head into the floor. An elbow and a strike with the butt of his rifle, and he stilled.

Kash had the other guy in some kind of choke hold, waiting until he went limp before grabbing her by the hand and pulling her to her feet. He picked up one of their rifles, offering it to her, but she shook her head.

"We can't risk it. He'll have trackers on everything."

"Seriously?" He cleared the door, nodding toward the brush. "You lead."

She took off, sprinting across the yard then onto the narrow trail winding through the trees. Shouts rose from the forest, bullets cutting through the walls of the cabin behind them. She veered right at the next junction, bounding over a few downed logs as the dirt bike appeared in the next clearing.

Kash swept the area, boots pounding up that same trail. Twigs snapped somewhere off to their right, branches and brush shaking against the weight of something. She opened one of the panels on the rear cowling — retrieved twin Berettas and a few mags.

He caught the key she tossed, straddled the bike, then kicked it on before looking back at her. "Are you gonna be able to hold on?"

She settled in behind him. "You just drive this baby like you stole it and let me worry about the rest."

* * *

Kash tugged Jordan in closer, rolled on the throttle then leapt ahead. Tires spinning. Engine growling. The bike bounced up the trail, cutting through the mud and brush. Bare branches whipped against their shoulders, threatening to drag them off as he followed the path through the forest.

Jordan held on, the grips of the twin guns pressing against his ribs. He wasn't sure what she thought they'd be facing. Nothing good, he supposed. Like the men who'd just infiltrated the cabin. Only they'd be in trucks or on bikes like theirs.

He hit a slightly larger track and opened the throttle, mentally mapping out where they were going. Their best bet was to double back and head into town — rendezvous with his team. Find a place to hunker down until Jordan came clean, and they could make a plan.

Branches cracked behind them, a few smaller trees crashing over as a couple SUVs swerved onto the trail, engines roaring. The massive machines eating up the distance. A guy leaned out of the closest one — took a few shots.

Kash bore left, turning onto what was little more than a goat path, ferns covering most of the ground. They bumped over a few rocks, ducking beneath an overhanging branch then shot onto a gravel road.

He picked up speed, two bikes joining the chase a minute later. Weaving through the underbrush then skidding onto the road behind them. Pushing them farther from town. He wasn't sure exactly where the road ended, but he had a pretty good idea they'd eventually hit the ocean. Probably pop out near that abandoned air strip.

Which meant, they needed backup.

"Call, Beck."

The unit in his ear hummed, Foster's cell ringing shortly after.

"Kash? This can't be good."

"We've got serious resistance on our asses. Heading southwest. We're gonna need air support and some overwatch." He took the next right fork, bullets eating up the mud off to their left — Jordan countering with a few trigger pulls whenever she got a chance. The engine noise faded behind them, the other cycles seemingly vanishing.

"Was that gunfire?"

Kash sighed. "You should be able to follow us through our shared location. It's gonna be close because I have a bad feeling we're gonna run out of real estate pretty quickly."

Foster breathed into the phone. "Mac. Call Atticus. Get him to push out the other chopper. We're on our way. Keep moving and don't fucking die on me."

Foster ended the call, the accompanying silence like a deadly premonition. Kash kept up the speed, still mapping it out in his head when those bikes shot out of another path in front, spinning toward them.

He hit the brakes, standing the machine up on its front wheel. Holding it all together as the bike roared to a halt, rear tire spinning. Smoke pouring out from the wheels. He kicked the back end to the right, hit the throttle as they bounced down, and tore off through the mud.

·

Jordan hung on, tapping his shoulder, pointing left as they popped out onto another road. He fishtailed it over, one of the SUVs barreling up behind them. A burst of gunfire echoed through the forest, mud spraying up from the impact.

That got Jordan moving. Swinging her leg over his hip — sliding in front of him. Her cheek next to his, her ass hugging the tank. She lifted both arms — put down more cover fire. Casings shot out the sides, the reports ringing through the trees. She dropped the spent mags, popped in some new ones then fired again. Finally doing enough damage the lead vehicle swerved off the road — bumping out of sight down an incline.

The other roared ahead, an identical creep leaning out the window. She pocketed the guns and grabbed the frag off his vest — the one he'd hoped was overkill — pulling the pin then tossing it before swinging back behind him a moment before it exploded.

It either took out a tree or the vehicle, the resulting crash sounding behind them. Kash veered down the next ghost of a trail off to the left, soaring over a log, then following the winding path as it paralleled the river. The water rushed past, nearly cresting the banks from all the rain — carrying branches and other debris downstream. Those bikes jumped into view on their six, bobbing and weaving through the brush.

The trail opened up in front, looking like more of

a proper road until a massive Hummer roared to a halt, blocking out the light.

No time to think. Kash just popped the front tire up and over a large rock, then took off along a downed tree hanging above the river. He wove the handlebars through the stabbing branches, tires slipping on the wet bark as a few stubby knots nearly sent them over the side.

A spray of bullets shot up chunks of wood, a couple hitting the rear cowling — taking it dangerously close to the edge before Kash manhandled it back. The entire tree rocked, a rough vibration rumbling up through the tires. Jordan wrapped her right arm higher on his chest then twisted. Three pops followed by one of those bikes revving louder for a few moments before water splashed off the right side. All the other noises cutting out.

They made it to the other side without dying, crashing their own path through a short section of mostly trees until they found a rough road. He headed right, then left, bouncing down an offshoot. A loud growl echoed behind them, blending in with the crunching gravel.

Hummer.

Had to be.

All the more reason to keep off the main tracks.

Until the bike sputtered, a couple gauges edging into the red. Smoke poured out from beneath the cowling, the entire machine finally chugging out its last breath.

"Damn it." Kash kicked out the stand, bending to give it a quick once-over. "A few rounds punched right through. The engine's toast."

Jordan didn't question his assessment, just grabbed his hand and took off running. One arm pumping. Feet flying over the ground. Only to stop when they broke out onto the side of a gully, a twenty-foot gap stretching between them and the other side.

Kash looked over the edge, shaking his head. "Climbing down isn't an option. There's probably a bridge along that road—"

Tires, splashing through mud, racing up the road, all the gravel and snapping branches cutting Kash off.

He stared at the gap, then back to Jordan. "Now that I look at it, it's not so bad. A running start and—"

"Are you insane? It's a good twenty feet. I've never jumped that far."

"Then, it's time for a personal best." He grabbed her shoulders. "You can do this. You just sprint, then jump. Let gravity help you out a bit. It's going to be fine."

"Kash..." She stared at the gap. At the smooth face and rocky bottom. "Fine. You go first."

"Oh, no..."

The Hummer's engine revved louder. Not that it could get all the way to the edge, but close enough.

Jordan fisted his vest. "I'm not going to ditch you. Or sacrifice myself. But I need you on the other side to pull some kind of ninth-inning-world-series-catch out of your ass if I don't quite make it."

"Jordan..."

"I promise. I'll be right behind you."

"You'd better."

A quick kiss and a curse, then he backed up. Focused on the edge. He took a breath, then ran. Arms pumping. Knees tucking in high as he threw himself off, soaring across the gap and rolling across the ground on the other side. Nearly impaling himself on a series of branches. His vest countered the worst of the impact, and he staggered to his feet, waving Jordan over.

She bit her lip, the Hummer's grill appearing at the other end of the trail. She looked back, then ran. No more second thoughts. No hesitation. She hit the edge going insanely fast, throwing her arms out just like Kash had done.

Whether it was that voice in his head or the look on her face he wasn't sure, but he grabbed a root and all but jumped off the ledge — looking like a damn starfish as he braced a boot on the side, stretched out his arm. Yanking on that root to get a bit more distance.

Her hand landed on his shoulder, sliding down his arm until he managed to lock his fingers around her wrist — stop her from falling the forty feet to the bottom. The force nearly ripped his hand free, Jordan swinging into the rock face below him. Grunting as she hit hard.

Her grip eased a bit, but Kash held on. Between him curling and her scrambling, he got her ass up and over the edge. She reached out — helped pull him up a second later. He crawled onto the ledge, whipping his head around when boots pounded on the other side of the gully.

The Hummer sat a good hundred yards off, the rear door hanging open. Some asshole in black skidding to a halt, a rifle lifting to his shoulder.

Jordan leaned over Kash, grabbed one of his K-bars and flicked her wrist. There was a flash of silver, then the guy's head snapping back as his feet kicked up. He got off a trigger pull, a spray of bullets cutting through the trees ten feet above their heads. Raining down pine needles and dead twigs. The tango hit the ground as his rifle landed in the mud beside him, legs twitching, body splayed out.

Some guy stepped out of the front passenger seat of the Hummer. Older. Dressed in black minus the body armor. Dark glasses shading his eyes. He didn't move or try to run up the path. He just stared at Jordan, lips pinched tights. Arms crossed.

Jordan's chest heaved against Kash's side, her breath panting across his neck. Her gaze locked on that asshole as if she'd seen a ghost. Kash scrambled to his feet, gave her a shove toward the track then raced behind her. Waves crashed in the distance, the air carrying a hint of brine.

They followed the trail, punching out onto a scrubby plateau. Seagulls dotted the sky, thick clouds filling the horizon.

Kash glanced at his watch, praying Foster was on his way as they headed for the edge. Not that he wanted to repeat his experience from the other day, but chancing the ocean sounded better than trying to outrun a few dozen bullets.

Until that rogue bike came roaring out of the forest, catching air as it got between them and the edge. The Hummer bounced along the adjoining road, mud flying out both sides. Engine whining. Drowning out what might have been a chopper echoing through the air.

Kash grabbed Jordan, ready to step between her and the inevitable spray of bullets when Foster's chopper rose like a wraith from below the cliff, side doors open. Zain already zeroed in on the SUV. The bird swung in closer, nearly blowing that rider off his bike when Nyx shot out the doors. She hit the ground going full out, eighty pounds of pure aggression crashing into the guy on the bike — toppling it over on its side.

There was growling and screaming, Zain popping off cover fire as the Hummer slammed to a halt. Kash had Nyx by the harness a heartbeat later, heaving her up and into the chopper. Jordan jumped in beside her, yanking Kash in when he reached for the frame.

Chase tapped Foster on the shoulder, and he slid the chopper over then dropped the machine off the cliff, screaming across the ocean then banking northbound. The wind howled through the doors until Chase snapped them shut.

Chase stared out the window, nodding toward the man standing beside the Hummer quickly fading into the distance. "Who's the dick in black?"

Jordan glanced back, closing her eyes as she leaned against the seat. "If he has his way, he'll be the reason we'll all end up dead."

CHAPTER NINE

Jordan sat in the helicopter, Rook's silhouette fading in the distance, all those voices in her head drowning out the beat of the rotors. How everyone else sat there — waited for her to elaborate. To say something that would justify nearly getting Kash killed. If Foster and the rest of Kash's team hadn't shown up...

Kash would have stepped in front of her — blocked the shots. No hesitation. The way his grip had tightened on her arm, the firm press of his mouth... He'd been about to dodge in front when his buddies had saved them.

Now, he sat beside her, holding her hand, looking as if he had nothing but time.

Chase huffed, then snapped his gaze to her. "Shit. Which one of you's hit?"

She frowned, some of the words getting highjacked along the way to her head when Kash cursed.

He twisted to face her. "Jordan?"

She stared up at him, drinking in the green of his eyes — his tousled hair and shadowed scruff. The man looked sexier than he ever had.

Kash turned fully, grabbed her jacket. "You're fucking bleeding."

She glanced down. Blood soaked through the left side of her clothes, a bit dripping onto the floor of the chopper. "It's probably just a graze."

Chase moved in close. "Oh, so you're a medic, too?"

"No."

"Then, maybe let me be the judge of what's a graze and what's a damn crater in your side."

"Trust me. It can't be worse than the last time I went up against him."

"Insightful, and yet not comforting." Chase waved his fingers. "Kash, help her out of her jacket so I can take a look."

Chase had obviously made that kind of request before because Kash had her jacket off and her body turned and braced against his before she'd even thought about moving.

She groaned when Chase started snipping through the fabric. "Scissors? Really? You couldn't just lift it?"

Chase chuckled. "You're never gonna wash out that much blood or fix all the ragged ends from whatever gnawed its way through. And lifting it hurts more."

"It's the only shirt I have."

"Then, it's a good thing Kash loves seeing you dressed in his."

Jordan glanced at Kash over her shoulder, then back to Chase. "That was before I nearly got him killed."

"Are you kidding? That just makes him even crazier about you." Chase peeled the sides of the shirt off her skin, sighing when she hissed out a breath. "Not a bullet wound, but you managed to skewer a nasty piece of wood through your side." He looked up. "Or am I gonna find some weird arrowhead at the end?"

Kash mumbled something then huffed. "No arrows, jackass." He leaned in closer, his breath warm against her neck. "You got that when you swung against the cliff, didn't you?"

"Pretty sure falling to the bottom would have left more of a mark." She pushed against him when Chase stuck a needle her side. "Damn..."

"I know. Freezing sucks." Chase moved it to another spot. "But it sucks less than me yanking out the wood, irrigating the wound, then patching it up without anything."

She snapped her gaze down. "You're freezing it?"

"Surely you've been treated by a medic before?"

"No."

Chase paused and glanced over her shoulder at Kash. "What happened when you got hurt in the field?"

"I hauled ass someplace remotely secure then patched myself up. If I didn't die, then I could ask the agency doctor to look at it later." She scoffed. "That rarely happened."

"You've got obvious bullet and knife scars."

She let her head fall back on Kash's shoulder. "No one's perfect, Chase."

"I guess as a spy, you can't wear a vest."

"I'm not..." She breathed out as he tugged against her skin, resting most of her weight against Kash. "I..."

"Damn. It's bleeding like a freaking faucet." Chase's voice sounded oddly distant. "Kash, hold her. Foster, I need you to set us down for a few minutes so I can deal with this without the turbulence."

"Jordan." Kash cupped her jaw — turned her head toward him. "Eyes on me, sweetheart."

Had he really just said that? Reminded her that less than twelve hours ago she'd been snugged beneath him, watching him as he made love to her as if he was just as lost as she was. That maybe, he'd fallen, too.

She blinked, eyelids heavy. Everything duller. Darker. Like they'd flown into a tunnel. And she swore it took twice as long to pry her eyes open. Stare up at him, again.

"Chase. Brother, she looks like she's gonna pass out."

"Working on it." Something clattered in the

background, Chase's hands tugging on her shirt. Slicing a line up her arm. "I've got saline and some plasma..."

Jordan closed her eyes, fading for a bit before blinking them open. An eerie quiet filled the space, only a hint of light glowing from a crack near the floor across the room. Definitely not the helicopter. Arms tightened around her shoulders, a steady thump beating beneath her head.

"Easy, sweetheart. Everything's okay. You just passed out." Kash pressed a soft kiss to her forehead when she tilted it toward him. "But you might want to limit moving for a bit longer. Your side's gonna be sore for a while."

"I'll take your word on that." She relaxed against him. "Where are we?"

"A client suite in Bodie's office. And before you lose your shit, it's probably the most secure building in town. We made sure no one followed us, and we've got overwatch and patrols. Chase wanted you to have a night to help restore some of your blood volume."

Kash sighed, eased her onto her back then pushed onto one elbow. He brushed back her hair, staring at her as if he hadn't thought he'd see her again.

She reached up — drew her thumb along his jaw. "Kash..."

"You scared me. Not the chase or the bullets or bleeding all over the chopper. You're insanely skilled, and I knew Chase would keep you breathing." He paused, swallowed. "When I realized I wasn't going to catch you on that bike..."

Her chest tightened, tears stinging her eyes. "I'm sorry." She placed her finger over his mouth when he looked as if he was going to interrupt. "For getting you and your team involved in this. For not coming clean. But more than anything, I'm sorry I ran."

She closed her eyes, cringing when a few tears slipped out. "It's not that I didn't trust you, I just... I've never had anyone care. Not without wanting something in return and I... God, I just didn't want him to hurt—"

He kissed her. Soft. Gentle. And it broke the last of her defenses. Had her gliding her fingers through his hair, holding on. Some form of anchor when she swore she'd shatter.

Kash stayed close when he could have eased back. Or shuffled off the bed. Maybe joined his friends now that he knew she wasn't going to outright die on him. "I know. And I'll admit, a part of me loves you for it. But the other part — the one that aged five years seeing that red taillight fade — it needs to know that you won't run, again."

"Are you sure that's in your best interest? Crazy or not, that escape was the easy part. Now that he knows what he's up against — *who* he's up against — it's only gonna get worse."

Kash tilted his head, looked as if he was

considering what she'd said. "What I know is that I got a glimpse of the future without you in it, and that hurt more than anything your agency can throw at us."

She drew her thumb along his jaw. "I won't run. As much as it kills me to say that, to put you in danger, I'm not strong enough to leave you, again."

He gave her a hint of a smile. "What about Ember? Is she strong enough?"

She froze, waiting for that familiar disconnect to wash over her. The one Rook had beaten into her. The core, he'd said, of what it took to be the best.

To be unstoppable.

She smiled and let go of any doubts. "There was a time I would have said yes. When I would have buried everything, taken off and never looked back. But the thing is..." She urged him closer. "Somewhere along the way, she fell in love with you, too."

She closed the distance — claimed his mouth. Opening for his tongue when he deepened the kiss. She wasn't sure how long they laid there before he finally eased back — allowed her to suck in a lungful of air.

He smiled against her skin, nuzzling her nose as he stared at her. "You're just so damn beautiful, I..."

He claimed her mouth, again, shifting over her as he tilted her head, got as close as possible without actually stripping them both down and making love.

She lost track of time, reveling in the way his

weight held her captive, when Kash grunted, shifting over to one elbow. She frowned at the furrow along his brow. "Kash?"

He shook his head. "I was crushing you into the bed. Chase is so gonna tear me a new one if you've reopened that wound."

"My side's fine, and you weren't crushing me. I like having your weight on me."

"You like not breathing?"

She smoothed her hand up to his jaw. "I like feeling safe. I've never had that before."

"You're determined to be the death of me, aren't you." He shushed her. "That wasn't a question." He shuffled until he must have found a compromise where he pinned her down without putting pressure on her side. "Sleep. We'll figure everything out in the morning."

"Your arms are gonna cramp if you stay like that."

"Pretty sure you'll be out cold before that happens, and I can roll you against my chest. Either way, I'm good."

She sighed, enjoying how his heartbeat eased the flutter in her stomach.

"And Jordan..."

She slivered her eyes open, again.

He just smiled. "It's okay if you need to become Ember for a while. If that's what it'll take to make it through. Because I love her as much as I do you."

She froze. Her breath lodged in her chest. Her heart somewhere up in her throat. She blinked, wondering if she was dreaming, or worse, dead. If she'd died in the chopper and this was her brain giving her one last pure memory. What could be heaven if it kept on playing.

Kash chuckled, the jerk. "Breathe, sweetheart. Or I'll have to call Chase in, and I'd rather not do that."

Breathe?

How was she supposed to breathe when he'd just blown her mind? Stopped her heart cold? She opened her mouth, closed it, then opened it, again.

Nothing.

Not a sound.

He sighed, dipping down and lingering in the kind of kiss that shattered barriers before nuzzling her nose. "Surely, someone's told you they love you, before."

She pursed her lips. "Will you freak out if I say no?"

Kash inhaled, swallowed — looking as if he wanted to rage war — she just wasn't sure against who. "Then, I'll make sure I say it often enough you won't forget."

"What's that saying? You never forget your first?" She smiled, eyes drifting closed for a moment before she forced them open. "I won't forget."

"Assuming you remember in the morning, which I'd say is a bit of a crapshoot with how fast you're fading." He shifted over, then tugged her in close, one hand under her head, the other snugged against her chest. "Rest. This might be the only chance we get for a while."

She closed her eyes. Allowed herself to fade into the warmth of his body — the strength of his arms. She'd trust his team to keep them safe tonight. Then, come morning, she'd lay it all on the line.

CHAPTER TEN

Kash leaned against one of the walls, watching Jordan stare out the window. Calm. Focused. Not quite how he'd envisioned she'd be while waiting for what would undoubtedly be a tough conversation with him and his team. He'd expected her to be edgy, aloof. Looking for the nearest exit in case all that training kicked in and she ran, despite her promise. That she'd become Ember. Operative, and the woman destined to be his undoing.

Jordan must have felt him staring because she inhaled, then glanced over her shoulder. And damn… The smile she flashed him. It had him pushing off the wall — closing the distance. Her head tilted back as she kept her gaze locked on his, still smiling when he stopped a breath away.

He reached out and tucked some loose strands of hair behind her ear. "You okay?"

She glanced at his teammates and Bodie as they

walked in from the other room and gathered around them. "Fine." She arched a brow. "No one's going to try and kill me, right?"

He chuckled. "Glad you've still got your sense of humor. Just remember… We're all friends, here. The guys can get a bit *intense* when they're talking shop. But it's because they care."

She scrunched her face as if she thought he was crazy. Or maybe it was disbelief that he'd said his buddies cared. That she was worth risking their lives for. Especially after she'd admitted that no one had ever told her they loved her. Not that he was truly surprised, but it had cut deep. Had highlighted how much trust and faith she'd already placed in him. What it had taken to give him that decryption drive. And he wasn't going to let her down.

A throat cleared behind him, and Kash glanced over his shoulder, nodding at Foster. The guy was still their unofficial leader, and it appeared as if he was ready to get down to business.

Jordan nudged him. "Guess your buddies are done waiting."

"Remember what I said."

"Right. All those gruff expressions come from a place of caring."

Kash sighed, then turned. He thought about venturing back to where he'd been standing but couldn't get the signals through. Instead, he gave her a hint of space, then whistled for Nyx. The dog trotted across the floor — settled between him and Jordan. As if she was showing her loyalty, too.

Jordan leaned over and gave Nyx a scratch. "At least Nyx doesn't look as if she's about to have a stroke."

Foster chuckled. "We'd be less uptight if we hadn't needed to swoop in and grab you two amidst a firefight." He gave her a pointed look. "And there's the part where you lost a liter of blood in the back of the chopper."

"Technically, the only person shooting at that moment was Zain. And I'm still breathing so…" She held up her hand. "But that's not the takeaway."

Jordan drew a breath, then straightened, and it was as if she'd flicked a switch. Just shifted into Ember in front of Kash's eyes. The way she stood, how she gazed around the room… It all seemed instantly different. Colder, maybe. Definitely more calculated. As if she'd lifted off the mask she'd been wearing.

Kash reminded himself it didn't matter what vibe she gave off. That under all the training and missions, she was still the woman he'd fallen for. That it was her form of body armor.

His teammates obviously noticed it, too. They responded in kind, standing taller, any hint of amusement gone.

Jordan looked at him, then at everyone else. "Before I lift the veil and let you see the other side, you need to be one hundred percent sure this is what you want. Because once I lay it all out, you'll be in the crosshairs, too. And there's only one way this ends with us still breathing. If we fail…"

She shoved her fingers through her hair, wincing when it obviously pulled on her side, before she blew out a rough breath. "We're either dead or on the run. And there's no corner of this Earth that's safe. No jungle hut or mountain cabin he can't find. So, be very certain you want to jump on this train because there's no getting off until we either burn them or die in the fire."

Foster stared at her for a few moments, then gazed at Zain, Chase, Bodie — finally ending with Kash. "I'm pretty sure we're already in the crosshairs. If our assumptions are correct, they've already been to the house. And it won't take a covert agency long to figure out who was flying the chopper, so… No one's getting off the train, Jordan. And we sure as hell don't plan on losing. So, tell us what we need to know to bring these fuckers down."

Jordan stared at Foster. The man seemed genuine. His eyes weren't shifting off to one side, and he hadn't looked at any of his teammates, or even Bodie, as if he was worried they'd overrule him. Sure, she knew Kash was onboard, but the rest of his team didn't owe her anything. Could write off the rescue to saving Kash's ass, with hers just being a lucky by-product. Yet, they all stood there, shoulders back, chins high. And she knew this was simply who they were. Men who'd spent their lives in the fray and who weren't afraid to jump back in.

She pushed down the riotous roil of her stomach — the ghostly echo of Rook's voice telling her she wasn't worthy of their devotion. That she'd never be anything other than Ember — the woman who'd sold her soul without question. "I think you're all a little south of normal to voluntarily jump in, but I could definitely use some of that."

She took a breath. This was it. A reckoning of sorts with her past on display, and she couldn't help but wonder if the truth would change their minds. "What do you know about Shadow Ops?"

Zain chuckled. "Damn, I hate when Kash is right."

She snapped her focus to Kash and inhaled at the hint of a smile beneath the stoic facade. He'd thought she was Shadow Ops all along? And he'd still asked her out? Taken her to bed? Said he loved her?

Kash leaned over. "Breathe, sweetheart."

She jolted back from her thoughts, sucked in an embarrassingly loud breath.

Zain grinned, and she had the urge to smack the guy up the backside of his head. "We know the basics. Deep underground. Highly secretive. Missions that skirt the line between what's legal and what's necessary, though, I suspect they lean far more toward the latter."

Jordan nodded. "The division I worked for

operates beyond standard intelligence channels. It specializes in missions that require surgical precision, zero oversight and complete deniability. Its operatives are considered assets, not people. Once they enter the program, their previous identities cease to exist. They're given new code names, new mandates and very few restrictions. Failure isn't tolerated on any scale, and if they make a mess or become too visible, they're disavowed and put on a termination list."

"How long were you with this agency?"

"Twenty years."

"Twenty?" Kash nearly choked the word out. "But you're thirty-two. That means you were recruited when you were twelve."

"From that group home you heard me telling Zain about."

Zain shook his head. "How the hell did this agency find you at a group home?"

"I had an uncle. He was an Army Ranger who'd reportedly died on a mission when I was two. Except, he wasn't killed, he was recruited. I guess he kept occasional tabs on me, and when he learned my parents had died and I was in the system…" She scrubbed her hand down her face. "He went looking. Got me pulled out on the condition I was indoctrinated into the organization, and the rest, as they say, is history."

"Jesus. How old were you when you went on your first mission?"

"Sixteen."

"Shit." Zain raked his fingers through his hair, making it stand up in every direction. "That guy in the Hummer. Was he your handler?"

She swallowed, barely keeping it down. "He was my entire existence, if I'm being honest."

Foster took a step forward. "I realize this can't be easy for you, but do we get to know his name? What agency you worked for? Or are we just gonna dance around it?"

She glanced at Kash, wondering if he'd heard of Scythe. If learning the truth would change his mind, too. Because despite Rook's efforts, she knew there were rumors of Scythe's existence, even if it was mostly an urban legend.

She didn't know if she'd looked at Kash funny or if the jerk had suddenly learned how to read her mind because he leaned in — got lover close.

"Nothing's going to change what we talked about last night. Promise."

"It's just..." How did she explain that it made it all real. That, once she'd divulged that last bit, she wasn't just Jordan, waitress and someone worthy of their trust. She was Ember.

Foster sighed. "Jordan. Let's simplify this. Did you roam the world killing people for the sake of it?"

She scoffed. "Of course, not. I was given missions, which included intelligence monitoring and retrieval, asset acquisition and, when required, elimination."

"Did you think these missions were sanctioned?"

"Yes."

"Then, however things went sideways isn't on you. But we need to know who and what we're dealing with if we have any hope of helping you."

She took a breath. Then another. Until she's pushed the last of the "new her" beneath the surface. Had finally made the transition back to Ember. "I worked for an agency known only as Scythe."

Zain inhaled, glancing at his buddies before shaking his head. "Scythe? Seriously? Shit."

She held her ground. "I assume you're heard of it?"

"Only rumors and damn... It's considered the original ghost cell. What every other shadow agency has strived to become and failed." Zain shoved his hands in his pockets as if he wasn't sure what else to do with them. "Who was your handler? Nathan McCoy? Or..."

Another raspy inhale at her continued silence as Zain scrubbed his hand through his hair. "Damn. Rook Donovan?"

"You know him?"

"Know him? The guy was a legend. Army Ranger. Green Beret. Transferred over to the CIA's National Clandestine Division then... vanished. As in record completely erased. Old mission logs rewritten. Every last trace of him — gone. A few of us suspected he'd gone dark. Heard whispers that it was to Scythe, but no one talks about him or Scythe unless they want to end up dead."

"Now you know why I was reluctant to say anything. Scythe isn't just an organization. It's a militarized cult with Rook Donovan as their leader. You either pledge your unconditional loyalty to him, or you end up on the wrong side of a bullet. There's no middle ground. No questioning his authority, and no backing out."

"So, what happened that made you stop drinking the Kool-Aid?" Chase held up his hands when Kash glared at him. "I'm not judging. In fact, based on how you ended up there, you weren't really given a choice. But you were obviously loyal to them — to Rook — for nearly twenty years, and I can't help but wonder what changed? What justified having him come after you, himself."

Jordan let her head tilt back. "I'd like to say it was me, but... I'd been questioning the validity of the missions for a while. Things were just off. Briefings were lacking vital intel. Targets seemed random, almost personal. And Rook went from micromanaging every detail to barely showing up, at times. Then, on my last mission, I was shown proof that Rook and Scythe had gone fully dark side. That they were using us to infiltrate cartels and acquire weapon systems for their own agenda. We're talking black market racketeering on an unprecedented scale. Hell, Rook had me neutralizing my own damn people. I saw that and..." She shook her head. "I knew I had to burn it all to the ground."

Kash reached into his pocket and removed the

drive she'd given him. "You said this is a decryption drive. So, where's the intel?"

"It's in a secure server at my last remaining dead-drop site. Not too far from here. Rook's beaten me to all the others I tried to access. Destroyed everything before I got the chance to download the evidence then run it through that program."

"What makes you think he hasn't done that already to this site?"

"Because he doesn't know about this one. It was my uncle's, and when he died for real, it activated some kind of Hail Mary protocol that sent me the access codes for it." She sighed. "He'd already linked our servers. Not sure how, but I've never been there. And my uncle wasn't Rook's subordinate. He was his equal. One of the first agents Scythe recruited."

Foster motioned to her. "What was your uncle's real name?"

"Cross. Thomas Cross."

"No, shit." Foster shook his head. "He was a legend, too. Ran maneuvers in Africa. Hardcore. Story was he went MIA during an op."

"No one gets to keep their past. I'm sure my mere presence caused him a bunch of backlash, but... He tried to save me, and for that, I owe him."

Zain cleared his throat. "Right, so, where's this dead-drop site?"

She sighed. "About that..."

"We're not going to like it, are we."

"It's in a cabin up in the forested hills about an hour outside of town."

Zain frowned, looking at his buddies. "And that's a problem because…"

"Because I haven't been able to easily access it. The only suggestion of a trail I could find was washed out. The forest is insane, even by my standards, and the whole thing's surrounded by steep, slick cliffs. And I suspect that once I do reach the place, there'll be surprises I'll have to disarm, or at least avoid, before making it to the door."

Jordan ran her fingers through her hair. "It's not that I can't, and given the right motivation, I will. But it could easily be a one-way trip." She shook her head. "Maybe several months on the outside has taken a toll. Maybe I'm not as savvy as I once was."

Zain chuckled. "Or maybe, your heart wasn't fully in it."

She glanced at Kash. Smiled. "That, too. Which is another level of crazy. Scythe and Rook have only two rules. Unconditional loyalty and no attachments."

Kash reached out and grabbed her hand. "Then, it's a good thing you're not with Scythe, anymore. And that the guy you broke that last rule for, has friends who fly helicopters."

She looked over at Foster and Mac. "Rook knows I'm here, now. He'll have satellites constantly scanning the area. I doubt he'll miss a chopper hovering over a secluded section of forest. I wouldn't put it past the man to have a damn Apache on standby."

Foster grinned. "Won't be my first encounter. Doubt it'll be my last, so… You worry about avoiding bombs and how you're gonna download everything, and leave getting there to me and Mac."

"Nyx will make short work of the bombs." Kash gave her head a scratch. "She's trained in various scent work, explosives being one of them." He nudged Jordan. "It came in handy grabbing assets from enemy strongholds. Which only leaves the tech side of things."

"Pretty sure I can handle that. I did spend fifteen years running missions." She tapped her head. "I know my way around a computer."

"Or, you can let me handle it." Bodie stepped up. He'd been noticeably quiet throughout the meeting, and she couldn't help but wonder how he fit in. "There's not much I can't hack my way into."

"I don't plan on this requiring any hacking."

"Which is your first mistake. There's always hacking."

She eyed Kash, then nodded at Bodie. "Are you saying that as part of this team or as Greer's deputy?"

Bodie arched a brow. "Does it matter?"

"I assume you have a different set of protocols depending on who's holding your leash."

"You really do see things differently. I'm just here to help out Foster and his crew. They pulled my ass out of a nasty situation once upon a time, and I still feel like there's red in my ledger."

Foster clapped the guy on the back. "We've been over this."

"And we still disagree." Bodie crossed his arms. "We good, Jordan?"

She eyed him for a few moments, but he seemed genuine. "Golden."

"Why doesn't that make me feel better?"

She simply shrugged, then looked Kash's crew in the eyes. "Not to be a broken record, but are you all sure..."

"Too late. We already know your secrets. No backing out now. Though... I do have one last question." Chase stepped closer. "What's your code name?"

She sucked at her bottom lip.

Chase sighed. "Sorry, I didn't mean to pry. You don't have to tell us."

"Ember." She pushed out a slow breath. "That's what Rook called me. He claimed I had a spark no one could tame. Said it made me uniquely qualified, which doesn't sound all that positive, now."

"Oh, I don't know. It kinda sounds like he suspected you might be the one to burn it all down." Chase pointed to her side. "I should check that before we head out."

He nodded at Kash then turned, the rest of the crew following after him, leaving her standing there, staring, until Kash reached out — took her in his arms. She melted against him, hoping he didn't let go.

He dropped a kiss on the top of her head, holding on until even she knew they were out of time. "It's going to be okay."

"You're damn straight because if it comes down to my life over any of yours, I'm making that call."

He pursed his lips and looked as if he wanted to argue before he nodded. "Then, let's see it doesn't." He stepped back — tugged her hand. "C'mon. We'd best catch up before Zain and Bodie devise some insane plan."

"I meant what I said, Kash. I can't live with more blood on my hands. If it were yours…" She wouldn't survive it.

"Men just like Rook tried killing us for twenty years. And despite his experience, his inflated ego, he's never faced a team like ours." He smiled. "Or an agent like you. We'll get that intel, and you're gonna see Rook and Scythe burn."

CHAPTER ELEVEN

Kash sat in the back of the helicopter, side doors already open as Foster skimmed across the trees, only the stars poking through the night sky as any source of light. Foster had night vision and instruments, but it still amazed Kash that his buddy handled the machine with such precision when Kash could barely make out Nyx sitting between his legs. Mac shadowed them in another chopper, making it look just as easy.

Jordan placed her hand over his and gave it a squeeze, silently asking him if he was okay. If he was still all-in. She'd been doing that all day, randomly checking in. And not just with him. Chase, Zain, Bodie, Mac. She'd given them all an out. Had suggested that Rook showing up was more than enough motivation to attempt the trek, alone.

A part of Kash loved her for that. For worrying about his brothers. About him. But they'd never backed down from a fight, and they sure as hell weren't starting now.

He looked over at her. "Still not bailing."

She sighed. "You realize it's not you or your buddies I'm questioning, right? I've just never worked as part of a team. I'm not sure I know how."

"Easy. You worry about doing your part and let us do ours."

"What if Rook shows up? I'm just supposed to let you handle him? Not step in front?"

Kash straightened — crossed his arms over his chest. "If you want to step in front, put on a vest."

"I've never worn a vest. Ever." She slapped the one he wore as if it might bite her. "I promise, if we live through this, I'll get used to one. But I can't face Rook without being the best version of me. And that means I need to move a certain way, which I can't if I'm wearing a vest."

"Which I promised you I understood. But you can't get mad when I jump in front of you if bullets start coming your way."

She frowned, staring at him for a while before shaking her head. "And you can't get mad at me if I eliminate any resistance before they get a chance to fire."

"You're determined to be difficult, aren't you?" He leaned over. Kissed her. "All you have to do is believe in us, and everything will fall into place."

She nodded, though he suspected she wasn't quite sure how that worked. Whether believing meant running beside them or allowing them to take half the risk.

His comms buzzed, Foster's voice coming through. "Infil site in thirty."

Kash rocked to his feet, placed his headset on the seat and had Nyx poised between his legs a second later. Zain and Bodie followed suit, keeping Jordan between them. She gave them each a raise of her brow, then settled in.

The bird banked over, evergreen branches whizzing past before Foster flared off the speed and brought them into a two-foot hover just in from the edge of one of the cliff sides. What they'd agreed was the fastest route while minimizing both them and the helicopter as a viable target.

Kash and Nyx jumped down — provided support as soon as the machine stopped moving, the rest of the team filing out behind him. Bodie and Zain ran ahead — took up point while Jordan moved in beside him. She wore boots and form-fitting everything with weapons tucked in places he didn't want to think too hard about. Nothing like him and his team. Black cargo pants and sweaters. Body armor with knives and frags for good measure. But he had to admit, she moved like a ghost, virtually floating over the ground. All but disappearing as soon as they entered the woods. Blending in with the shadows until he had to focus just to bring her into view.

Bodie and Zain cleared the path until they neared the cabin — dropping to one knee as they waved him ahead. Kash moved up with Nyx, keeping the pace steady but not rushed. Nyx scented the ground, moved ahead, then scented, again. Continuing toward the cabin before stopping. She tilted her head, gave him a whispered bark. Not loud enough to carry, but he heard it.

"Stay." He moved in beside her, scouring the forest floor. Needing a second pass to pick out the thin silver wire woven through some ferns to some rough IED strapped to a nearby log. What would have taken one or two people out — made one hell of a heat signature for anyone with IR-capable satellites scouring the area.

Bodie darted up. Disarmed the thing in all of ten seconds. Kash wasn't sure if the man had been an ordnance specialist or if he'd learned some new tricks as part of his deputy status. Either way, they moved on in under a minute.

Nyx identified two more at the edge of the small clearing encircling the cabin. Though, clearing wasn't really the correct term. More like the cabin had been slung beneath a chopper and plopped into a space barely large enough to fit everything.

Bodie disarmed one, left the other in case anyone came in behind them, then waved Kash ahead. Kash quickstepped to the door, allowing Nyx time to fully scent it before motioning the rest of his team forward.

"Quite the lock for a hut practically hidden in the

middle of nowhere." Kash looked at Jordan. "I assume he sent you the codes."

"God, I hope so." She moved in, studied the lock then hit four numbers, waiting until it flashed green twice then put in four more.

The lock clicked over, a steady green light illuminating the wood for a moment before it winked out. She turned the handle, cracked it open maybe half an inch before stopping.

She handed Kash a mirror from one of her pockets. "I think it'd be best to run that along the floor."

Kash crouched — slipped the mirror beneath the frame. "Clear. I'll check the rest, just to be sure."

He took an extra few seconds to slowly slide it between the open door and the frame, once again nodding. "All clear there, too."

"I'll swing it open, but Nyx should probably scent our way across. Raider was one paranoid SOB."

"Your uncle's code name was Raider?"

"It fit."

"Like Ember?"

She smiled, though it didn't quite reach her eyes. "Let's hope Rook was right about the spark."

Rook had been right. No doubt in Kash's mind. Jordan definitely had a fire inside her.

He whistled to Nyx — let her scour the room. "Clear."

Bodie headed straight for the computer setup, switched on a dim lamp, then got everything humming a heartbeat later. Zain scoured the forest. That overwatch that was ingrained into his DNA. Jordan typed in the appropriate access codes, then Bodie started flying through screens and folders, mouth slightly open as he grunted several times under his breath.

Kash alternated his focus between Jordan and the rear windows, the hairs on the back of his neck prickling. And he knew, this wasn't going to end with Foster simply picking them back up.

"I've got all the files located. There's just one catch." Bodie glanced over at Kash, then Zain. "Jordan's asset rigged the upload so that once we copy it off the server, it's permanently erased. Also, that decryption algorithm she has needs to be run twice. Once here in order to copy the files over. Then we can run it the second time back at my office."

Zain huffed. "How long?"

"A good five minutes."

"Shit. Do it, just be prepared for resistance. My freaking sniper senses are off the charts. We're definitely being watched." Zain focused on Jordan. "Guess Rook knew about your uncle's cabin, after all."

"If that's true, then…" She kicked at the floor. "Damn it. It means Rook's been corralling me here this entire time because he needs me to remove all that intel from the server, first, so he knows it's been permanently erased. That he considered this site his best option."

She muttered more obscenities as she paced. "Now, I'm thinking that asshole, Bart Conrad, *was* part of Rook's little test, only when he realized Rook was going to double cross him, he gave me the actual files."

A growl. Low. Throaty.

Kash glanced at Nyx. She stood alert by his side. Hackles raised. Teeth bared. She took a step. Muscles primed and ready to pounce. "We've got company."

"Bodie?" Zain didn't even bother turning around.

Bodie killed the lamp — the glow from the computer still shining through the room — then tossed the answer over his shoulder. "Three minutes."

"That's likely two more than we've got."

"I doubt they'll open fire until Rook's certain we've got the files, which suggests they'll wait until we try to leave." Jordan scoured the room. "No way someone like Raider didn't have another way out of here. One only accessible from the inside."

Kash moved over to her. "You thinking trapdoor?"

"Some creepy ass tunnel sounds about right. It doesn't have to go far to pop up in the woods."

"Nyx. Scent." Kash walked her across the floor. "It's not going to be airtight. Nyx might pick up on the airflow bringing in a different smell."

Nyx had her nose on the floorboards, going over each one. Moving around the cabin until she stopped behind Bodie. Another whisper bark, and her pawing at the floor.

Jordan arrived at Kash's side a second later, feeling along the area next to the wall, smiling when a small piece lifted up, exposing another keypad. She input some codes, and a section of the floor hinged downward, exposing a dark, narrow tunnel. "Definitely creepy. But it's probably better than what's coming through the doors in the next sixty seconds."

"Kash, you, Nyx and Jordan get moving. Secure the exit." Zain waved at Bodie. "We'll be right behind you."

Kash stared at Zain. "You know I hate it when you do that, brother."

"That thing looks pretty damn narrow. We'll need to go single file so get your asses moving or none of us are getting out of here. I've got movement in the trees."

Jordan looked about as happy as Kash felt, but she swung her legs into the hole then slipped in. She clicked on an insanely dim red light, then disappeared. Kash jumped in behind her, scooted over then whistled for Nyx. The dog crowded next to him as they started crawling along the passage, going mostly by feel.

They'd traveled maybe thirty feet when they reached a small hatch. It opened inward, then Jordan popped up — cleared the space. She waved Kash out just as gunfire erupted behind them, what sounded like that IED Bodie had left untouched exploding off to the left.

Kash jumped up and out, sweeping the area, guarding the hatch. Limbs off to their right shook, some asshole in black slinking out of the dark. Nyx was on him before he took another step, jaw locked around his arm, dragging him backwards. Kash cracked him in the head with the butt of his rifle before he managed to scream for help, pulling Nyx close when a loud bang ripped through the air.

"Get down." Kash dove on top of Nyx, covering her a second before the cabin exploded, debris shooting out in every direction. The resulting percussive wave sent branches toppling to the ground as smoke and ash covered the area.

Shit!

Kash staggered to his feet, ears ringing, the ground shifting beneath him. He managed to stumble to the hatch without puking, head still spinning when Zain and Bodie climbed out of the ground, tripping onto their asses as soon as they were out.

Jordan braced her weight against a tree, shaking her head as she waved at them. "We need to move before the entire squad realizes we aren't dead, yet."

They took off. Not running, but at least they were moving. Painfully slowly and not quite in a straight line, but they managed to put some distance between them and the wreckage. Jordan hadn't been exaggerating. The forest was thick, every inch between the trees packed with brush and bramble that clawed at their legs — tried to trip them at every turn.

They'd only been traveling for about ten minutes when Nyx froze, blocking Kash from continuing forward, a low growl sounding around them. He held up a fist, crouching behind a thorny bush — scanning the dense forest.

Tree.

Maybe fifty meters up and to the right.

Some asshole dressed in black. Nestled in the crook of a couple branches. Assault rifle sweeping the shadows. Jordan twirled her finger, pointing to the guy.

Kash shook his head, mouthed, "I've got this," then motioned Nyx to wait.

The dog mimicked Kash's crouch as Kash shifted over, then slowly picked his way toward the tango. Placing each footfall. Staying low. Signaling Nyx once he was in position.

She took off, bounding over the brush like a freaking deer, barely making a noise. Covering the distance in all of five seconds. Leaping and kicking off his back before her paws hit the branch. She barely slowed, barreling into the gunman — wrestling with him for a few moments before they tumbled out the other side.

Kash darted over — caught her before she hit the ground, then kicked the creep in the head. Gave Nyx a quick once-over before falling in behind his buddies. They hadn't taken more than a few steps when automatic fire lit up the forest, branches and needles raining down on them.

That was all the motivation they needed to take it up a notch. Lay down cover fire then hoof it through the trees. Jordan palmed stumps and vaulted over logs like some extreme parkour junkie, firing off a few rounds without missing a step. They found what passed as a deer trail and picked up their speed, Zain keeping anyone behind at bay with short, controlled bursts — Bodie joining in whenever Zain needed to reload.

Nyx veered left when their trail branched off, neither path looking remotely inviting. Kash didn't question Nyx's choice, just kept running, clipping what must have been a sentry when the guy popped up. The forest brightened slightly up ahead. What Kash hoped was some sort of break in the foliage.

They hit the clearing going full out, a distant whop whop whop echoing through the trees. Only, it didn't sound like Foster or Mac's choppers. This was lower. The whine of the transmission sending a chill down his spine.

He'd heard that exact noise before. Shadowing their every move that fateful night. The buzz of the machine guns. The unrelenting beat of the rotors. Foster had pulled some insane save out of his ass — flown the bird through a literal hole in the mountainside — but Kash would never forget the chase. Or the wet gurgle of Sean's last breath. How Rhett had looked over at him and Zain before he'd passed out.

Zain darted up beside him — pointed to the far

side as they all sprinted for cover a moment before a black Apache rolled over the trees, lighting up the night with a spray of gunfire cutting through branches and brush. Kash grabbed Jordan and shoved her and Nyx beneath him. Though, with the caliber of that gun, it'd likely eat right through his vest.

The machine moved in to hover when Foster's chopper came screaming out of the night, Chase popping off some shots out the door — hitting the Apache's tail section and sending it spinning. The pilot regained control, then banked off, following after Foster as he threw his aircraft up and over the rise off to the right, disappearing into the darkness.

Kash pushed to his feet just as Mac flared into the space, somehow fitting her helicopter into the clearing without chopping down trees or burying the tail rotor into some brush. Zain went to one knee, laid down suppressive fire — kept the rest of Rook's men diving for cover. He didn't budge until they were already on board. Then he sprinted for the side, all but diving in as Mac lifted the chopper while banking over — skimming across all those trees then peeling off toward the ocean.

Mac glanced at them over her shoulder, banking hard to the left. "Buckle in. This isn't going to be pretty."

Kash sighed. She'd definitely been flying with Foster too long. Was starting to sound like him. "Is there more than one attack chopper?"

"There were two, but..." She shook her head. "Is

Foster always that intense? I mean, I knew he was but damn, you get another chopper in the mix, and he becomes someone else — something else. I swear that man has hollow bones."

"You realize, the rest of us think you're both equally crazy."

"I've picked up a few tricks." A ping sounded through the cockpit. "Looks like our friend's back. Or maybe this is a new one. I have no idea how many choppers Rook Donovan has at his disposal."

Jordan grunted. "As many as he deems necessary. This is why I ran. Why I didn't want to ask for help. He has the full backing of Scythe."

Mac shrugged, tipped the aircraft forward and picked up speed. "And you've got the best damn team I've ever worked with. Zain. Bodie. If I do this right, sooner or later I'm gonna serve this asshole up on the starboard side. Feel free to use extreme prejudice when I do."

Zain checked his weapon, readying the doors. "And here we didn't get you anything. Just count it down."

"Roger. We'll head for the ocean. Let's see how well our friend does five feet off the water as we slalom around some rocks."

Some tracer fire lit up the night left of the chopper, but Mac simply shoved the nose forward — got the helicopter screaming over the trees. Not quite as low as Foster pushed it, but damn close. She wove toward the water, mimicking the undulating landscape until they hit the cliffs. Then, she was all-in. Pegged the bird that five feet she'd talked about, weaving it along the shoreline, narrowly missing rocks and outcrops as she skimmed the cliff, then banked over — headed for a large rocky island just offshore.

She climbed over the top, then dropped in behind, bringing the helicopter into an aggressive hover, before backing it around the towering stone — lining Zain and Bodie up for that kill shot. "Less than ten…"

The Apache roared around the rock, banking hard to the right in an effort to avoid a collision and opening up their side just like Mac had promised.

Bodie and Zain didn't miss a beat, hitting the engine and rotors as the machine sailed past. Smoke poured out of the cowlings as the chopper limped back toward shore, vanishing into the night.

Mac peeled off, heading back toward the hangar. "Foster just took care of the other helicopter. He'll be sweeping behind us — ensuring there aren't any more surprises. Though, this won't be close to over until you decrypt that intel, Jordan. I just hope it's as damning as you thought, because I have a bad feeling your handler isn't going to take this loss sitting down."

CHAPTER TWELVE

Jordan reran the evening's events, the night rushing past the window in a ghostly blur, as Mackenzie started her approach to the hangar landing pad. A layer of fog hung above the water, the thick clouds gathering on the horizon promising more rain.

Unease slithered down Jordan's spine, roiling through her stomach in nauseating waves that had nothing to do with Mac tossing the chopper around or the firefight she'd left behind.

Something was off.

Despite their apparent victory, Jordan couldn't shake the scratchy feeling between her shoulder blades. That voice in her head nattering that it had been too easy.

Or maybe, too predictable.

Sure, Rook was meticulous and exacting, and she'd been running missions for him long enough to know his different strategies intimately. And this one wasn't sitting right. Especially if he'd known about the cabin. In fact, the more she replayed everything, the more it struck her how little Rook had accomplished, other than assuring the intel had been downloaded. That it was now on a piece of tech he could acquire, instead of stuck on her server.

Kash nudged her, Nyx at his feet. He brushed a few wisps of hair back from her face, his knuckles lingering against her skin. "Hey. You okay? I kinda thought you'd be a bit more relaxed now that we have the intel, but you look as if you might crawl out of your own skin."

She could lie. Tell Kash exactly what he wanted to hear. That it was leftover adrenaline. Or having to work as part of a team. Give herself time to figure out what was eating at her and how to fix it.

Except, where he'd trusted her. Had her back with little more than his gut instincts that she wasn't the one with the deadly agenda.

That she wasn't the monster.

"Okay, now you're scaring me." He inhaled, started patting her down. "Were you hit? Are you bleeding—"

"I'm fine. You're the one who shoved me to the ground when that Apache started firing. If anyone got hit, it was you."

Kash frowned as he straightened. "Vest, sweetheart. I'd already told you I'd be jumping in front if bullets started flying. So, what's wrong? And don't tell me nothing because your nose gets these adorable creases when you're trying to figure something out."

"It's nothing concrete, I just..." She huffed and ran her fingers through her hair. "What's his backup plan?"

"His backup plan?"

"Rook never does anything without backup plans for all the ways an op could play out. And one of them was us making it back, alive, with the intel. So, what am I missing?"

Any hint of a smile faded as Kash looked at his buddies, then back to her. "You think he had enough resources that he might have a squad waiting at the hangar when we land?"

"All I know is that this feels wrong."

Kash turned and tapped Mac on the shoulder. "Is it too late to do a fly by? Jordan's concerned we might have a fan club waiting for us."

Mac peeled off, banking the chopper over as she soared above the hangar — giving them a clear view of the parking lot below. Then she followed the long twisting driveway before angling it back. "There's an SUV at the end of the drive. That could be trouble."

She hit another button — started talking to someone else. "Okay, Foster's close. We'll land together, and you can storm the hangar while we're shutting down."

Mac circled around, Foster's machine coming in hot beside them before they flared off the speed and planted the machines on the tarmac.

Kash and his buddies jumped out before the aircraft fully touched down, hoofing it toward the hangar door. Jordan trailed behind, watching their six. Ensuring Rook didn't have a squad camped out on the rocks beyond the property, waiting for the right moment to climb over the edge and open fire.

Zain showed the countdown on his fingers, then they busted in. Zain and Bodie going high and left, Kash, Nyx and Chase going low and right, leaving her to just barrel up the middle. Face any threat head-on.

Darkness filled the massive space with only a couple dull emergency bulbs adding any hint of light. Jordan headed straight for the door leading to the main office, ready to slide along the floor or kick off a wall if some asshole in black tactical gear came bustling through. Reaching the other side without a suggestion of trouble didn't sit well. Had those voices in her head screaming.

Something was definitely off.

Kash darted through the doorway a moment later, his weapon sweeping the area, Nyx primed for a fight. He cleared the room before shuffling over to her, his gun still notched in his shoulder. Muscles tense. "Hangar's clear. Zain and Bodie are checking the perimeter."

Jordan moved to the door, peeking out the

window without presenting enough of a target someone might cap her through the glass. "I know you probably think I'm crazy…"

"You're not crazy. If your gut's telling you we've missed something, then we treat every location as if it might have been compromised."

She stared at him, wondering if he was real or if she'd fallen into a coma somewhere between that compound back in the Catskills and Raven's Cliff. If this was all in her head because she'd never had anyone put their faith in her the way Kash did. And despite wanting to brush it off to the by-product of their night together, she doubted any sex was great enough to account for his actions.

That he'd actually meant what he'd said before.

That he loved her.

Kash sighed, lowered his weapon, then brushed his thumb along her cheek. "Still doubting everything, huh?"

Jordan glared at him. "Would you stop reading my mind? And no, I don't want to know when you were suddenly gifted the ability. But it's annoying, in case you were wondering."

"I'm not reading your mind. More your expression. And the fact that I know you. Which I'm sure you're going to claim isn't possible. That you've barely told me anything about your past, and what you have is only a small part of it."

"Which is why it's impossible."

"Sweetheart. I know all the important details.

That you're strong. Intelligent. Insanely skilled. That you're willing to put your life on the line in order to do what's right. You could have walked away. Left that intel rotting on your server — disappeared into the ethos. I know you said nowhere's truly safe, but I'm betting some beach hut in the Maldives would have been exponentially safer than hanging out here in the hopes you'd get a chance to take Rook out."

"Hate to burst your bubble, Kash, but I didn't hang around this long out of honor."

The jerk grinned. "Which is the most important trait of all. No one with utter darkness in their heart, would risk it all over coffee dates and a kiss that shifted the Earth's axis."

Jordan reached up and brushed his jaw. "You're more than worth the risk. So, don't freaking die on me, okay?"

"You're not getting rid of me that easily."

He kissed her forehead, holding her close when the rest of his team walked into the room.

"You know, if you two are going to make out whenever you think people aren't watching," Zain thumbed at Foster, "just like Foster and Mac, I'm gonna start carrying my taser."

Jordan merely smiled at him. "I'm disappointed you aren't already. And we weren't technically making out."

"Trust me, Kash was only a breath away." He nodded at Bodie. "Perimeter's clear. We should head over to Bodie's office — decrypt this intel. But we'll all keep our damn heads on a swivel because I agree with Jordan. Something's off."

"It's the air." Jordan stepped back and wrapped her arms around her chest. "It's heavy or has a hint of… something."

"That's just Kash pumping out the pheromones to let everyone know you're his." Chase dodged Kash's slap. "Your side okay, Jordan?"

"Fine. Really."

Chase shook his head, then followed the team out, constantly scanning the area, his gun just a breath away from being ready. Kash waved Jordan on, trailing behind, always guarding her six. As if he thought it was easier to take a bullet meant for her if she wasn't watching him. But she couldn't take her gaze off him. Not overtly, but it always drifted back like the tide following the moon.

They reached Bodie's office, cleared it like they had the hangar with pairs of them moving through the building and circling the perimeter. They'd gathered in the main room when Bodie's phone rang. He frowned, answering it as he turned — got a bit of distance. Just enough his words didn't carry.

That voice in her head started shouting, again, and she knew, this call was the part of Rook's plan she'd missed.

Bodie returned, mouth pinched tight, eyes narrowed. "That was Greer. She wants all of us over at the Lighthouse Café. Said it's urgent. And no, she didn't give me additional details. I got the impression she either didn't think it was safe, or she simply didn't have enough to share."

Jordan's stomach dropped. "Shit."

Kash turned. "What?"

"It's him. It's Rook."

"You don't know—"

"Yes. I do. I said I'd missed something, that he always had a plan for every eventuality, and this is it." She shook her head, any hope of a future fading into the realization that she wasn't getting out of this alive. That she'd always been destined to pay for a past she couldn't change. "I never should have stayed."

"Hey." Kash stepped in front, gave her no other choice but to meet his gaze. "If this *is* Rook, then we'll deal with it, and him, like we always do. As a team. So, get that thought of facing him alone out of your head. We all agreed on the plan. If we missed something, then it's on all of us."

"My handler." She tapped her chest. "My mistake. While I love you for trying to bear this weight, if he hurt anyone, it's on me. And sooner or later, you're going to have to accept what I've known all along." She pushed past him, stopping at the door. "There's only one way this ends — bloody."

"Jordan…"

She kept moving. Walked out the door, headed to Zain's truck then waited. Half-considering just hoofing it all the way to the café. Anything to stem the restless roil of her stomach.

This was bad.

She felt it.

The hint of something that had been lingering in the air in the hangar. She recognized it, now. Licorice. The same scent as Rook's gun oil once it sat for a while. She'd gotten so used to it, she barely noticed it anymore. But it had clung to the surfaces inside the hangar. Waiting, like him.

Kash marched out a moment later, each step marking his displeasure. He stopped behind her, knuckles cracking. A measured exhale breezing past her.

She glanced at him, noting pinched lips and narrowed eyes. Slashes of red across his cheeks. "I promised you I wouldn't run."

"I came out here to finish our talk, not because I thought I'd have to chase you down."

"I thought about it. I..." She let her head tilt back. "I don't know how to do this. How to be Jordan and take on Rook. How to be part of team when every instinct wants me to face him alone. To end it by whatever means necessary."

She took a breath, met him head-on. "How to love you without hurting you."

He closed the distance. "How about you start by living? Because that's all I need you to do. We'll handle whatever this is. If Rook hurt people? We'll make sure he pays. But sacrificing yourself when we have options isn't the answer."

"And if we run out of options?"

"Let's see that we don't." He turned when his teammates bustled out of Bodie's office, sporting only sidearms. What she assumed was necessary in order to meet Greer without looking as if they'd just waged war.

Kash focused on her, again. "We'll listen to what Greer has to say. Go from there. However, it might mean bringing her into this."

Jordan opened the door. "If this is Rook, she's already part of it. Might as well give her a fighting chance at making it to the other side."

Jordan scooted over, absently scratching Nyx when she wedged her way between Jordan and Kash, as if the dog needed to be connected to both of them to settle. Another kick to Jordan's heart because she'd fallen for the mutt, too. Found Nyx's presence oddly calming, despite her skill set. A fact that made Jordan acutely aware of how human she'd become.

Greer stood outside the café doors as they pulled up, silently watching them pour out of the vehicles. Her gaze landed and held on Jordan, the unspoken weight nearly tripping her.

She'd been right.

The way Greer shifted on her feet. The unwavering focus. How she took in Bodie as if she already knew where he'd been and what he'd been doing. Hell, maybe she did. Maybe Bodie had confided in her. Or maybe the woman was simply that gifted. Sensed they'd all been recently engaged in a tactical maneuver. Could all but smell their heightened awareness and the inevitable edginess that persisted after a fight.

Greer nodded at Bodie. "Thanks for bringing everyone. Though, I get the feeling you were already together."

Chase stepped forward. He was the group's go-to where Greer was involved. It was obvious Chase wasn't the only one who was interested. Greer seemed equally taken by Chase, with his boyish good looks and easy charm. He was definitely the most laid back of the bunch, though Jordan suspected he merely hid it better. That he kept it coiled inside and sooner or later, something or someone would make it all snap.

Chase motioned to the diner. "Everything okay? Bodie's message sounded cryptic."

"That's because it's a freaking puzzle. First, there's no obvious indication anyone's been hurt. Which is damn curious because the second part is there's a burner cell in there, sitting on the counter with a flame drawn out of blood beside it." Greer's gaze shifted to Jordan. "I don't suppose that means anything to anyone?"

Nothing.

Not a hushed breath or a glance her way.

Just Kash's team standing strong. Waiting for her to decide if she wanted to let it all slide or confront the obvious answer that Rook had called her out.

Greer huffed. "Look, I know there's way more

going on here than you've let on. So, someone better start talking—"

"It's for me." Jordan took a breath and stepped forward. "But you already knew that."

Greer didn't so much as blink. "You take down bikers and trained military men like they're barely a speed bump along the road. You have the situational awareness of a squirrel on crack, and I know, if I did a real deep dark dive on you, Jordan Archer wouldn't have existed until seven months ago. So, yeah, I think it involves you."

"Technically, you'd find a pretty convincing backstop, seeing as I made it myself, but you're right." Jordan crossed her arms over her chest. "Now, we can either talk about it out here, where any asshole with a parabolic mic can hear us, or we can go inside, and you can let me assess what level of fucked we're at. Your choice."

"I want the truth."

"You really don't, but you deserve it." She nodded at the café. "I just need to know what he left before I drag you down that rabbit hole."

"And when you bolt on me?"

"She won't." Kash moved in beside her, Nyx hugging his leg. "You have my word."

Greer eyed Kash, then looked at Chase. "What about your word? Because your buddy's obviously in love with her and can't see past his heart, bleeding out on his sleeve."

Chase shrugged. "If Jordan wanted to ditch us,

there's nothing any of us could do to stop her. She chose to ride over here, with us, instead. Offered to bring you into the fold if it was necessary. She's good."

"All right." Greer backed up and opened the door. "I'd appreciate it if no one touched anything, though, I doubt a forensics crew would find anything useful. Right, Jordan?"

Jordan sighed. "Nothing you'd want to run through AFIS or any other database without gaining the attention of the kind of agencies who shoot first, worry about who they'd buried, later."

"And to think I was told working in a small town would lower my blood pressure."

"Sorry. If it makes you feel any better, I'll take care of the issue. That's a promise."

"*We'll* take care of it." Kash gave her a pointed look. "I know. You're still new to this team gig."

"Or maybe, I'm trying to remind all of you that you're crazy." Jordan groaned when he simply stood there, unyielding.

She gave his hand a squeeze, then drew herself up — walked inside. Nothing looked out of place, other than the phone sitting near the front. Which only emphasized that this was Rook. That he was playing with her.

"The owner says it was the strangest thing. He got a notification that his freezer had lost power so, he came over, opened the rear door and went inside. He did a quick once-over of the place, swears that,"

Greer pointed to the cell and blood stain, "wasn't there. He checked the freezer, found it working so, he did one more round, and in those thirty seconds, someone had left that behind."

Jordan walked over. Nothing telling, just a standard burner cell she knew Rook would call her on later, and that fire emblem written in blood. His way of addressing his message, she supposed. "Has anyone touched it?"

"Seriously? For all I know, opening it sets off a damn explosive. I'm curious about the flame, though."

"It's my code name."

"Flame?"

"Ember."

"I see." Greer shuffled over to Jordan. "I'm starting to think you're not with WITSEC like you'd hinted at. In fact, I'm betting it's much darker. One of those agencies you said shoot first."

Jordan didn't answer. She didn't need to. Besides, she knew they'd discuss it, *ad nauseam*, back at Bodie's. "The cell's not rigged."

"How do you know?"

"Because he's going to call me on it, later. Which makes me wonder... Why this seat? He had all of them to choose from, and the one at the end is closer to the rear door, especially considering he only had thirty seconds to get it set up. But he chose this one, specifically."

"I assume this mystery guy doesn't do anything by chance?"

"Never." Jordan ran through the past several months — all the people she'd put into memory. The regulars who, like Kash's team, always picked the same seats, when one image hit her hard.

She inhaled, replaying all the times he'd sat at the counter, chatting. Friendly, without being overbearing. Like he knew she'd weathered hard times and understood she wasn't ready for anyone to push. He'd had a look when they'd first met, as if he'd just seen a ghost, but it had vanished just as quickly.

"Jordan?" Kash was at her side, letting Chase grab her arm — take her pulse. "Sweetheart, breathe because you look like you did back in the chopper a moment before you passed out."

She gazed up at him, his words not quite making sense as she sorted through her memories, again — prayed she was wrong.

Fingers snapped in front of her. "Jordan!"

She blinked, tumbling against the counter once her lungs finally remembered how to suck in some air — clear the dots scattered across her vision. She glanced at his team, and she knew this was it. The straw that would break them. That she'd never recover from.

Chase shook his head. "Keep breathing, Jordan, or you're gonna face plant."

How could she breathe when her next words would ruin them?

Foster obviously recognized the look because he stepped forward, kept his gaze locked on hers. "Whatever you need to tell us, just say it."

She swallowed, nearly puked, then focused on Foster and Mackenzie. "Mac, do me a favor? Call Atticus."

CHAPTER THIRTEEN

Call Atticus.

Two words Kash knew would change the entire scope of the mission. Either band them together or isolate Jordan even more than she'd attempted on her own. What she obviously assumed would happen based on how ashen she looked. How she'd fallen against the counter when she'd gotten stuck in her own memories — shifted through all the faces she associated with that seat. The fact it was Mac's father…

To her credit, Mackenzie didn't panic. Didn't rip her jacket in an effort to remove her cell. She simply dug into her pocket, palmed her phone, then hit her dad's number. His phone rang over her cell's speakers, going to voicemail after several tries. "He always answers."

She took a step forward, the corners of her mouth twitching, the hand holding her cell shaking slightly.

"Did Rook take my father?" She pointed at the counter. "Is that his blood? Jesus, did I get him—"

Nyx growled, cutting off Mac and snapping Kash's attention toward the door. A couple stood just inside the entrance, feet braced apart, backs straight. Obviously law enforcement. Kash just wasn't sure which branch.

The massive guy looked at Mackenzie. "Your father's not dead. At least, not yet. But he's definitely Rook's bargaining chip."

Mac inhaled. "How do you know that? Do you work for him? Who the hell are you?"

Kash darted in front of Jordan as she pulled her piece — managed to stop her from simply firing. "Sweetheart, we don't know if they're friends or enemies, yet."

She didn't let up. "Anyone I don't know is an enemy until proven otherwise."

"Seriously, Cannon? This is why you don't just barge into the middle of a situation." Bodie turned to Jordan, looking as if he'd tackle her if she made a break for it. "Jordan, for the love of God, put the gun down. And don't vault over the counter and start chucking knives or plates or whatever's handy at them, either. They're here to help."

"Help? You told them about me? About Rook? Are you nuts?" Jordan holstered her weapon then took a step, stopping when Kash matched her movement — kept himself between her and everyone else. "You said I could trust you."

"Easy, sweetheart." Kash grabbed her shoulders — squeezed them. "Let's hear him out."

"You can, it's just… Can everyone take a breath?" Bodie glanced back at the guy — Cannon. "I told you to meet me at my office."

Cannon didn't seem fazed. Hadn't gone for the gun hiding beneath his jacket. He just stood there, his arms crossed over his expansive chest. Looking as if he could have stopped the bullet simply by flexing. "Why, when all the action's over here?"

"Because I hadn't gotten around to telling everyone about you and Jericho, yet? As you saw, Jordan's in more of a shoot first, kind of mood, than waiting to see if you might be trustworthy." Bodie scrubbed a hand down his face, still looking ready to dive at whoever broke ranks, first. "We'll go over proper introductions later, but… This is Rick Sloan, aka Cannon. He's ex-military. Spent a decade leading a Delta team. He has a high-tech security company in Seattle called Wayward Souls. His partner, in all aspects, is Jericho Nash. U.S. Deputy Marshal, to be exact."

"You called the Marshal Service?" Kash turned and closed the distance — got up in Bodie's personal space. "You'd better start talking, brother, because we vouched for you, and I'm a breath away from being the one you need to worry about."

"Easy folks." Cannon cleared his throat. "Bodie only called because he knew you'd need some reliable help dealing with this situation without ending up in

Leavenworth. We've been in similar circumstances, and our official contacts know, firsthand, not every scenario can go through the proper channels. So, everyone take a breath, like Bodie said. We'll explain everything in detail back at his office, because we have far more intel on this issue than anyone knows, even you... It's Jordan, right?" He didn't wait for a confirmation. "Kash, can you please ask your dog to stop growling at me? I take that personally."

Kash sized up Cannon, considering his options before whistling. "Nyx. Guard." She backed up two steps but kept her focus on the newcomers. Not quite growling, but she wasn't backing down. Was ready to launch at them if Kash gave her the command.

He glanced at Jordan and damn, she wasn't masking her feelings, now. Eyes narrowed, mouth pinched tight with red along her neck and cheeks, she looked like she had when she'd still been riding the adrenaline high after taking Tucker down.

She took a calculated step forward. The kind Kash's gut told him preceded a precision strike. "Give me one reason why I should even consider trusting you."

"Me. I'm the reason, love."

Kash cursed under his breath when another guy strolled in as if this was a freaking party. Tall. Leaner than Cannon, who Kash swore could take on a tank and win. This new guy was suave, almost pretty despite the vibe he gave off. Nothing like the death one rolling off Cannon. Similar to what Mac accused

Kash and his teammates of projecting. This was honed. The same kind of tightly wound energy Jordan emanated, only a thousand times more lethal. Add to that the British accent, and Kash swore the guy had double O written all over him.

Kash instinctively stepped between the Brit and Jordan before he realized he'd moved. Not that he didn't think Jordan could handle herself, but he'd promised her he'd have her back, and he wasn't failing her, now.

Jordan closed the distance, staying somewhat behind him. A fact he'd have to thank her for later. She tilted her head, staring at the guy before she grunted. "Miller?"

The guy — Miller — grinned. "Awe, I told Cannon you'd remember me. Though, I *am* a hard bloke to forget." He nodded at everyone else. "The name's Gibson Miller." He glanced at the phone, then at Kash, before focusing on her. "I see you finally broke both of Rook's rules, and in brilliant fashion, as always. The dog handler's a bit of a surprise. I always pictured you as more of a cat person."

"Jordan?" Kash gave her a quick glance. "We good?" *Or are we throwing down?* He didn't say that part out loud, but she got the message. Shifted closer and gave his arm a squeeze.

"Miller's good. Not convinced about the other two." She stabbed Bodie with a death glare. "Or Bodie, right now."

"Cannon and Jericho are mates, love. And Cannon

seems to think Bodie's an okay bloke, as do most of your friends so..." Miller waved at her. "Let's go back to whatever secure flat you've got and chat, yeah?"

Kash held his ground. He didn't care if Miller knew Jordan because she was still primed for a fight. Still on that razor's edge between control and execution. No one moved, and Kash suspected his teammates felt it, too. An electricity in the air that only needed a single spark to get it all firing.

Greer held up her hands. "All right, boys, everyone zip up. We've got more pressing issues than who's the real alpha dog. Like what you think's going on with Atticus."

Jordan sighed. "Cannon's right. This is all part of a larger plan that requires Atticus to stay breathing. At least, for now."

Greer nodded. "What level of fucked are we talking?"

"Well past holy, but not quite royally, yet."

"And you're sure this cell isn't going to blow up in my hands?"

Jordan shuffled over and grabbed it. "It'll be for me, anyways."

Kash glanced at Chase. "Chase? Buddy do me a solid and let me borrow your truck. Jordan and I need a few minutes. We'll meet you all at Bodie's in five."

Chase dug into his pocket and tossed Kash the keys. "Don't take too long, brother."

Kash nodded, waiting for everyone else to leave

before turning and pinning Jordan with his gaze. "All right. Out with it."

She frowned. "Out with what?"

"All the stuff whirling around inside your head. I can practically hear it. We both know you're not going to tell the team everything, so… Talk to me."

She pinched the bridge of her nose then leaned against the counter. Eyes closed. Everything clenched.

Kash moved over to her — brushed back some of that silky brown hair. "Jordan. Sweetheart, I know you think this is your fault—"

"It is."

"No, it's Rook's, but I understand where you're coming from. So, answer me this. Do you really think Atticus is still alive?"

"Rook won't kill him until he has what he wants."

"Are we talking you or the intel?"

"Honestly? Both. I made it personal. He's not going to just let me walk away."

Kash nodded, appreciating her honesty as he worked out how to bring Rook down and keep her breathing. "Who's Miller? Is he someone I need to be jealous of?"

She snorted. "You're jealous of Miller?"

"Not yet, but the fact you seem to trust him…"

"It's not like that. He got outed on a mission. I was working the same cartel, and I broke ranks to get him to safety." She shook her head. "I got hit a few times in the process, and he made sure I didn't die in return. No reason for you to feel anything, other than maybe gratitude."

"Sounds like one hell of a beginning."

"And ending. Besides, I didn't say I trusted him, I said he's good. That I don't think he's going to try to kill me. But there's only one person I truly trust, with your team being a close second."

He smiled, that warm fluttery feeling in his gut bubbling to life as he reached up and ran his thumb along her cheek. "Then, trust me to help you find a way out of this without you dying. I know you're going to have to face Rook. I've made peace with that. But it doesn't have to end with your sacrifice."

She sucked in her bottom lip, and he knew she was trying not to lie to him. To tell him what he needed to hear. "I can't lose you to him."

"Good, because I don't plan on losing. That includes you."

He leaned in, kissed her. Lost himself in the smooth press of her skin, the glide of her tongue as she tangled it with his. Her fingers landed in his hair, holding him close until Nyx growled as someone coughed behind them.

"Enough snogging, love. We've got work to do."

"No reason, huh?" Kash gritted his teeth, glancing back at Miller as the guy leaned against the door frame, looking way too cocky for his own good. "You sure it wasn't like that?"

"Let me put it this way. Out of everyone, I'd say Zain's his type. Only, there's something different about him, and I get the feeling Miller might already have his sights set on someone."

Miller chuckled. "I heard that."

Jordan raised a brow. "Am I wrong?"

"Are you two ready? I need a lift."

"So, I'm right. What's his name?"

"You always think you're right, love."

Kash turned. "Why didn't you go with everyone else?"

"Because I know Ember..." He sighed. "Sorry, Jordan, and she looked ready to bolt. Since she obviously fancies you, and you're gobsmacked over her, I thought you two might make a break for it. Figured someone should knock you both up the side of the head if needed."

"You MI6?"

Miller grinned. "When needed."

Kash nodded. "We should go before Chase comes looking for his truck."

They headed out, Nyx squishing in beside Jordan as they made the short trip back. His buddies stood outside Bodie's office. Waiting.

Miller slipped past them, chuckling to himself before disappearing inside. Leaving Kash and Jordan to face the rest of his crew.

Kash stopped in front of his teammates. "Call me crazy, but you all look as if you didn't think we'd come back."

Foster crossed his arms. "Between Rook snatching Atticus, Bodie calling in reinforcements he neglected to tell us about, and some fellow operative showing up, we figured there was a good forty percent chance you'd simply head to wherever Jordan thinks Rook is holed up and leave us hanging."

"You had forty percent, Foster, because you tend to give people the benefit of the doubt." Kash motioned toward Zain. "No way Zain picked anything under seventy-five."

Zain shrugged. "Closer to ninety, actually, because it's what I would have done if I were in Jordan's shoes." He clapped Kash on the back. "I'm glad you both proved me wrong because I'm seriously done with this Rook asshole. He's crossed a line, and there's no way I'm not getting some payback."

Foster huffed. "You'll have to take a number, Zain, because I have first dibs."

"Actually, boys, I have first dibs." Jordan matched Foster by crossing her arms over her chest. "And last, really. I might let you take out some of his disciples. Which is crazy because you should all be standing there, insisting I fix this on my own."

Foster scrunched up his face, looking at her as if she'd lost her mind. "What kind of men would we be if we did that? Besides, we both know this is going to be an epic shitshow. The kind with wet squads and impossible terrain. No way you can handle all the men Rook's going to have waiting and hand him his ass without backup."

Jordan just shook her head. "Like I said... Crazy." She pushed past them, stopping a foot inside.

"Thanks. I'm gonna need all the crazy I can get if we're going to finally put Rook in his place."

Kash stood there after she'd disappeared inside, glancing at his buddies. "We good?"

Chase huffed. "Just don't get any bright ideas about ditching us for real."

"And miss you and Greer giving each other awkward longing glances?"

"You're an ass."

"I love it when you talk dirty to me."

Chase rolled his eyes and headed inside, Zain trailing behind.

Foster lingered, toeing the cement as he blew out a rough breath. "If this goes poorly..."

"Jordan's confident Rook won't hurt Atticus until he has her and the intel. Honestly, the bastard's too smart, and far too cocky, to risk eliminating his only bargaining chip."

"I meant, Jordan, too. We've all seen how you look at her. How this has been months in the making. Just... Don't fucking die on me."

Foster turned and marched off, his words hanging in the air. It wasn't as if Kash wanted to die, either, but if he had to choose between his life and Jordan's...

Nyx nudged his leg, tail wagging. Eyes bright. She'd help him see this through. And once they'd taken care of Rook and Scythe, he'd do whatever it took to show Jordan she had a future in Raven's Cliff.

CHAPTER FOURTEEN

Jordan leaned against the far wall, plotting. She just wasn't sure which to act on first. If she should strangle Bodie, disappear and hunt down Rook, or march over to Kash and kiss him.

She brushed the back of her hand across her mouth. She still tasted him on her lips. The hint of coffee and spice mixed with something innately him. Heat or maybe ice. She only knew that she was addicted to it. To him.

Footsteps echoed through the room as Foster walked in, giving her a small smile before heading for Mac — tugging her into a firm embrace. Jordan had expected Mac to yell. Maybe throw a punch. But she'd been oddly quiet.

"I know that look." Kash moved in beside her, Nyx choosing to sit between them, again. "No one in here blames you."

Jordan nodded at Mackenzie. "You sure about that?"

"Mac's upset. Scared. Undoubtedly angry. It's just not at you, which is the real issue." He bumped shoulders with her. "Give it time. You'll get used to having people care about you."

Jordan bit back the part where she wasn't convinced she'd live long enough to get accustomed to anything when Cannon stepped forward, his mere presence commanding attention.

Cannon shoved his hands in his pockets, which only made him seem even more imposing. "I could stand here and give you all a laundry list of reasons why you can trust us. Missions. Connections. But the truth is, trust is earned, not given. So, let's cut through the bullshit and just get down to facts."

He nodded toward Bodie. "Bodie called me a couple days ago, after the incident at the café involving Tucker Grant. He knows we've got a tech analyst who's…" Cannon chuckled. "To say she's scary good with a keyboard is an understatement. She also happens to be NSA—"

"You involved the National Security Agency? God, do you all have a death wish?" Jordan ignored Kash's hand on her arm. "Do you have any idea how dialed in Rook is? He's got people watching *every* agency. He gets just a suggestion that someone is searching for him or Scythe…"

Dead.

They were all dead. Sure, she suspected Rook

already knew her location before Tucker had waltzed in and outed her, but that incident had sealed her fate. The fact someone from the NSA had gone digging after meant Rook would be more suspicious. More prepared.

Cannon glanced at Kash then back to her. "Trust me, Becca Tate doesn't leave trails or traces. She's you, only with computers. A ghost."

"If I was half as good as you seem to think, I wouldn't be in this mess."

"You've avoided Scythe for seven months on your own. And yeah, I know exactly who and what they are. Had a buddy go dark with them. He discovered something he shouldn't and tried to leave. Only made it a week before he had an 'accident'. So, you do the math." Cannon rolled his shoulders. "Bodie's going to get Becca on a secure video chat. You really need to listen to what she has to say because this goes so much deeper than just Rook Donovan."

Cannon nodded at Bodie, and the man started hitting keys, mumbling to himself before light flickered over his face and he smiled.

"Hey, Becca. Great to see you, again. Give me a second, and I'll spin the monitor." Bodie turned it, then walked around to the other side of his desk. "Quick introductions. The guy with long hair is Foster Beckett, and the woman on his right is Mackenzie Parker. It's her father, Atticus, who's gone missing. Next to her is Zain Everett, then Chase Remington. Finally, over here," he waved at Jordan and Kash, "we've got Kash Sinclair with his furry sidekick, Nyx, and Jordan Archer. You know her through your digging as Ember."

The woman on the screen — this Becca person — smiled. "Nice to meet everyone. Circumstances suck, but that's usually how these things go, and time is never a luxury we have so, let's get to it. Jordan... I assume you're not going by Ember any longer?"

Jordan snorted. "I'd hoped I'd buried her in the past, but we can't really do that, can we." She hadn't phrased it as a question, and Becca merely nodded.

"Well, you've done a pretty kickass job of staying off-grid. Which is saying a lot considering how many resources Scythe has invested in finding you. They've got agents monitoring cell phones and CCTV footage. Anything they can hack from dash cams to ATMs to traffic cams. Any sort of photo or video that makes it online. Hell, they have agents just driving through small towns live-streaming on the off-chance they'd catch a glimpse of you. I'm impressed it took them this long."

Jordan shuffled on her feet. Being praised for simply surviving then putting people she cared about in harm's way didn't sit well. "In the end, the result's the same. Cannon says this is about more than just me pissing off Rook and threatening to post the intel."

"First off, I'm running all of my programs remotely through Bodie's setup, so nothing was transferred over. You still have the intel on your end.

Speaking of which... What you downloaded." Becca whistled. "I'm assuming you didn't have a chance to go through all of it?"

"Rook sent an RPG into the bunker while I was attempting to extract the asset. So, no, I didn't have time."

A growl. Low. Gravelly.

Jordan glanced at Nyx, then Kash, but she couldn't tell if it had been the dog or the handler.

"Sounds like your team's the same as mine. Which is lucky because you're going to need every ounce of skill they have." Becca tapped more keys, had images and manifests scrolling down the screen. "I'm betting you're familiar with all the weapons and drug dealing, the intelligence smuggling and asset elimination. But that's all under Scythe's jurisdiction. The reason Rook's so hellbent on getting his hands on this is what I suspect you weren't aware of. What do you know about an agency called Sandman?"

Jordan frowned. "I've never heard of it."

"It's Rook Donovan's own creation. I guess running a ghost agency wasn't enough. He needed to create his own within the company."

"Wait. Rook created his own ghost squad? Is running his own missions?"

"Seems he handpicked a few agents from Scythe and started sending them on unsanctioned ops about three years ago. Nothing too obvious at first, but they got riskier and crazier over the last year you were with them."

"Is my name on that list?"

Becca looked over Jordan's shoulder at Kash. "You *are* the list. Well, there's one other who pops up a lot. Icarus."

"I'm not familiar with that operative, but we always worked alone."

"It's a bit strange. I haven't been able to uncover anything about them, other than the code name. It seems they were recruited differently. I'll keep digging until I have an answer, but you were his go-to. Looks like you didn't disappoint."

"Not exactly something I should be proud of." Jordan pinched the bridge of her nose, just like back in the diner. Hoping to stop the spread of pain through her temples. "Why didn't I figure this out sooner? Hell, at all. I thought it was just about the drugs and the weapons, but…"

"He hid it well. Got one of his IT guys to route everything through the Scythe mainframe — made it look legit. I'm impressed you picked up on anything because *this* is a work of art."

"So, that's why he won't let it slide. If Scythe finds out he's been playing them — possibly trying to replace their agency with his…"

"I imagine it wouldn't end well. Even for someone with his connections and status." Becca pursed her lips, looking at Cannon then Kash. As if she'd already figured out Jordan was intimately involved with him.

Jordan sighed. "Whatever else you need to say, just spit it out."

Becca folded her hands on her desk. "You're not the first agent who uncovered the existence of Sandman. There were two others. Both met with untimely accidents."

Jordan glanced at Cannon. "Was one of them Cannon's friend?"

"Dwayne Goodman. Code name, Hopper. This was after you left. Rook cut back on the number of missions. My guess is, he couldn't find anyone to fill your shoes. But he sent Hopper on half a dozen before one of Rook's cyber guys got careless and left a bit of a breadcrumb for Hopper to follow. He'd been a communication specialist and..."

"The other?"

Becca's jaw clenched impossibly tighter, some of the color draining from her face. "He was a year before you."

Jordan waited, but Becca just kept staring, until everything shifted into place. "Raider."

"I'm sorry. I think that's why he sent you all those coded messages—"

"All? I only got one regarding his safehouse. How to access it. A subtle hint that if I ever had to bail, I should head here, to Raven's Cliff. That I might find some sort of salvation."

"Raider sent you over a dozen, but I imagine Rook intercepted the rest. As for Raven's Cliff... Turns out, Raider, Thomas Cross back then, knew Atticus Parker. Ran missions for him before shifting over to Scythe."

"Is that why Rook targeted Atticus? It wasn't because of my connection to Foster's team but because of my uncle?" She fisted her hands, wanting to punch them through the nearest wall. "Did Atticus know about me, all along? Did he... Was he the reason I got the job at the café without intense background checks? How I was able to rent that cabin with little more than a simple form? Did I put him in Rook's crosshairs the second I set foot in town? Jesus."

"Jordan." Mac's voice echoed through the room, and Jordan had to fight not to cringe. To look the other woman in the eyes when all she could think was how she'd ruined everything.

Mac held her head high. "It doesn't matter why Rook took my father. All that matters is that we get him back and take Rook down. All things considered, you're our best shot at that."

Jordan stared at Mac then slowly made her way through the rest of Kash's buddies, finally ending with Kash. She didn't deserve the unyielding faith staring back at her, but she'd take her wins where she could find them.

"Becca? If I give you some parameters, can you search the area, say an hour or two in any direction? Maybe we can narrow down a handful of locations Rook might be hiding in. Get a jumpstart on some kind of strategy because I know him, and he's not going to give us any time to adapt once he calls."

Becca beamed. "Girlfriend, I can do you one

better. I can list all the areas in order of probability based on everything you give me. More is better here, and..."

An alarm sounded throughout the room. Not a siren, like Jordan would expect if there was a fire or an inbound missile. This was just a few pings, then silence.

Becca inhaled. "Whoa. What the..."

She tapped more keys, windows and folders flying across the screen. Too fast for Jordan to make out any of the words. Becca seemed to follow everything. Clicked her way until she had blueprints of the building superimposed on the monitor. "I'm not sure what's going on, but someone just pinged a tracking device inside the room."

Bodie shook his head. "No way. Not a chance Rook's men infiltrated my office without setting off something. I might not be at your level when it comes to hacking, but I know how to secure my own damn building."

Becca frowned, her fingers still racing over the keyboard. "It's odd. It's more of a homing beacon. Very low range, no more than a few hundred feet." More typing. "There's some sort of code embedded in the transmission. Give me a minute, and I can probably source it..."

She froze, gaze locked on her screen before lifting to look at them. She swept the gathering of people, lingering on Jordan. "I'm sorry, but it's you."

Jordan frowned, studying Kash's team before

coughing. "Me?" When Becca just stared at her, she shook her head. "It can't be me. These aren't even my clothes, and I haven't been close enough to any of Rook's men for one of them to have slipped a tracker on me. It must be something else." She held up the cell. "The phone?"

"Not to sound vain, but I'm pretty damn good at what I do, and this isn't coming from a cell. The signal would be stronger, and the coding would be different. I honestly don't know what this is. I've never seen anything like it before."

"I think I'd know if Rook implanted…"

The answer hit her. Took her breath away. Left her standing there, mouth gaped open, lungs refusing to inflate. She turned to look at Kash, but he'd obviously already arrived at the same conclusion.

He raked his fingers through his hair, tousling strands across his face. "Shit. Your implant."

"I had a private doctor inject that. I never trusted anyone remotely associated with Scythe unless I was dying."

Kash took a breath — grabbed her hands. "And were you ever close to dying since you had your last one replaced?"

"I…" Everything locked down tight. Her throat, her lungs, her damn heart. Frozen. Just like Becca had been a few moments earlier.

Kash moved in close. "Relax, sweetheart. Just breathe."

"Breathe? God, what if…" She rolled her

shoulders, wanting to claw out of her own skin. "I need a knife. Now."

"Easy..." Chase darted over. "No one's getting a freaking knife. Just, talk me through it. Obviously, you both think you know what kind of implant Becca's talking about."

Jordan met him head-on. "It's supposed to be for birth control, because God forbid one of Rook's *assets* did something as insane as get pregnant. I had it replaced a year ago, but a month before I ran, I had a mission go seriously sideways. Barely made it to the extraction site before I passed out. It was one of the few times I'd ever been thankful Scythe has its own physicians. I never thought..."

Chase merely nodded, thanking Zain when his buddy handed Chase his medic bag. What Jordan assumed was always waiting in Chase's truck. "I assume nothing changed to make you suspect it had been swapped out?"

Jordan resisted rolling her eyes. "I was always in that fifty percent who didn't get any additional benefits other than the obvious, if you get my drift."

"No need to say more. Is the implant under your arm?"

"Scapula. I get hit too often in the arm to risk putting it there."

Chase didn't have to ask her to lift her shirt. She had her form-fitting sweaters off and her tank yanked over to one side before he could open his bag and remove a scalpel.

He probed the area, hissing out his next breath. "Damn."

"What?" She tried to look over her shoulder, but he tsked.

"This'll go a lot smoother if you don't move. And whoever put this in went way too deep. It's supposed to sit just under the skin, not in your damn muscle."

"I don't care if you have to shove a sword in there, just get the freaking thing out."

"Spies." He removed a syringe. "Let me freeze the area a bit. And no, that's not up for debate. You don't have to muscle through me slicing a six-inch groove in your back to prove you're tough. We already know."

Jordan stood there, picturing all the ways she'd strangle Rook once she got her hands on him, when Chase sighed. She chanced another glance, when he held up the unit. "That son of a bitch."

"It's definitely *not* for birth control." Chase dropped it into the palm of her hand. "Let me get some skin adhesive on this before you try to kill anyone, okay?"

Jordan stared at the device, wondering how she'd been so naive. Why she hadn't thought to check. If this was the first time Rook had made the swap or if he'd used the handful of other times she'd been medically compromised to insert similar implants.

Which brought up another issue, but she could worry about the unprotected sex with Kash, later. Assuming she was still alive.

Chase taped a bandage over her back and gave her arm a pat. "I don't get it. Why would he exchange your implant with a tracker that has such limited range?"

"Because he's an obsessive, manipulating, narcissistic bastard." She resisted the urge to punch the nearest wall. "Damn. Did he get a lock on me?"

"I jammed the signal before he would have gotten more than the general area." Becca sighed. "But I'm sure he already knows where you are."

"And everyone wonders why I have trust issues. Can you—"

The burner cell rang.

Becca started tapping keys, again. "I'll do what I can to trace it but…"

"Don't worry. He's going to tell me exactly where to find him." Jordan took a breath, then answered, putting it on speaker. "Rook."

He chuckled. "Ember. Or do you prefer Jordan, now?"

"If you knew where I was, you could have just knocked on the door so we could have this chat in person."

"What's wrong? Miss me, already?"

"I promised you I was going to stick a knife in your back. I can't do that unless we're in the same room."

"I thought the point of shifting into Jordan was to reduce your violent tendencies?"

Jordan laughed. "I guess you just bring out the vengeance in me. I want to speak to Atticus."

"He's fine."

"Then, put him on."

Rook breathed heavily into the phone. "You know how this works. He stays alive as long as you follow the rules."

"This isn't about rules. This is about which side of me shows up for the meeting. Now, put him on, or I'll assume he's dead, and I'm not sure you have enough men on hand to wage that war."

Rook huffed, then the sound changed.

"Jordan? Don't you dare make a deal with this bastard."

Mac inhaled as her father's voice echoed through the room. Rough. Definitely edged with pain.

Jordan fisted her hand, using the bite of her nails against her palm to ease the jumpy feeling in her gut. "Are you okay, Atticus?"

"Don't worry about me. I promised Thomas I'd keep an eye on you if you ever showed up. Don't make a liar out of me. You need to run—"

Everything cut off, just the rustle of fabric — something heavy hitting the floor in the background.

"Parker always was the sentimental type. You have your proof. Now, I assume you've decrypted all the intel." He took a breath — let it rasp over the line as he blew it out. "I'm gonna need that back."

Jordan swallowed past the lump in her throat. "Where and when?"

"What? No counter proposal?"

"We both knew there was only one way this was ever going to end. Do you have a location, or am I picking it?"

The phone dinged, a text popping up in the window.

"I just sent you the coordinates. It's a bit *off* the beaten path. Let's say, midnight. I'm afraid that won't give you much time to strategize before you have to leave. And that's assuming you get your new friends to give you a lift. You can bring two plus the pilot to retrieve Atticus. If I see even a suggestion of anyone else, he's dead, along with all those *friends* you've put in my sights. And I trust you know enough to come unarmed."

"You just keep your end of the bargain."

"Don't insult me. I don't renege on my promises."

"Then, I'll see you at midnight."

"I mean it, Ember. Try to double cross me, again, and I'll drown Raven's Cliff in their blood."

"I get it. And Rook..." She pressed the phone against her jaw. "This ends. Tonight."

She hung up, hating the fact her hand shook. Not much and not something any of Kash's team might notice. But she did. Each tiny vibration reminding her of how far she'd fallen. That she wasn't the operative she'd been when she'd limped out of that warehouse. That somewhere along the line, she'd started caring.

Kash moved in beside her. He was the reason she'd changed. Not because he'd asked her to, but because he'd dared her to move beyond her comfort zone. To be more than just an asset for Rook to manipulate.

He'd dared her to become Jordan Archer. Ex-operative, and the woman in love with him.

He nudged her shoulder. "You okay?"

She looked over at him. Memorized his face. Let the love gleaming back at her burn into her psyche. "I…"

What could she say? That she wasn't close to being okay? That a part of her wanted them to let her do this alone? To die while he still looked at her like he was right now. As if she wasn't the person who might destroy his family.

Instead, she glanced at Becca. "I know you've already got those coordinates locked down. How screwed are we?"

Becca frowned. "I do, but… I honestly don't know. It looks like it's in the middle of nowhere about half an hour south of here along to the coast. I'm just not sure what I'm looking at."

Foster cursed. "I think I know where the bastard's hiding. Can you put the map up on the monitor?"

Becca hit a few keys, then the map popped up.

"Damn it. There are a series of interlocking caves and lava tubes all along that stretch of coastline. My dad used to take me and my cousin, Keaton, there to explore when we were kids. But the constant punishment from the Pacific Ocean eventually causes the roofs to cave in. A couple kids were killed farther south, and the forestry service pretty much buried their existence. Locals know but... I had no idea any of them were still useable."

Jordan nodded. "Can you get us there?"

"Getting there's easy. Landing..." He raked his hand through his hair. "Since Rook's expecting us, I can plant the skids on that stretch of rocky shore. But there's no way I could get a backup crew anywhere close without him knowing with how sounds get amplified by all the rocks."

Zain edged forward, tapping his chin as he studied the landscape. "You know what that reminds me of? The shoreline by Cascade Head where Striker had Mac and Kash held hostage."

Foster turned to Zain. "Is that your subtle way of suggesting we call a friend?"

"It wasn't subtle, and if anyone could pilot a boat amidst those rocks and shoals without getting us all killed, it's Saylor."

"No." Jordan took a few steps their way. "We've already got Greer over there, itching to call in her old friends from the Bureau. Cannon, Jericho and Miller looking as if they've got a plan they haven't told us about trying to claw it's way free, and all of you signing up to be Rook's next casualties. We don't need to add anyone else to his hit list."

"I realize we haven't worked out all the logistics. How we'll concede to Rook's demands without leaving you hanging. But regardless of what we decide, it'll involve getting a team in close that Rook isn't aware of. And the only way to do that is by boat. Which means, we'll need Saylor." Zain stopped her from interrupting. "She's ex-Coast Guard. She can handle herself."

"I don't care if she's an ex-assassin. This is crazy. I should go. Alone." She turned to Kash. "I know. That's not how teams work but... Damn it, Kash. Rook's *the* ghost operative. Practically wrote the book on modern shadow ops. He'll know all of your team's background, and he'll be prepared to fight *you*. Not some arbitrary people I might have roped into helping me. You. Specifically. And the men helping him will reflect that."

Jordan looked him in the eyes. "Please don't ask me to send you all there to die."

Kash glanced at his buddies, including the others, then slowly made his way over to her. He didn't take her hand, just stood there. Calm. Determined. "We really need to work on your team-building skills. Ah," he placed a single finger over her lips, "my turn. We don't care how many men Rook has or how skilled they are. We've all humped our way through missions to hell and back, and we're still here. So, this is what we're gonna do. We're going to take a breath, then hash out a plan that provides you with a ridiculous amount of backup while hopefully keeping everyone alive. You heard Rook. You need Foster or Mac to get you there. And we'd just follow, anyways, so..."

She leaned into his hand. "You do realize I'll kill any of you if you don't come back."

"I'd expect nothing less."

She sighed, wishing she had the strength to push past them and figure it out on her own. But she'd be lying if she didn't admit she wanted the help. That for once in her life, she knew she couldn't complete the mission alone.

"Fine. But I mean it. Die, and I'll kill you." She turned to Cannon, Jericho and Miller. "Before we start calling people and readying boats and helicopters, I want to know what your angle is. Because it's obvious you have one."

Jericho grinned. "I like her. And you're right. Rook's undertakings have gotten the attention of a few high-level players inside the Department of Justice. They'd really love to have a chat with him so, if possible, we're here to take him in. Alive. Along with all that intel. Make sure he doesn't slip through the cracks and end up reinventing himself for another agency."

Jordan eyed them. "You can have the intel if it survives the meeting. But I can't make any promises about him not dying. He's not likely to give us many options."

Becca cleared her throat, drawing their attention. "I can't help you regarding Rook, but with respect to the intel... I think I can tweak the coding on the drive so it sends all the information back to my server when Rook tries to access it while erasing what we give him. A version of what's already embedded, so to speak. Unfortunately, that won't solve the issue if he decides to simply destroy the thumb drive."

"It's better than what we have now."

"I'll get started, while you all work your strategizing magic."

Jordan grabbed Kash's hand. "Fine. We can talk it over. See if there's a way to beat Rook at his own game. Just know this. I meant what I said. Whatever it takes. Whatever the price. It ends here."

CHAPTER FIFTEEN

Kash stood in Bodie's office, brooding. A mixture of anger and fear and, damn it, love burning beneath his skin as his teammates stood beside him, looking as if they found it equally hard to breathe. To work past the part of the plan where Jordan gave Rook exactly what he wanted.

Her and the intel.

Alone.

Kash understood her reasoning. What seemed like a compromise between her going solo and having that backup they'd talked about. Except where there was a thousand ways the plan could backfire, and very few where she didn't end up sacrificing herself.

Miller stood next to her, occasionally nodding. The only one among them who seemed onboard with any of it. What was obviously a spy mentality because even Cannon and Jericho frowned, shifting restlessly on their feet as if they couldn't quite contain the nervous energy strumming through the air.

Miller paused for a moment and scanned the room before chuckling. "If I ever needed proof that operatives and military blokes see the world differently…" He gestured at how everyone, but him and Jordan, had gathered together, leaving them isolated. "I've got it. Kash. You look like you have an opinion you'd like to share, mate."

Kash glanced at his teammates, then focused on Jordan. "Everyone already knows my opinion. I hate the plan."

Zain nodded. "You're not the only one, brother."

Cannon shuffled as he blew out a rough breath. "I gotta admit, I'm not fond of it, either. We're just assuming Rook will hand Atticus over instead of simply shooting everyone point blank. Call me crazy, but I'm not that trusting."

Miller held up his hand. "Granted, I'm not chuffed about it, either, but Jordan knows Rook better than anyone. We need to keep that in mind."

"I'm not suggesting we don't." Kash took a step forward, his gaze locked on Jordan's. "But there's got to be a better option than a string of Hail Marys all stitched together."

The room fell silent, Kash's last statement lingering in the air. Hanging like a mist about to rain down over them.

Jordan scanned the meager bits of intel Becca had unearthed about the cave, then focused on him.

Mouth pinched tight. She looked as if she wanted to say something, then sighed, defeat rounding her shoulders.

Kash closed the distance. "Jordan…"

She huffed. "I don't like it either."

"Perfect. Then, we'll scrap it."

"But it's the only way to get Atticus back." She held up her hand. "I know. You don't want me to face Rook alone. Don't trust that he won't grab the intel, then put a bullet between my eyes. And I get it. That's what you'd do. You all neutralize the threat, then move on. Except, he's not like you."

"The man was a Ranger and a Green Beret. That kind of mentality doesn't get erased just because he moved to Shadow Ops."

"That's not what I mean." She raked her hand through her hair. "I'm not a threat. Not in the way you're thinking. He doesn't want to kill me."

Zain snorted. "So, blowing that cabin…"

"His men were close enough to track me. They knew I wasn't inside. The same thing with my rental. They didn't fill it full of holes until the first team failed, and Kash and I were clear. I'm not saying if they'd terminated me, Rook wouldn't have shrugged and gone on with his life. But now that he has Atticus — has that leverage over me…" She blew out a heavy sigh. "I'm worth more to him alive."

Zain shook his head. "That's great in theory, but you rebelled once. What's to keep you from simply bailing? I get that in his eyes, he's invested twenty years in your training, and it's obvious you're his go-to agent. But how could he ever trust you to complete a mission when you'd likely bolt at the first chance?"

Jordan stared at Zain before her gaze skipped over to Kash.

Kash cursed. "Me."

She simply smiled.

"You honestly think he'd be able to sustain a threat on my life for the next twenty years?"

"It wouldn't just be your life. Zain, Chase. Foster and Mac — anyone else who happens along. Rook has virtually endless resources. He's the type of guy who'd have a handful of men infiltrate the community, just waiting in case I ever went rogue." She walked over — took his hand. "You're all willing to die for me. How can you expect anything less in return?"

"Getting killed while executing a sound plan is one thing. This…" He leaned into her palm when she rested it against his cheek. "This feels like a surrender."

"That's because you're choosing to overlook the part where I'm counting on all of you to save my ass. I know Rook. He's not going to grab me, then hop on a boat or a chopper you could easily follow. He'll drag my ass through those tunnels to that giant cave in the center. He'll be expecting me to have a plan, and that's where he'll try to outsmart me. Where you'll all be waiting to stop him."

"That's assuming those tunnels still exist. That they haven't caved in."

Jordan pointed to one of the few images Becca had found online. "That photo was taken last fall. I see at least three openings. And Becca did a search. She couldn't find any evidence of seismic events that suggest there's been any large-scale cave-ins."

"Which is great until you're standing in that chamber, waiting for us to pop out, but we can't make it more than twenty feet down the tunnels."

"I know this isn't how you like to plan your ops. Rook's a lot of things, but he's a man of his word. And if we don't follow his instructions, he'll kill Atticus, then hold true to his other threat. And I can't..."

Tears glistened in her eyes, and she turned, but not before a few slipped free — one shattering on the floor the way Kash's heart cracked at the thought of how much this cost her. That this wasn't her running. It was her begging them to help her stay.

He moved in close, pressing his chest to her back. "Sweetheart."

"I've never had a family. Never felt as if I belonged... Until now. Until you and your team." She glanced at him over her shoulder, cheeks damp. Eyes glassy. "There's nothing I won't do to protect this. I'm not asking you to give me up. I'm asking you to bring me back. Because I know, no matter what odds you face inside those tunnels, you'll come out on top. And you'll be there, waiting, just like we planned."

Kash pursed his lips, glancing at his teammates then back to her. "You're sure he's not going to kill you?"

"As sure as I can be. He'll want me to suffer. I can't do that if I'm dead."

"And we're confident we'll be able to receive the tracker signal underground?" The thought of Chase putting it back in place irritated him. Knowing Rook would be tracking her, too. But having that invisible lifeline definitely eased a bit of the rawness raging inside Kash's head. What might edge the odds in their favor.

Becca chimed in. "Are you doubting my ability to hack that thing? I'm actually hurt."

Kash sighed. "I'll assume that's a yes."

Becca merely stared at him. "It's good to go. I've increased the strength of the signal, and I've sent the tracking app to everyone's phone. As long as you don't stray more than half a mile away, it should work, regardless of where you are."

"Then, we'd better finalize this because we're out of time."

Cannon shook his head but scoured over the map with the rest of Kash's team, divvying up their resources. The somber mood followed them out as they headed for their respective trucks. Mac would take Chase and Greer with Jordan, leaving Foster and Bodie to man their overwatch as the rest of them rendezvoused with Saylor — made a beeline for the tunnels south of the where Rook would be waiting.

Kash held up his hand as everyone piled into the vehicles, holding Jordan's gaze. She pursed her lips, then launched herself at him, eating at his mouth when he caught her — held her until he was sure he'd used up all their extra time.

She wiped her thumb across his mouth. "Don't die."

"And risk having you kill me a second time? That's crazy." He held on a bit longer when she went to push free. "I know this needs to end, but you living is worth more than Rook dying."

She smiled, though it didn't quite reach her eyes. "Don't be late."

She jumped in, still watching him as Foster drove off. Kash climbed into Zain's truck, absently stroking Nyx as they headed for the marina.

Saylor stood beside one of her boats, arms crossed, toe tapping the dock. "Just once, it'd be nice if these life and death missions didn't crop up with a storm front baring down on us."

Zain grinned. "What's the fun in that? Besides, I think you miss the adrenaline rush you got in the Coast Guard." He leaned in close. "Face it. You love this shit."

She rolled her eyes, waving everyone onboard. Miller cast them off as Saylor worked the throttle, got the boat through the surf then headed south. White caps rolled across the ocean, the beginnings of the incoming front already kicking up the wind and the spray. Clouds thickened around them as the vessel cut through the water, rising and falling with the increasing swells.

Nyx pressed against Kash's leg. She obviously sensed his unrest, staying closer than usual. Alert. Ready to react at the first hint of trouble. He tried to tamp it down, but all that looped through his head was the look in Jordan's eyes as she'd disappeared into the night. That the kiss they'd shared outside Bodie's office would be their last.

Kash scrubbed a hand down his face. There was plenty to be concerned about, the fact her implant hadn't been the kind they'd counted on was right up there. But they could worry about that if they lived past tonight. If the future was more than a black hole threatening to suck them both over the event horizon.

Zain sat beside him, blinking against the stinging spray. "She'll be okay."

Kash nodded. Not because he believed it, but because he wasn't about to jinx the mission before it began. Put any possibility other than success out into the universe. He'd tempted Fate enough, lately. No sense pissing her off. "It's not just her I'm worried about. If anything happens to Atticus…"

He wasn't sure how Mac would take it. How any of them would. Despite the fact Atticus was opinionated, ornery and a giant pain in their asses, he was the heart of Raven's Watch.

"The old coot's too stubborn to die."

"Let's hope you're right."

"I'm always right, brother." He grunted when the boat tipped up then dropped down, shooting water out both sides. "Looks like that storm's moving in fast."

"Then, it's a good thing our captain seems to thrive on the challenge." Kash nudged him. "You ever gonna ask her out?"

"Who says I haven't?"

"Nyx would know if you were *entertaining* anyone, and she'd rat you out."

Zain chuckled. "Maybe I'm just waiting to see how your experiment in love goes, first. Because I can't tell if you're on cloud nine or paddling down the river Styx."

"Ask me, again, once this is over."

Zain clapped him on the shoulder, then moved to Saylor's side. She gave him a quick glance, lingering a bit longer than necessary before pointing at something in the distance. Kash squinted against the utter blackness. Large rocks rose out of the frothing surf, slashing against the inky sky like jagged scars. Waves beat against the sides, shooting into the air only to rain down over the boulders, swirling with the churning water before flowing out — starting the cycle all over again.

Saylor reduced the throttle, looking back at everyone across her shoulder. "This is where it gets tricky. There's nothing but rocks and more rocks between us and our only viable docking location. I had the option of running the boat aground last time. We don't have that luxury here."

"Wait." Cannon waved at the boat. "You crashed last time you did something like this?"

"I didn't crash. I made a painful decision. Which isn't an option. So, everyone get ready. I only get one shot at this."

"And if you miss?"

"Then, I hope everyone knows how to swim." She turned away, then quickly gazed back. "Everyone *does* know how to swim, right?"

She didn't wait for an answer, hitting the throttle and lurching the boat ahead. It danced over the waves, rising and falling amidst the rocks until Kash wasn't sure how they were still in one piece. How she maneuvered the craft in the dead of night, the wind howling around them as the water raged against the hull, spitting and gurgling as if it was taking its last breath. Like Sean had that fateful night in the helicopter.

Kash pushed the memories aside and tightened his grip on Nyx's lead. He couldn't afford to get distracted. To be anything less than two hundred percent invested. He'd already lost family. He wasn't losing anyone else.

Saylor spun the wheel, toed the boat into the waves, then allowed them to push her back, aligning her with that docking spot she'd mentioned. More like the only flat rock in the entire area. A massive, craggy spire protected it from the worst of the surge, but getting there wasn't going to be easy. Zain moved over to the side, line in hand, not an ounce of fear as he readied himself to jump.

Kash pushed to his feet, snagging Zain's arm. "What the hell do you think you're doing?"

Zain shrugged. "Someone needs to jump over. Saylor's exceptional, but she can't do this alone."

"Then give the line to Nyx. She can make the distance in her sleep."

"Sorry. Pretty sure we need someone with opposable thumbs for this one. To properly secure it while everyone disembarks. Preferably before Saylor's boat gets battered into kindling."

Kash didn't have time to argue before Zain climbed over the rail, timed the next upswell, then launched off. He landed dead center, catching his balance against a wash of water across the surface, when a larger than normal wave knocked the boat hard to the left.

The line pulled taut, dragging Zain to the edge, then over. He managed to wrap one arm around a small rock, barely hanging on when the next wave hit.

Kash unclipped Nyx's leash, put his back to her, then waved her on. "Go."

The dog took two bounding steps, kicked up and off Kash's back then over to the rock, sliding across the slick surface a foot before spinning and zeroing in on Zain. She grabbed the line in his other hand — started tugging and grunting. Using all her strength to slowly pull Zain up and over the edge. He crawled onto the rock, shaking off the next spray before giving her a scratch.

It took a few minutes to maneuver the boat into the tight space and secure it enough everyone else could climb over without falling. Nyx darted back to Kash the moment he jumped onto the rock, hugging his leg.

Zain clapped him on the shoulder. "Thanks for the save. I owe Nyx a steak, or ten."

"She's gonna hold you to that." Kash motioned to the boat. "You sure you don't want to take Miller's place and stay with Saylor? Be the one to sweep through the tunnels once Saylor makes it around to the main entrance?"

"Not a chance, brother. Miller will keep her safe on the trip over. We've got family counting on us."

They already had their pairings. Kash would go in one direction with Nyx and Zain, while Cannon and Jericho took the other. Saylor had found a few old maps of the area she'd brought with her from the Coast Guard, and they confirmed the branching passages converged on the main cave farther south.

Assuming nothing had changed.

Saylor frowned, looking as if she wanted to suggest altering the plan — sneaking through the tunnels with them instead of circling around to the main entrance. But she stayed in the boat, nodding her thanks when Zain tossed the line to Miller and gave the vessel a hefty shove to get it moving.

She managed to back up, turn and disappear into the massive graveyard of rocks in under a minute, the incoming clouds quickly closing in around them.

Cannon motioned to the twin tunnels. "We'll take the right passage. If Saylor's maps are accurate, we should pop out on the southwest side of the main structure, with you three gaining access to the upper northwest section. Just remember, any amount of noise will carry, even suppressed fire."

Zain nodded. "Isn't that why we all brought knives?"

"God, you're just like Miller. Try not to die. Jericho has her boss on speed dial. He's got a unit on standby once we've got the situation under control. Until then, we're on our own."

They took off, vanishing into the complete darkness of the adjoining tunnel. Zain turned on his flashlight then motioned Kash ahead. Kash followed suit, letting Nyx lead. He kept the light level as low as possible without risking a broken ankle. Still, the beam seemed overly bright as it bounced along the slick walls, casting odd shadows as they moved down the tunnel. The kind of attention that would get them killed if they didn't detect any viable threat before a bunch of highly trained assholes started firing.

Kash checked his watch, then the tracker app — eleven fifty-five. Another five minutes, and he should pick up the signal — have visual proof he hadn't lost Jordan, yet. That if he hauled ass to that chamber, he could still save her.

Nyx worked her magic, scenting the air then scrambling ahead. They climbed over rocks, then crawled under rocky shelves, the massive walls groaning and creaking. Bits crumbled off and crashed onto the solid floor, landing with an echoing thud. The kind of noises that preceded cave-ins.

Zain muttered under his breath, staying close. "I really hate being underground."

Kash nodded. "I hear, ya. At least, we haven't come across any bats, yet."

"Seriously, Kash?" Zain rolled his shoulders, pursing his lips. "Why did you have to jinx it?"

"You know I'll deal with them if it comes down to it, right?"

"Just find this main section before we get swarmed."

Kash snorted, when Nyx growled, staring into the darkness, teeth bared. The line of fur along her back raised. He killed the light, pressing his shoulders into the rock as they stood there, straining to hear anything above the distance drip of water. How the wind still howled through the rock formations.

Nyx held firm, tilting her head before taking a cautious step forward. She paused, sniffed, then moved. One step at a time — Kash sliding his hand along the wall to keep from tripping over his own feet — until they reached a bend in the tunnel.

The dog scented the rush of air, growling again. Lower. Deeper. The vibrations strummed through the rock as she pawed the ground. He chanced a quick peek. A hint of light brightened the far end, a lone shadow cast along the wall.

Kash held up one finger, then pointed down the tunnel. He inched out, gun and one of his KA-BARs at the ready, Nyx hugging his thigh. They moved in sync, closing the distance, keeping to the darker shadows when a guy stepped into the tunnel. Gaze still focused on someone or something off to his left. His rifle resting against his chest. Available, but not ready.

Bastard didn't get the opportunity to use it when Nyx barreled down the last twenty feet, looking like a damn bullet streaking through the air. She hit the guy full force, bounced him off the wall then onto the floor. He landed hard, obviously dazed, head rolling side-to-side. Kash whistled, calling Nyx off as he quickstepped over — knocked the bastard out.

Voices echoed in the other chamber, footsteps heading their way.

Kash pressed his back into one side of the wall, Zain the other. Waiting until the men's muted shadows appeared in front before stepping out — engaging them point blank. Kash didn't have Jordan's ninja skills, but he held his own at hand-to-hand. Deflected the guy's strikes, then landed half a dozen of his own — ending it with a firm hook to the creep's jaw just as Zain's tango landed in a heap beside Kash. His buddy bound and gagged the men, then waved Kash on, still taking point.

They cleared the open chamber then continued

down the tunnel on the far side. Keeping the light low until they reached another junction. Kash showed the countdown on one hand then popped out, sweeping the area. Bright light illuminated the end of the corridor, odd shadows dancing across the floor.

They jogged down the path, constantly checking their six until they reached the end. Zain went first, this time, taking a breath then darting out.

"Holy shit." Zain cleared the immediate area, shaking his head as he took in the row of lights disappearing down a larger tunnel. "This wasn't some last-minute decision. Rook's been here at least a couple days. More likely a week."

That voice inside Kash's head started yelling as a shiver worked down his spine. "I don't like how this is shaping up."

"Me, either. Has me rethinking the past few weeks."

"I know Jordan said Rook always had backup plans, but this feels like he's operating on a whole other level. That he's got multiple ways of getting her out."

He grabbed his cell and studied the app. A blue dot flashed near the entrance, the rhythm reminiscent of a heartbeat. Except, he had no way of knowing if Jordan was alive or not. If they'd already made the trade or were facing the bastard down. Just that light pulsing against the darkness.

Zain looked over Kash's shoulder. "Game on." He

nodded when it started moving. "Looks like she knows Rook as well as she claimed. They're on the move."

"He'd better not hurt her."

"That's why we're here. You ready?"

Zain took off, hoofing it down the lit corridor. Back rigid. Multiple weapons at the ready. He rounded the corner, stopped, then took off. Vaulted over an outcropping before he caught another tango as he bolted out from an adjoining path. The guy bounced off the rock, blood splattering across the stone before he rolled to his feet. Zain had a knife slicing through the air before the guy fully recovered. It hit him in the shoulder, just outside his vest. Sent him careening backwards.

He crashed into the wall, sliding down with an eerie groan — leaving a bloody trail across the rock.

Kash joined Zain on the opposite wall, checking the tracker, again. "They're closing in fast."

Zain rolled his shoulder. "I realize this is all going to plan but…"

"Yeah, I feel it, too. Murphy sitting on our shoulders, just waiting to screw it all up."

"If we get any closer before Rook enters…"

"They'll see us."

Zain gave him a pat on the arm. "Dig in, brother. This op's about to… Get down!"

Zain tackled Kash to the floor, taking Nyx with them as automatic fire popped to life, cutting through the air as bullets whizzed overhead. They ricocheted off the stone, one hitting Kash's vest before Zain rose — emptied a full clip at the men.

They grunted then hit the floor before something clattered along the tunnel.

Grenade.

Too close to avoid.

Instead, Kash tugged Nyx closer and covered her head — braced for impact as the unit skidded along the corridor then exploded. Rocks and dust shot through the tunnel as smoke billowed through the air. The walls shook, parts of the ceiling crashing to the floor as more explosions sounded in the distance.

Zain grabbed Kash's shoulder as he patted him down, the ground still rumbling beneath them. "Shit, are you hit?"

Pain flared through Kash's ribs, the dull ache clearing some of the ringing in his ears. "Vest stopped it. Nyx?"

"No blood, but I'm sure her head's spinning, too."

Kash nodded, hating the way it amplified the pounding through his temples. "The tunnel?"

"What tunnel?"

His buddy climbed over the debris as Kash finally managed to push onto his hands and knees — stared at the remains of the corridor.

Zain ran his hands along the edge of the rocks. "There's a hint of daylight, but…"

Kash dug for his cell, staring at the blue dot pulsing less than a hundred meters away, when gunfire echoed through the walls. Shouts rose beyond the mountain of stone, followed by the unmistakable rattle of a flash bang. "They're already in the chamber. We don't have time to go around."

Zain nodded, tossing pieces of rock to one side. "We'll never clear it in time." He glanced back at Kash then removed one of his own frags. "Maybe we can blow it out of the way?"

"Or bring the rest of the cliff down on top of us."

"It's either this or we backtrack."

Kash glanced at the dot then over to Zain. "Blow it."

CHAPTER SIXTEEN

Three figures.

Standing in the shadows. Just the hint of their outlines silhouetted against a dull light burning somewhere deeper in the cave. Two heavily armed. The other...

Rook.

While Jordan couldn't see his face, she recognized the way the air shifted. The heaviness to it as he stepped out. That sense of foreboding that sucked out all the available oxygen — made her stomach roil from the sheer thickness of it.

She stood near the edge of the shoreline, Greer and Chase on either side. Backs stiff. Weapons just a draw away. They inched closer as the men moved out from the mouth of the cave, looking as if they'd shield her if anyone opened fire. Which they probably would. Just like Kash.

Chase shouldered in closer. "Remember. Don't engage Rook until you've got backup."

Jordan smiled. "God, you sound like Kash."

"The man's like a brother. And it's obvious he's stupid in love with you so, don't make him have to live through another loss. The last one just about broke us."

"I wasn't planning on dying today, Chase."

"You don't have to die to rip out his heart. I know you want to make the ultimate sacrifice if one needs to be made. See that it doesn't."

She merely nodded, drawing herself up as Rook finally moved into the glow of the helicopter's landing light. "I thought you said you didn't renege on your promises? Because I followed your instructions, and yet, I don't see Atticus."

Rook chuckled. "No, hello? How are you? Really, Ember, what would your uncle think?"

"That I didn't leave soon enough. Or maybe he'd be disappointed I didn't put a bullet between your eyes the moment you appeared, consequences be damned. Just like you did to him."

Rook's smile faltered. "Someone's been reading up. Who's your hacker?"

"Where's Atticus?"

"Close. I wanted to make sure you didn't have your team hiding nearby. That you came unarmed."

"They're not hiding, and I'm not stripping. You're just going to have to take my word." She reached into her pocket and removed the thumb drive. "Are we doing this, or what?"

Rook motioned with his fingers. "I want to make sure it's authentic, first."

"And I wanted to be left the hell alone, but we don't always get what we want. You can have it once Atticus is safely on his way to the hospital."

"And if it's a fake?"

"Then, I guess you get to kill me." She huffed. "It's not fake, but that doesn't matter because you know," she tapped her head, "I've got it all up here."

Rook laughed. "There she is. Fine."

He snapped his fingers, his gaze still locked on her. Two more men materialized out of the darkness, Atticus slung between them. Each shouldering an arm as they dragged him toward the chopper like some drunk at a bar.

"I told you not to hurt him."

"No, you told me to keep him alive." He waved off her scowl. "It's just a dose of Ketamine. The old dog wouldn't shut up. He'll be fine once it wears off."

Jordan bit back her reply, waiting until the men got within twenty feet of them. "My people will take it from here."

Rook shrugged. "Be my guest."

Jordan nodded at Chase, and he and Greer darted over to Atticus. Chase gave the older man a quick once-over, then grabbed one arm as Greer took the other. They helped him along, finally shuffling him into the helicopter.

Chase stopped shy of getting in, looking at her across his shoulder. "Are you sure this is how you want it to go down?"

Jordan smiled. "I'm good. You just focus on Atticus."

Chase frowned but jumped onboard, still staring at her as Mac spooled up the engines then took off, banking up and left before disappearing into the night, the flash of the nav lights quickly fading.

Rook tsked. "I have to admit. You seem to have found the kind of loyalty I'd hoped to have instilled in you. And he's not even the dog handler." He moved in closer. "I can't help but notice he wasn't part of your entourage."

She scoffed. "Did you really think I'd bring him for you to use as leverage? If you're going to test my skills because you're worried several months on my own has deteriorated them, at least make the challenges worthy of my time."

"It never hurts to ensure you've still got a solid foundation. I could do with a little less attitude, though."

"Then, you shouldn't have threatened the people I care about because you got caught with your pants down."

The corners of his mouth quirked before he leaned in dangerously close. "Just because I'd rather take you back alive doesn't mean I won't snap your neck if given the right motivation. You're already looking at months of retraining. You might want to keep that in mind before you say something you'll regret."

"Are we going inside or waiting on a boat?"

He held out his hand. "The intel."

She placed it in his palm. "It's all there. But, that's only part of the reason we're here. You really just hate to lose."

He snarled then spun, waiting for her to move in beside him before heading inside like a man on a mission. The wind howled across the entrance, the roar slowly fading as they traveled farther inside. A string of lights hung from the ceiling, the bulbs dancing in the strong breeze.

She glanced over at him, noting the deep lines around his mouth. He looked older than she remembered, and she wondered if the months had taken a toll. If losing her had been a thorn in his otherwise exemplary career. "I didn't expect the lights. How long have you been down here?"

He slowed a bit, turning right at the next junction. "Long enough to get a better understanding of who Jordan Archer is." He cocked his eyebrow. "A waitress? Really?"

"I'm sorry, were you hoping I'd become a mercenary, instead?"

"At least, it would have put your skill set to good use. Do you even remember how to eliminate an asset?"

"Are you volunteering as a test subject?"

"I've already warned you about the attitude."

"Then stop asking inane questions. If you believed I was anything less than the Ember you trained, we wouldn't be talking. Which brings me to the real topic. Sandman. Does Scythe know you're trying to oust them? Or are you simply killing off the execs one at a time. Like that op in Virginia you sent me on before I went to the compound."

The corner of his mouth twitched. Not much, but she noticed. "We'll talk about Sandman after. First, I want to hear more about this dog handler. I have to admit, of all the rules, I never thought you'd break that one. Allow yourself to care."

"I already told you not to waste my time with these amateure-ish games. You know exactly who he is."

Rook studied her for a while, then sighed. "Kash Sinclair. Ex-Army Ranger and SAR specialist. He and his crew all work for Raven's Watch. Not that I'm surprised. Atticus always drifted toward like-minded people. Tell me, how did Kash take it when he learned who you really are?"

"Surprisingly well. But then, he already suspected I was Shadow Ops. I guess I'm not as good as you at hiding who I really am." She paused for a moment when two more men joined their procession. "Why did you create Sandman? Wasn't running Scythe enough for you?"

"There's no such thing as too much power. You know that. While Scythe had promise, the current administration is too weak. Too worried about protocol and accountability to do the work that needs to be done. I'm not."

"Then, why not just tell me? You recruited me once. You could have officially brought me over."

Rook laughed. Hard. "I think this situation speaks to the reason. You were always destined to turn on me, Ember. To outgrow your leash. I couldn't afford to have you go rogue while under my umbrella. This way, you're still Scythe's asset. And they had no problem issuing a kill order." He grinned. "At my insistence, of course."

"Of course." She shifted her gaze, checking over her shoulder. "Too bad the men they sent kept missing the mark."

"Enough." Rook stopped at the entrance to that large cavern. "I let you have a taste of freedom. Proof you don't belong out here. Now, it's time for you to come in. To come home."

"Home? Scythe was never home. You never cared about me. Not really. You took advantage of that little girl who was so starved for attention, she didn't care what kind she got." She laughed, but it wasn't because it was funny. "Like I said. You only want me back because you hate to lose."

"You know how this works. There's no future for you without Scythe in it. Without me."

"Then, I guess you're going to have to kill me, after all."

"Something's... *off* about you. And it's more than just the taste of freedom." His eyes widened before he laughed. "You actually fell in love with him, didn't you? I knew you cared but..." He shook his head. "You really don't want him to get hurt."

She glanced into the chamber, wondering if Kash and the others were in position or if they needed her to buy more time. If the tracker really was broadcasting her position or if their op had already gone sideways. "If you give me your word that you'll leave Kash and his teammates alone — that you'll never set foot in Raven's Cliff, again — I'll walk out of here with you. Spend what's left of my life running whatever missions you want. No questions. No lies."

"You'd do that? Just to save him?"

"Not just him. His team. Atticus, too. I want them all off-limits." She twisted enough she could dive for cover when everything erupted into chaos. "What do you say? It's a good deal."

"Except where your heart wouldn't be in it. And sooner or later, Kash would come looking for you."

Jordan stared at Rook — at the way his left eye twitched as the corner of his mouth quirked — and she knew. Even if he'd agreed and she'd willingly walked out with him, he'd had no intentions of letting anyone on Kash's team live.

That he'd never be satisfied until he'd broken her.

Rook narrowed his gaze, glanced at the chamber, the tunnel, then focused back on her. "If you're waiting for the cavalry, I don't think they're going to make it in time."

She smiled as everything clicked into place.

"Really? Because by my calculations, they're already here."

Gunfire echoed up the path behind them, Miller obviously taking the initiative as explosions rocked through the cave a moment later. Everything shaking and rolling — parts of the tunnel collapsing around them.

She grabbed a couple canisters off the guy to her left, kicked him in the groin, then dove into the cave, clearing the entrance as more of the structure fell. She pulled the pin, then launched the first one across the floor. Thick gray smoke filled the space, adding to the already dense air as rocks and dust rained down from above. Rook stepped through the increasing cloud, fired off a couple rounds, then disappeared amidst a swirl of gray.

Jordan tripped to one knee, a deep groove grazed down her ribs before she scrambled for cover, tossing the other grenade out for good measure. It clicked across the stone, stopping close to the entrance before erupting in a display of light and sound. The concussive wave caved more of the roof in, covering the entire front half of the chamber in a mountain of rocks. Not quite sealed off, but close.

Gunfire continued in the distance, followed by an eerie silence. Pain teased her senses, but she pushed it down, listening for any hint of movement. Rook's muffled curse echoed around her before all traces of him vanished.

Just like that. As if he'd fallen through the floor or been *beamed up* by aliens.

This was the true version of him.

The man who'd spent more time as a ghost than he had being alive — being visible. The operative who'd completed more missions than most teams combined.

Other than her.

Because she'd learned from the best, and she could vanish, too.

Jordan quieted her mind, sensing her surroundings more than simply seeing them. How the smoke curled off to her right, a hint of that licorice wafting toward her. The slight press of a boot followed by a rustle of fabric as his gun brushed against his jacket.

Rook lunged out of the smoke, Sig level with her chest, his finger already inside the guard. She spun into him, eliminating any chance at a shot before slamming his hand against a rock. A quick hit to his elbow and jaw, and the gun clattered to the ground.

She kicked it away, ducking his left hook before shoving him back — gaining a bit of distance. That only enabled him enough time to draw his KA-BAR — brandish it in the glow of the smoky lights before slicing it toward her in long sweepings arcs. He caught the rock above her shoulder as she dropped — swiped at his feet. He managed to jump out of the way, but he recovered a heartbeat later, stabbing at her. Landing a hit to her arm. Blood splattered across the stone, looking almost black in the eerie light.

Rook tossed the blade into his other hand, twirling it a few times as he shook his head. "Maybe I was right? Maybe seven months in the real world made you soft?"

She stepped to her left, keeping her limbs out of reach. He couldn't afford to throw the knife with her this close, aware she'd counter before he drew a second. She studied the way he moved, noting the stiffness in his right knee.

"Actually, it gave me a whole new perspective. Allowed me to focus on the bigger picture. Like your knee. You've had it replaced."

She blocked his next strike, then kicked the inside of that knee — buckled it. Not enough to drop him, but she landed half a dozen hits to his arm and ribs before the knife fell, bouncing a few feet away.

Rook grabbed her, countered the way she tried to lower her weight then bodily lifted her. He spun, slammed her into the stone, then wrapped his hands around her throat. Her airway cut off, black dots quickly eating up her vision.

He leaned in, his breath washing over her face. "I'm starting to think I was wrong about you. That you were never the protégé I'd hoped for. I guess I should have focused more on Icarus, after all."

She clenched her jaw, palmed his head with her left hand and shoved her thumb in his eye. He shouted, easing up just enough she connected her elbow to the side of his head — knocked him back.

That was all the opening she needed. She grabbed his jacket, kicked off the rock and jumped onto his shoulders. It wasn't pretty, both of them still reeling from the after-effects of the grenades, but she managed a couple strikes to his head before he stumbled backwards, arms flailing trying to catch his balance. They hit a rock and tumbled, crashing to the floor as an explosion sounded off to their right.

Jordan hit hard, her head bouncing on the stone — adding to the wooziness blurring her vision. The impact had the floor tilting left and right. The scenery spinning, then stopping, only to whirl, again. Even the air seemed louder, ringing in her ears as the smoke curled around her. She staggered onto her feet, fighting to find any semblance of balance when Rook lunged out of the gray light, his Sig grasped in his right hand. Not quite pointed at her, but close. All he needed was a few more seconds to get his muscles to respond, and he'd have her. No way to miss that close.

Kash's face flashed in her head. She wasn't going to lose.

Not this time.

Not to Rook.

Her reflexes kicked in, and she stepped toward him, deflecting his arm as she slammed her palm against the grip — ejected the magazine. Her momentum carried her into his chest, knocking him to the ground. Dropping the Sig into her hand. She flipped it, pointed it at him, the chambered bullet a pull away from hitting his heart.

Rocks crashed in the distance as she stood there, chest heaving, blood dripping onto the ground. Each drop echoing through the cave. She just wasn't sure if it sounded like victory or failure.

She blinked back sweat and smoke, staring him in the eyes. "Who's Icarus?"

Rook chuckled, pushing up enough to lean against a rock. "All this time and you never looked beyond the obvious. Never considered anyone who wasn't already part of the system." He grinned. "I named him, too."

"Him?" She inhaled. "Is Icarus your son? Is that what the code name means? Like the myth? Did you send him to hurt Kash?"

Rook's eyes widened. "Why don't you ask him?"

A single footstep sounded behind her before twin reports boomed through the space. Bouncing off the walls then moving through her. Pain shot through her shoulder, everything shifting left before she hit the ground.

A silhouette passed above her, haunted brown eyes staring down at her. Something stabbed her neck, a burst of icy fluid burning through her veins before the scenery swam and everything faded to black.

CHAPTER SEVENTEEN

Kash held his breath as the frag exploded, nearly bringing the entire tunnel down on top of them. Two distinct shots sounded in the distance, the deep reports like a knife to his heart. There was something about those last rounds — the eerie finality to them that stole his breath. Had him waving off the smoke then booking it to the end of the tunnel. He chucked a few larger rocks out of the way, then scrambled over what remained of the debris, squeezing through the narrow opening before tumbling into the chamber.

He staggered to his feet, squinting against the burning smoke. The stench of propellant hung in the air, a layer of ash covering half the cave.

It couldn't end like this.

After all they'd been through — all his promises — he couldn't lose her.

Kash zeroed in on Jordan — her limp form swaying over Rook's shoulder — then took off. Hauled ass across the large cave, completely focused on closing the distance. Cutting it down with each driving step.

He got halfway across — had already worked through how he'd outmaneuver the bastard without compromising Jordan's safety — when the junction to the tunnel exploded. Just blew up, raining rock and dust down around him. The resulting wave knocked him and Nyx back, tumbling them ass over head a few times before skidding to a halt.

Kash groaned. Every muscle cramped. Every bone hurt. The room spun, though he wasn't sure if it was his head or just the smoke. Nyx managed to regain her balance, first, stumbling over to him, then licking his face. He gave her a pat as he tried to get everything to stabilize.

"Jesus, Kash." Zain dropped to his knees beside him, skin smudged with dust and soot, a fresh cut across his forehead. "The way you flew backwards…"

His buddy swallowed, coughed, then gave Nyx a quick once-over. "Can you move everything? Do you need me to carry you out?"

"I need to find a way to follow that bastard."

"The rest of the crew's looking. Cannon had to blow his tunnel to get through, too. And Miller all but excavated the entrance to get inside. I'm actually surprised the whole cave system hasn't collapsed." Zain scrubbed a hand down his face. "It looks like that other tunnel's completely blocked."

"Shit." Kash pushed onto his elbows, nearly fell

back when the world did a full three-sixty, but he managed to hold it together. "Help me up."

"Can you give yourself a freaking minute before you try to wage war?"

"Jordan doesn't have time for me to wait a minute."

"I thought I'd find you and Nyx packed full of shrapnel, so cut me some slack. Besides, if Rook wanted her dead, she'd be in the rubble. The fact he carried her out implies he wants her alive, just like she said."

"Just, give me a hand."

Zain shook his head. "Damn, you're stubborn."

Kash clapped Zain on the shoulder, though, even that small movement hurt. Increased the jackhammer pounding away in his head. Made him acutely aware of the ringing in his ears. Zain helped Kash up, stayed close in case Kash face planted the moment he moved.

Miller whistled from across the cave. "I found Donovan. He's been shot with what looks like a forty-five, has multiple contusions, but he's alive. Not sure how long he might stay that way if we don't get the prick to hospital, soon, though."

"What?" Kash picked up the pace, half-tripping his way over to the edge of the debris, Zain keeping him upright. "If that's Rook, who the hell took Jordan?"

"Let's ask the prat." Miller gave Rook a shake,

slapping him when he blinked. "Donovan. Chum. Who took Ember?"

Rook grunted, coughing when Miller shook him, again. He squinted, looked as if he was going to pass out, then sighed. "You're too late."

"Who took her?"

He laughed, drops of blood dribbling out of his mouth. "You'll never find her, now."

"And you're dead unless you start talking."

Rook snorted. "I win." He slumped against Miller's hold, barely moving when Miller released him.

Kash stared at the rubble. His heart somewhere up in his throat. His chest so tight it took all his effort just to move it an inch — suck in any air. He needed to think. Except where that jackhammer kept derailing any thought. Sent it off on some tangent as soon as it formed. "We can't just stand here. We…"

He inhaled, then dug for his cell, brushing all the dirt and grim off the screen. He opened the app.

Nothing.

No pulsing dot.

No way to follow her.

"Damn it. The tracker's not working."

Miller cursed as he picked up a bloody bandage. "Looks like whoever snatched her removed it then smashed it."

Zain grabbed Kash's arm when he took a stumbling step toward Miller. "Brother, you need to stop trying to crack your head open until Chase gets a chance to look at you."

Kash shook his head, regretting it when pain shot through his temples. "I heard two shots. If Rook's only hit once..."

"That doesn't mean Jordan got pegged with the other. Let's focus on what we can do, right now."

"I'm a hundred percent focused. I..." He reran what Becca had said earlier, one thought making it all the way through. "What was that name?"

"What name?"

"The other agent who ran missions for Rook's company, Sandman?"

"Icarus." Cannon cocked his head to the side. "Do you think that's who took Jordan?"

Kash palmed his head, squinting to keep from puking. "I don't know Donovan, but we all know his type. Does he strike you as the kind of guy to assign his most important mission to just anyone? If he'd planned to take her back to Scythe all along, then he gave her to whoever he trusted the most after her. Or maybe Icarus double crossed him. Either way, I bet my ass it's him."

Cannon had his cell in his hand a second later. "Damn cave's blocking the signal." He jumped when another section crashed behind them, more dust billowing into the air. "We can't stay. This whole place is compromised. I'll get Becca on it, though, I don't think she ever stopped looking into Icarus."

"We can't just leave." He grabbed another frag off

his vest, nearly dropping it twice as his vision blurred. "I say we blow the fucker open."

"Kash." Zain had him by the shoulders. "I know how badly you want to go after her, but I don't think this place can take another round of explosives. Everything's still creaking and rolling. One more will likely bring it all down."

Kash looked at the rocks blocking him from following that bastard down the tunnel. "What if there's another tunnel and he's going to backtrack? Or he got caught up in the explosion? What if that's the last time I see her?"

"It won't be. We'll get her back. Whatever it takes." Zain shifted closer, his face fading in and out of focus. "We can't save her if we're all dead."

Kash remained silent, allowing Zain to help him stumble across the cave and into the tunnels. He picked up speed as some of the fogginess lifted. Or maybe he'd just gotten accustomed to the constant shifting. How the walls all looked as if they were at a forty-five.

Bodie met them at the bend before the main entrance, eyes wide. Mouth pinched tight. "Jesus, what the hell happened?"

Zain grunted. "Bomb. Atticus?"

"Foster just talked to Chase. Atticus was dosed with Ketamine, but his vitals are strong. He should be fine once the drug wears off. Which is more than I can say for Kash. Can you even see straight?"

Kash waved him off. "I need you and Foster to

take Rook and get the bastard to the hospital. He's the only one who knows who took Jordan—"

"What do you mean, who took Jordan?"

"Just, keep him breathing if you can. We'll need the bastard alive if we can't find her."

Bodie darted off, leaning over Rook once Cannon placed him on the ground.

The air strummed to life with Foster's chopper spooling up — Bodie and Miller shuffling Rook onboard. Saylor kept her boat from crashing onto the rocks as waves broke against the shore. Non-stop movement that had Kash's head spinning. His stomach threatening to empty right there on the rocks.

Foster took off as the first raindrops splattered across the ground, the machine disappearing into the night. Taking any chance of following after Jordan in the aircraft off the table. At least, not until Foster dropped everyone at Providence — got his ass back to the cave.

But they needed Rook alive if...

Jericho darted over, cell in her hand. "That task force I mentioned is inbound. They'll deal with the cleanup, for now. Cannon will hang out with me, just in case there are any stragglers who think firing on us is a good idea. We'll catch a ride home with them. Cannon's on with Becca. Said he'll be over in a minute with an update."

A minute.

Jordan didn't have many of those left. A fact that ate at Kash until he wanted to scream.

Zain held firm. "Brother, I know this is killing you, but if we go off halfcocked, we might waste what little time we have. So, breathe. We'll get her back."

Kash pushed down all the riotous feelings until they were stone cold. "I never should have lost her in the first place."

Zain opened his mouth, then closed it, looking up at Cannon when he marched over. "I hope this is good news."

Cannon held up his cell. "I've got Becca on the line. Becca? You're on speaker with Kash and Zain."

"Now, before everyone tries to interrupt and demand I get to the point, I'm downloading Icarus' personal file as we speak. But I have to continuously change that location so we can't be traced, which means it takes a bit longer."

Cannon groaned. "How the hell did you gain access to that file?"

"I hacked Scythe."

"Jesus."

"Don't worry. It'll never come back to us. Besides, we didn't have time for me to scour every inch of the dark web searching for a scrap of intel that wasn't scrubbed when Rook moved over to Scythe."

Something pinged in the background.

"Got it." She breathed into the phone for a few moments. "Wow. There's quite a story here, which we can get into later. But Icarus is really Gavin Troy. He's thirty-one. Was institutionalized from the age of twelve for suspected Dissociative Identity Disorder. It seems Rook liberated him a year later. Gavin's been on medication to help mediate some of the symptoms ever since, but during a recent Scythe assessment, he showed signs of schizophrenia. The doctor recommended immediate removal from the field, but Rook overruled it. Claimed the issues made Gavin the perfect candidate for missions with unfavorable survivability rates. His current location is marked as unknown."

She tapped on keys, the sound echoing through the phone. "I'm searching for a photo that isn't blurry or beyond recognition… got one. Sending it through to Cannon's phone."

Cannon's cell chirped, and he swiped over to the image.

"No fucking way." Kash pulled the cell closer, blinking a few times to keep it in focus. "Do I really have a concussion or is that freaking Tucker Grant?"

Zain practically growled. "You definitely have a concussion, buddy, but you're not seeing things. That's Tucker. Damn. Did he know who Jordan was all along? Was this a setup?" He looked at Kash. "Did he purposely try to kill you and Nyx that day?"

"I don't know, but I'm sure as hell gonna ask him. Becca? Any chance we can track this guy? Maybe a chip like Jordan's?"

"From what I can tell, he never had one. But assuming he's not a former Coast Guard guru like Saylor, he must have a vehicle nearby. I've got satellites searching anything larger than a goat trail. He can't avoid me for long." She paused. "I know we don't have any time to spare but give me a few minutes to scour the area. I'll call you right back."

The line went dead, just like Kash's heart. Nothing but empty weight in his chest as he stood there, willing the phone to ring. Time ticked past as that storm front swept over them, kicking up the wind and the waves until Kash wasn't sure they'd have any other option but to wait for Foster or Mac to return.

He should have listened to Jordan. She'd been skeptical that Tucker was simply a coincidence, and now she was paying the price.

Cannon muttered under his breath. "I'll call her back—"

The cell rang in his hand, cutting him off.

He swiped his finger across the screen, holding it out so everyone could hear. "Talk to us, Becca."

"I've got a dark SUV barreling out of the forest northeast of you onto some old two track twenty minutes ago. It's headed northbound, with two confirmed heat signatures onboard. I can't guarantee it's Icarus or whatever his name is but, seeing as it was the only vehicle within the parameters, I think it's a safe bet."

"How close is he to Raven's Cliff?"

"About five minutes. He'll have to jump onto a highway if he wants to go anywhere east or south. If it's safe, I'd hop back in the boat and head that way. Maybe plan to grab a truck at the hangar. I'll keep you posted."

"Gib's tagging along with them. Ring Miller the moment you know which way that bastard's going. And keep Jericho's boss, Art, updated. With Tucker's questionable mental state, I think it's safer to let him get where he's going. If we set up roadblocks, it might set him off."

"I'll be in touch."

Cannon stared at his phone, then at the ocean. "Water's getting pretty rough, but something tells me you don't care. That Saylor won't care much, either."

Kash took a step, swayed, then caught himself before he landed on his ass. "I can't let Jordan down, even if I have to pilot that boat, myself."

"Are you nuts? You'd have us capsized in a heartbeat." Saylor moved in behind him. "Zain's already searching for possible venues that asshole might target if he continues north. And we're wasting what little good weather we've got, so…"

Kash grabbed her arm. "Are you sure? I…"

She smiled. "Endeavor to do more, Kash. Or we can go by your creed and lead the way. Both work. Just try not to puke. You look ten shades of green already."

She took off, jumping onboard as if the boat

wasn't rocking like a damn Tilt-A-Whirl. Had spray shooting several feet in the air as waves crashed over the side.

Cannon snagged Kash's elbow. "You sure you're up to this? Saylor's right. You look like shit."

"Not dead yet."

He nodded. "I know the feeling."

Kash clapped the man on the shoulder. "Thanks for all your help. I owe you."

"Anytime, brother. I'll see you at the hospital when this is all over because you're gonna get her back."

Kash merely nodded. He wouldn't say it. Wouldn't jinx it, just like he hadn't in the boat. Instead, he headed for the vessel, Miller shadowing him — looking as if he'd catch Kash when he inevitably tripped. Making it all the way to the boat without landing on his ass was a nice surprise. Not that he thought it would last, but he'd take the wins wherever he could find them.

Kash grabbed Nyx's harness, handed her to Zain then practically fell onto the deck. Zain grabbed him before he continued all the way to the floor, tsking as he helped him over to a seat — pointed at him to sit.

"Keep your ass in that chair until we get to our destination. You hear me?"

"I'm fine, just... Do you have any idea where he might be headed if he stays his course?"

Zain thumbed at Saylor. "Saylor does."

Saylor glanced over her shoulder at them as she

revved the engines, clearing of the shoreline as she flew over the waves. "There's an old, abandoned Coast Guard supply depot about twenty miles north of town. It hasn't been used in over fifty years and is mostly accessible by boat. There's a path down the cliffs, but it's treacherous in the best weather. Though, with Tucker's unstable mental state, I'm sure he'd risk it." She sighed. "Assuming I'm right."

"It's as good a place as any and in the right direction. We'll just hope that Becca gets an update before we get there."

The boat bounced along the water, rising and falling with every swell, every breaker, until Kash thought he really would puke. Anything to relieve the constant pounding in his head. How every motion got amplified by the next. He grabbed ahold of the rail, doing his best to ground himself as rain poured from the sky, the horizon a thick gray mass of unforgiving clouds.

Zain kept looking over his shoulder, shaking his head and muttering under his breath. Kash knew his buddy would have pulled rank if Jordan's life wasn't hanging in the balance. But Zain had similar demons haunting his conscience, and he'd never ask Kash to step aside with one of their own on the line.

Gibson's cell rang.

Miller answered it, nodded, then ended the call, staring at the screen before handing it to Saylor. "It looks like Saylor's intuition was spot on. Becca followed the vehicle to the top of the cliff overhanging that depot. Said it looked as if the driver jumped out then hoisted the other person over his shoulder and headed down. She lost them once they went inside. And despite all the movie hype, she can't see through the walls."

Kash nodded. "Then, we'll do this old school."

Which, he had to admit, felt right. Knowing it would come down to their skills against Tucker's. And he'd put his faith in his team, any day.

The wind picked up as they roared past the lighthouse and the hangar, then continued up the coast. The waves crested higher, battering the boat despite Saylor's attempts to literally dance through them. His fingers cramped from holding on, the searing cold cutting through his resolve until simply existing seemed to take all his strength.

Saylor kept them upright and on course, piloting the boat the way Foster flew a chopper. She didn't seem the least bit fazed when a wave nearly toppled them. She simply angled into it — shot out the other side smiling. She worked the throttles, timing each burst until the old metal depot appeared through the veil of clouds, sitting on the precarious rocky shore like Olympus atop its peak. A lone, rickety dock stretched out to one side, rising and falling with every surge.

She eased back on the throttle, using it and the surf to get in close until Zain jumped out, Miller right behind him. They did a quick sweep of the area with their weapons, then tied off the boat.

Kash tripped to one knee as soon as he stepped onto the dock, the platform rising and falling beneath him. He just didn't know if it was really moving or if it was all in his head.

Zain pursed his lips but didn't call Kash out. Instead, he gave him a hand, then took point. Miller followed suit, the two of them quickstepping up the dock and over to the main structure, Kash and Nyx trailing behind. Gibson showed the countdown on his hand, then shoved open the door. Zain went high and right, Miller low and left. They cleared the immediate area then waved Kash and Saylor inside.

Zain pursed his lips, searching the area, again, before sighing. "Saylor? I know you're gonna hate this, but we need you to stay here." He held up his hand to stop her from interrupting. "I know you're more than capable of guarding our six. But you're the only one who can pilot that boat, and we have no idea if Foster will be able to rendezvous with us in time. Which means, it might come down to you and that ocean."

Miller nodded. "Knowing our exit's secure would be nice, too. If you're okay with that, love."

Saylor narrowed her eyes but nodded, taking up her position by the door. Looking as if she could take on a full wet squad on her own.

Miller scanned the room. "We've got more doors than blocks. It's your op, mate. What do you want to do?"

Kash frowned. "I'm betting there're bombs."

"Yup." Miller sighed. "Probably other forms of traps, too, but nothing we haven't faced before, yeah."

Kash glanced at Zain, then Miller. "As much as I'd love to stay together, my gut's telling me Jordan's out of time. And I didn't come this far to fail now."

CHAPTER EIGHTEEN

Light.

Cutting through the darkness in random flashes.

A wall. A boat. The unmistakable roll of the ocean. There'd been gravel and metal, then the whir of a ceiling fan spinning endlessly above her.

Jordan blinked, groaned at the crushing pain moving through her shoulder and into her chest. Derailing any effort to suck in more than a sip of air. She turned her head, blacked out, then resurfaced to that same red-hot pressure. The only indication she wasn't dead.

The room spun, again, nearly took her back down, but she pushed through. A hum sounded in the distance. A generator or maybe a boat. Some kind of engine chugging along. The deep vibration shaking the entire room.

A voice mumbled off to her left. Disjointed. Obviously distressed.

She managed to twist just enough she could shift her gaze — focus on the silhouette hunched over a table. A hint of light illuminated his face, the familiar curve of his jaw hitting her hard. "Tucker?"

He froze, some kind of tool in his hand before he turned — looked at her. His eyes widened, all that white seemingly glowing amidst the muted light. "You're alive. That's… good."

Jordan let her head roll back, the strain of simply holding it to the side draining her. She closed her eyes, prying them open after God knew how long. That fan still spinning above her.

Tucker sighed. "I hooked up a generator. Not too big. Just enough to move the air around…" He tapped the desk. "Provide a bit of light. Do you know how to rig a generator?"

She did her best to focus on him, blinking when everything kept shifting. "I do. Did Rook teach you?"

That set him off. Had him jumping up — raging around the room. Kicking the heel of his palm against his forehead as he shook his head. "Don't say his name. Don't say it! He's…" Tucker cackled, shushing himself before staring down at her. "I saved you from him."

She nodded. Nothing more than an inch up and down, but he understood. "Where are we?"

"Somewhere safe."

"Are we by the ocean?"

She smelled it now. The heavy scent of brine, mixed with rust and day-old sweat. Something coppery. Maybe blood. Or maybe just years of decay on the metal walls.

Tucker looked around but didn't answer. Instead, he lowered onto the edge of the cot. "Do you know who I am?"

"You're Icarus, right?"

He grunted. "No. Icarus..." He swallowed. "He's away. I mean *me*."

She frowned. "Tucker?"

"No! Yes! Damn it." He jumped up, chewing on one thumbnail as he shook his head. Body shaking, eyes wild. "Do you know I'm your brother?"

"You're my..." She coughed, closed her eyes against the pain, then pried them open. "Brother?"

He nodded, leaning in so close she tried to push into the cot. "Not by blood. But after..." He snarled, glancing over his shoulder as if someone stood in the far corner, watching. "*My father* got me out of that hospital, he told me he wanted me to be just like you. That you were my big sister, and I needed to mimic everything you did."

"Rook told you that?"

"I told you not to say his name!" He pounded his fist on the cot then raked his hands through his hair, looking as if he was going to pull it out.

"But that's why..." She wet her lips. "Why you went on all those missions."

"I had to prove myself. *You're nothing but a hack!* Am not!" Tucker pointed to the empty corner. "Don't listen to him. He hates us."

Jordan glanced at the shadows, wondering if she'd imagined Tucker's voice dropping an octave — the way he'd stilled, seemingly in complete control for those few moments — or if it had been real. If he was in the midst of some kind of psychotic break. Just like that night in the café. "Is that Icarus?"

Tucker's eyes darted back and forth. "You see him, too?" He glared at the shadows. "*He* didn't want me to bring you here, but I had to." He nodded several times. "I had to."

"Can I... I need to talk to him." She pushed out a breath when he glared at her. "Just for a moment."

"I... I don't know. He's... He's not very nice."

"It'll only be for a minute, then you can come back. You're my brother, right?"

Tucker stood, paced the room for a minute then stopped and stared at her. Eyes focused. Completely distant. "What the hell do you want?"

She pursed her lips. "Is Rook dead?"

The guy, Icarus, she assumed, shrugged. "No idea. I hope so. The bastard's lost his edge. Ever since you left, it's been find Ember. You have to locate Ember. Ember, Ember, Ember." He lunged at her, getting in close. "I fucking hate Ember!"

Jordan breathed through the surge of pain when he jostled her, doing her best to hold his gaze. "Me, too."

He tilted his head, then eased back. "You look like her, but Tucker says you're not."

"I'm not. Not anymore."

"We'll see." He glanced at that table when something pinged. "Looks like we've got company. They made better time than I thought."

"Who? Who's here?"

"Who do you think? That bastard, Kash and his teammates." He laughed. "I had the asshole right where I wanted him. Strung out on the side of a cliff. Nothing but honor between him and death. Then, Tucker had to get all sentimental. Wanted to *save* him." He rolled his eyes and slammed his fist against the wall, a dull thud echoing through the air. "He wouldn't let me finish him. But he won't stop me, this time."

"Icarus, please..." She tried to push onto her elbow — fell back without gaining more than an inch. "You don't have to hurt them. You can leave. You're free."

"Free?" He laughed harder. "That's the illusion. None of us will ever be free. Whether Rook's alive or dead — whether we're with Scythe or Sandman. We're just pawns. But if I kill everyone..." He smiled. "Then... Then I might escape. Wait here. I won't be long."

He walked out then shut the door, the metallic clang resonating through the room. A series of chirps sounded beside her, what looked like a monitor panning parts of the building.

Talk about a screwup.

She licked her lips — took stock. Her right shoulder was useless. Nothing but pain and that numb feeling she knew stemmed from a traumatic injury. The vague recollection of a gunshot. Or had there been an explosion?

It hurt too much to puzzle it out. Not that it mattered. Either way, just moving would take all her focus and a healthy dose of luck. Maybe some kind of sacrifice because it seemed beyond her.

She tried.

Clenched her jaw, palmed the cot with her left hand and shoved.

It took several tries repeating the same motion before she stayed upright — swung her legs over the edge. Another half a dozen of trying to stand before she did more than just rock back and forth — finally got her feet beneath her enough to trip her way over to the table. She crashed into it when the scenery swam, everything sliding left and right. But she breathed through the worst of it, leaning against the wall when it all stopped moving.

She wouldn't get far. She knew it. In fact, she'd consider it a miracle if she did more than kiss the floor the moment she opened the door. But she'd go down fighting. She'd do everything she could to warn Kash and his teammates before Tucker unleashed some kind of attack. He'd obviously been here a while. He could have IEDs or traps set all over the area. And with the generator only powering the emergency lighting throughout the building, they'd be lucky to spot anything before it was too late.

Jordan sighed. She'd push herself one last time. Then, she could rest.

* * *

The place was a maze.

Whether it had always been like that or Tucker had been there long enough to do some rearranging, Kash wasn't sure. Just that every room led to two more.

He stuck to the edges where the shadows were thickest. Anything to stay hidden. There wasn't much light, but even the dim glow of the emergency bulbs could give him away. Tucker was watching. Not that Kash had spied any cameras, but his shoulder blades twitched. The same kind of warning he'd experienced in the service. And he wasn't about to ignore his training, now.

Nyx stopped, ears twitching. Back rigid. She didn't growl, but something had her attention. He gave her some slack, following her as she sniffed the floor, stopping at the next door. She sat, looking back at him as she gave a hushed bark.

"Wired, huh?"

Which they'd already suspected. He just hated being right.

Kash bypassed that exit and headed for the other, allowing Nyx to take lead — steer him around any other surprises. There were two more hidden wires, but he made it into the adjoining corridor without setting anything off.

The whole building creaked, the howling wind echoing through the hallways. Some kind of motor hummed in the distance, suggesting Tucker had hooked up a generator. Which made sense if he'd been living here for a while.

A hint of movement stopped him cold, Nyx pressing back against his legs. Kash waited, breath held, gun at the ready. He wouldn't take a lethal shot unless he had no other options. Not until they'd located Jordan.

The floor creaked as a shadow moved beyond the doorway. Slow. Methodical. Disappearing off to the right. Kash shuffled forward, boots silent against the weathered flooring. The scenery dipped a few times, but he pushed through, stopping at the threshold. He drew a breath, then slipped inside and cleared the area, when Nyx backed into him.

He hit the ground, covering her as bullets cut the air, ricocheting off the metal walls — whizzing way too close to his head. He laid down a few cover rounds, grabbed Nyx and retreated back into the other room.

"Hey, Kash. I know that's you, buddy."

Kash cursed under his breath. "Tucker?"

"Sorry, Tucker's not here right now."

Kash motioned for Nyx to stay then chanced a peek out, hoofing it across the open space for the far wall when Tucker didn't outright fire on him. If he kept the man focused on him, he could turn him around then spring Nyx on him. Take the guy down without killing him.

Kash moved through the next door, circling to his right. "I'll assume you're Icarus."

"Bravo. You figured it out. I'm impressed." He laughed, the sound bouncing all over the place. "I'm afraid your teammates are on the other side of the building. I made some modifications over the past month. Installed a few doors so I could isolate different sections. It'll all be over by the time they double back."

"Look, Icarus. I don't want to hurt you. I just need to see Jordan. Make sure she's okay."

"She's been better. But then, bullet wounds tend to leave a mark." He'd moved off to the left, farther from the doorway.

Kash clenched his jaw, biting back the urge to barrel ahead, guns blazing. But if Tucker really had made modifications, they might need him to find Jordan before she bled out.

Kash cleared the next area, then turned back, that thick feeling between his shoulder blades stronger than before. "Did you shoot Rook, too?"

"The man's a monster. Always pushing. Never satisfied. Nothing was ever good enough. Except Ember. She's *all* he ever talked about. Be like Ember. Think like Ember. Well, screw Ember! I'm his son. I should have been his favorite."

Boots scuffed off to Kash's left. He'd been right. Tucker had backtracked.

Kash inched ahead. "That must have been frustrating. Always being in her shadow. But she was a victim, too. Why do you think she left?"

"To make my life hell! Do you know what Rook did to me when she slipped past me at that compound?" His voice trailed off, a solitary sob sounding in front of Kash.

"Nothing good, I'm sure."

"She said I could leave. That I'm free. But I'll never be free… Until I kill everyone."

He stepped out of the shadows off to Kash's right, rifle notched in his shoulder. A burst of gunfire preceding each step.

Kash dove to his left, clipping Tucker in the leg before whistling — keeping the man at bay with a few well-placed shots just shy of hitting him but enough to make him retreat. He took two staggering steps back, blood blossoming through his pants, when Nyx hit him full force from behind.

They crashed to the floor, landing hard as Nyx shook her head, yanking on Tucker's arm — dragging him back. Tucker shouted and kicked then grabbed his knife when Kash called her off.

She released him, circling around to Kash's left side as Kash stood over Tucker. Feet braced apart. His weapon centered on Tucker's heart. Even with his head still spinning, the room tilting, he wouldn't miss. Not this close.

"Where's Jordan?"

Tucker glared at him, still brandishing the knife, but too far away to get in a viable hit. And Kash would have a bullet through his chest before the man could throw the blade. "Probably already dead."

"Tell me where."

"Or what? You'll kill me?" He laughed. "Looks like your 'not yet' is going to be your 'not ever'."

Tucker moved, shoving the knife in his side, then twisting. Kash dove at him, knocking him out with the butt of his weapon before Tucker could yank the knife out and stab himself, again. But it was already critical, blood quickly pooling beneath his side.

"Damn it, Tucker." Kash went to his knees, stabilized the knife as much as possible when Zain and Gibson barreled around the corner. They cleared the area then rushed over, staring at Tucker.

Miller toed the floor. "What the?"

Kash grunted. "He freaking stabbed himself. I…"

"Did he tell you where he has Jordan?"

"Not a word. But if Becca was right and he carried her in…"

"Nyx can get her scent off him." Zain peered over Kash's shoulder. "Well?"

"Guess we'll find out."

Miller nodded. "I'll take Tucker to the boat. If you arses aren't back in five, I'll come looking for you. See that I don't have to."

Kash sighed. He hoped they wouldn't need help,

either because he wasn't sure Jordan had that much time to spare. "Nyx. Find, Jordan."

Nyx took one more sniff of Tucker's clothes, then bounded off, limping across the floor and through one of the doorways. Kash followed, bouncing off the walls a few times when his balance shifted, but he kept up. Trailing after her as she went deeper into the building. She stopped at an open door, sniffed the lip then headed inside.

Kash braced himself, then ran in, staring at the empty bed. Blood stained the sheets, the sheer amount stealing his breath. "Shit. Where the hell is she? That's way too much for her to be vertical."

"A normal person, sure, but Jordan." Zain scoured the floor just outside the doorway. "I've got directional blood drops. Can Nyx track her that way?"

"Hell, yeah." Kash moved to the door — pointed to the blood. "Nyx, find."

The dog made a few passes then took off. Not running but walking fast. She paused every few feet, then continued, weaving back toward the entrance when something clattered to the floor ahead.

Kash took off, racing down a corridor then through a doorway, scanning the room when a silhouette lunged at him from the darkness, nearly tripping him up before he spun — grabbed an arm. "Christ."

CHAPTER NINETEEN

She looked like a ghost.

Skin deathly white. Deep smudges beneath her eyes as she trembled against him, a length of pipe in one hand. Blood soaked her sweater, the excess dripping onto the floor.

"Easy, sweetheart."

Jordan fisted his shirt, her grip stronger than he'd thought possible. "It's Tucker…"

"I know."

"He's Rook's son." She collapsed against him, nearly taking them both down when the scenery swam for a moment.

Zain stopped Kash from tripping onto his ass, possibly hurting Jordan in the process, cradling her head as Kash eased her onto the floor.

Kash checked her pulse. Thready, but there. "Jordan? Eyes on me."

She smiled, or at least, tried, only one corner of

her mouth lifting. "You know what that phrase does to me."

"Which is why I keep saying it." He lifted the bottom of her shirt then rolled her enough to expose the bullet wound on her scapula. "You really outdid yourself. A knife wound and a forty-five to the shoulder blade."

"I..."

"Shhh. Let me get some pressure on this, then we'll head back, okay?"

"Rook?"

Kash huffed, thanking Zain when he handed Kash his tee. "Still breathing the last time I saw him."

She nodded, then frowned. "You're hurt."

"And yet, a far sight better than you."

"What..."

"I'll tell you everything once you're coherent. Which is my subtle way of telling you to stay with me." He leaned in. "You promised me you wouldn't run. I need you to keep that."

"I'll..."

Her head lolled to the side as she faded, eyes falling shut. He rechecked her pulse — breath held, heart a dead weight in his chest until a weak strum fluttered against his fingertips. "We're losing her."

Zain crouched low. "Brother, I know how much you want to be the one to carry her out, but it might complicate things if you end up on your ass on the way. Let me take her."

Kash cursed under his breath but nodded. While

he wouldn't admit it out loud, he wasn't sure he *could* carry her. Not without doing exactly what Zain had mentioned.

Zain gathered her in his arms, maintaining the pressure on her back before making a beeline for the exit. Kash trailed behind, using Nyx and the wall to stay upright and moving.

Miller already had Tucker on the boat by the time they reached the dock, the weather infinitely worse than when they'd ventured in.

Saylor waved them on, holding up her radio. "Foster just left Providence. But with the freezing level so low, he has to go around a few of the bigger hills. It'll add another ten minutes to his flight."

Zain winced. "I don't think she has that to spare."

"Which is why I told him we'd meet him at this out-of-the-way marina south of here. I called ahead, and they'll let me dock my boat for the night. Honestly, I think they were more surprised anyone was out here. There's enough room for Foster to squeeze the machine next to the dock. It should buy us back that time."

"Are you sure it's okay to be out on the water?" Zain shook his head. "I'm not gonna lie, Saylor. It looks bad."

"I've been in worse."

"And if this ends up beating that?"

Saylor glanced at Jordan. "I'll never be able to look at myself in the mirror if we don't try. I've lost teammates, too. I'm not losing another."

Zain looked at Kash, then back to her. "Then, let's go."

Zain motioned for Kash to plant his ass on one of the seats, then placed Jordan in his arms. "I figure you'll be okay as long as you don't try to stand."

Kash held Jordan against his chest as Saylor maneuvered the boat away from the dock. She hit the throttle and leapt ahead. Not as insane as before, but faster than she probably should, considering the conditions. Zain hadn't been exaggerating. White caps covered the surface, lashing at the hull as each swell lifted and dropped them several feet. The wind roared past, lowering the temperature until Kash had to focus on keeping his teeth from chattering.

Saylor never wavered. Kept the bow pointed south, despite how her hands shook against the wheel. Even from several feet back, he noticed the way she shivered. Zain stepped up behind her, shielded some of the spray, but it was only a matter of time before they all succumbed to the cold.

Having the marina appear amidst the pouring rain and heavy clouds gave Kash a glimmer of hope. If they could just make it to the dock, Jordan would have a chance.

Saylor spun the wheel, working the engines as the surf attempted to capsize the vessel. But she held firm, guiding it in without crashing, which looked like a distinct possibility with everything rocking and tilting.

Or maybe that was his head.

Regardless, Saylor had the boat snugged into the pier just as Foster soared overhead, the downwash rocking the vessel before he banked to the left, wrestling the chopper into an aggressive approach. He hovered a foot off the ground, making it look easy despite the gusting winds and driving rain.

They clambered onboard in record time, shutting out the weather. Chase had an IV and some plasma hooked up to Jordan's arms before Foster lifted off. Had her on her side — her wound exposed. Chase didn't falter, coating it with clotting powder then wrapping it tight. He double checked her vitals then moved on to Tucker.

Kash didn't know how Chase did it. Held their lives in his hands without batting eye. Just staring at all the blood, how her skin was practically transparent, had Kash fighting not to puke.

Chase shifted back, pushing meds into her before handing Kash a bag. "If you're gonna hurl, brother, do it in that. And count how many times, because I have a bad feeling that concussion I heard you got at the cave has gotten a whole lot worse."

Kash waved it off. "I'm fine. You just worry about Jordan…"

The room spun, and he bent over, emptying whatever was in his stomach into the bag. It took three bouts before he managed to stop, the ever-present jackhammer even louder.

Zain tsked when Kash tried to straighten. "Don't

even think it. You look like a damn corpse. Just… stay like that. We'll be landing in a couple minutes."

They were already at the hospital?

The machine shook, voices echoing around him, every word like a knife to his skull. He blinked, blacked out, then came to lying on a stretcher. He rolled his head enough to follow the rush of white coats past him. One straddled the gurney, pumping on Jordan's chest, yelling for more blood and to clear an operating room. Kash grabbed the railing, but Chase leaned over him — got up in his personal space.

His buddy sighed. "I know it looks bad, but she's in good hands. If anyone can bring her back from the brink, it's this staff. And you breaking ranks and trying to stagger down the hallway will only add you to the critical list."

"They can't…" Why did talking hurt? Cause lights to flash behind his eyes as his stomach roiled, threatening to empty, again.

"I'll make sure they do everything they can. You have my word. Just, keep your ass on this gurney."

"I'll make sure he stays put." Foster appeared off to Kash's right, arms crossed. Looking every inch the leader he'd always been. "So, don't even think about testing me."

Kash groaned. "Nyx?"

"There's a twenty-four-hour emergency vet just down the road. Zain insisted on getting her checked. The vet's doing some x-rays and running a few more tests, but she's pretty confident it's nothing serious. Just a few cuts and a pulled ligament in Nyx's shoulder. Zain said he'd call if anything changes. I suspect he's going to detour and grab her a cheeseburger once she's cleared."

"If I didn't know any better, I'd swear she was cheating on me with him."

Foster laughed. "You know he sneaks her bacon every night, right?"

"At least, he doesn't rub it on my pants like someone I know. Who still thinks it's hilarious when she won't stop sniffing my ass."

"It's the little things in life, Kash."

"Right." He closed his eyes, wondering how the light simply followed him. "Jordan…"

"Is gonna pull through. The girl's a fighter."

"She needs to know…" More pain, stabbing through his skull, pulling him under.

"You can tell her you love her once you're both stable. Assuming you haven't already. Either way, rest. We've got your six."

* * *

Had breathing always hurt this much? Like fire burning beneath her skin every time she managed a small inhalation?

Jordan blinked, slivering her eyes open only to close them against the punch of light. The resulting pain dragging her down. The pressure held her under, finally allowing her to resurface minutes, hours, maybe days later. The light still bright but not blinding.

It took a while for the scenery to sharpen, a steady beeping sound adding to the headache arcing across her temples. She shifted her gaze, groaning when the entire room dipped.

A voice tsked next to her. "It's way too soon for you to be conscious. Sleep, sweetheart. I'll be here."

Kash.

She wasn't sure she said his name or if it just materialized in her head. But it soothed the edgy feeling prickling her skin. Lulled her back to sleep.

The light seemed duller, the pain less intense when she pried her eyelids open, again, that steady beep still teasing her senses. She managed to gaze at some of the room without it spinning.

A wide couch occupied most of the available space, a couple pizza boxes stacked on top of a makeshift coffee table. She looked to her right and froze. Kash sat in the narrow chair next to the bed, his hand lightly brushing her left arm. Long lashes rested against creamy skin, a scattering of bruises marring his face and neck.

She must have moaned or mumbled something resembling his name because he jerked awake, his gaze snapping to hers. She smiled, or at least, she tried, only one corner of her mouth lifting before she bit back a grunt, pain pulsing through her chest.

Kash sighed then leaned forward, taking her left

hand in his. "I'd say, welcome back, but you don't look like you're quite here, yet. How's the pain?"

She swallowed, coughing against the dry rasp of her throat before smiling her thanks when he offered her some water. "Where…"

One word, and she was exhausted.

He brushed some hair back from her face. "Providence. You had surgery to remove the bullet from your scapula. It was shattered, by the way. You've got a plate and some screws holding it all together. The doctor said it went well. Expects you to make a full recovery, though, it'll take some rehab to get all the mobility back."

Kash leaned in closer. "Looks like you'll be stuck here for a while."

"Good." She tried to push through her memories, but it was all a jumbled mess. "Atticus? And did we…"

Five more words, and she was ready to sleep.

"Atticus is fine. Had a rough night from the Ketamine and a lot of his time with Rook is blurry, but all-in-all, no worse for wear. Mac's insisting that he takes a full week off. Needless to say, there were some colorful words exchanged. And if you're asking if we finished the job… Rook's in custody, as is Tucker. Shit's hitting the fan with regards to Scythe and Sandman. All-in-all, it's been one hell of a few days. But we'll talk about that once you're stronger. For now, all you need to do is rest. Trust me to have your back."

"You know I do..." She sighed. "You promised you'd say it often. So, say it again."

Kash smiled, and her heart gave a hard thump. "I love you, Jordan."

"Love you, more."

"Not possible, but I'm sure you're gonna prove me wrong. Sleep."

She faded, his words bouncing around inside her head until they finally connected and she woke with a start.

"Whoa, easy, sweetheart, or you're gonna pull out the IV and everything else."

She blinked, groaning against the pain. Better than before, but still there. Still raw.

Kash leaned in — cupped her face. "I knew you'd be waging war once you woke for good. So, now I can say it for real. Welcome back."

Jordan accepted the water, downing several sips before relaxing against the pillows. "You said something about it being a tough few days. How long have I been out?"

"Five days."

"What?"

He shushed her, keeping her from bolting upright with gentle pressure on her left shoulder. "You nearly died. Actually, you did die. Right in front of me on some crappy gurney. They worked for ten minutes to get you back, and only because Chase threatened to kick their asses if they gave up before he thought they'd tried everything." Kash raked his fingers through his hair. "The fact you were hypothermic probably helped, too. That old saying that you're not dead until you're warm and dead. Still..."

She nodded at the bed, smiling when he raised the back until she was level with his face. "I'm sorry."

"Just don't scare me like that, again."

"Are you gonna tell me what happened?"

"Soon, just..." He rested his forehead on hers. "Give me a second."

She lifted her left hand and palmed his cheek. "You can have them all."

She closed the distance — kissed him.

"Sheesh, leave you alone for five minutes, and you're already making out." Chase stood at the end of the bed, arms crossed, toe tapping the floor. "Give the girl a chance to breathe on her own before you compromise her airway."

Kash laughed. "It's called kissing."

"The way you do it, it's more like resuscitation."

"You'd know, buddy." Kash made kissing noises as he puckered his mouth at Chase. "Everyone else on their way?"

"Grabbing food, which Jordan might appreciate." Chase moved to the other side of the bed. "How's the pain?"

She sighed. "Better."

"That's not saying much when you admitted you've treated your own wounds."

"Let's put it this way. I've done complete missions hurting far more than I am, right now."

"Again, not a benchmark I'm looking for." Chase motioned toward her back. "May I?"

"From the way Kash tells it, you're the reason I'm still alive, so, knock yourself out."

"Kash tends to exaggerate. I simply kept the staff motivated. Reminded them of all the transfers Raven's Watch does on their behalf." Chase checked her shoulder blade. "Everything looks good, and your vitals seem stable. You keep this up, and we can bust you out sooner than expected."

"I'm ready."

"Relax, *Houdini*. The doctor's coming 'round in an hour or so. Let's get at least one more assessment before we're breaking ranks." Chase looked up when the rest of the team walked in. "Food's here."

Foster rolled his eyes. "I swear you're always thinking with your stomach." He smiled at her. "Look who's back from the dead."

Kash grabbed her some food, and she nibbled on a couple fries, drifting in and out as his buddies chatted, their voices soothing that rawness. They'd finished eating and changed places, maybe changed their clothes, when she roused, again. Clearer than before.

Kash cozied up to the bed, leaning over her as he brushed his fingers along her jaw. "You're awake, again. That's good."

Jordan frowned. "Again?"

He laughed. "You ate two fries then passed out, which was to be expected. Feeling any stronger?"

"Ready for you to bust me out."

"Easy, tiger. Let's see if you can stay awake for more than five minutes before we make a run for the border."

"Or, I can just sleep all the time in our bed."

Kash's lips quirked. "You said that on purpose to sway me."

"Is it working?"

"More than you know." He twisted when footsteps sounded in the doorway. "Greer's here. She's been hoping to chat for a couple days but didn't want to push. You up to talking for a few minutes?"

"That depends. Does she have handcuffs?"

Someone laughed, then Zain moved in beside her. "Nothing in your size. I'm pretty sure Kash has a pair with pink fur if you're interested, though."

Kash groaned. "You're such an ass."

"I'm sorry. Is the fur blue?"

"Don't listen to him. He's sore because Nyx insisted on sleeping at the foot of your bed last night instead of curling up beside him on that couch." Kash grinned. "And the fur's purple. I'll get you some water."

He reached behind him, offering her more water as Greer shuffled over, Bodie at her side. They both wore uniforms, looking alarmingly official, despite Zain and Kash hinting that they weren't there to arrest her.

Greer tilted her head. "I gotta say. I wasn't sure you were gonna make it based on how pale you were a few ago. Glad you proved me wrong. You sure you're strong enough to talk?"

Jordan winced when she shifted. "I can't promise I won't black out on you, but..."

"I'll risk it." She glanced at Kash and Zain, then sighed. "That was quite the adventure. Do you remember everything that happened?"

Jordan relaxed against the thin mattress, easing when Kash held her hand. "Up until Tucker shot me. After that, it's fragmented." She frowned. "It was Tucker, right? I didn't imagine that?"

"You didn't. Which puts a whole new spin on that night in the café. Guess I should have locked him up, after all."

"You couldn't have known who he really was. I didn't know."

"But you picked up that something was off about him, other than the obvious. Anyway, he's being moved to a high security psychiatric facility in a few days. I doubt he'll ever leave."

Jordan nodded. "And Rook? Is he..."

"That's where things get a bit trickier. I'm sure it's no surprise that every agency has gotten involved. Wants their piece of flesh or to have him defect to their side. It looks like the CIA might get final custody of him. I can't promise you it'll be the kind of ending he deserves, but Jericho and Cannon are pulling out all the stops. They'll keep me posted. Which is why they and Miller aren't here, but they said to call if you need anything. Miller also left you a message. Said if he ever made a go of it with that guy you joked about, he'd bring him around for a visit." Greer motioned to Kash and Zain. "It might be wise if you stuck around for a while. For safety purposes, of course."

"Will that be an option? Or do I have few of those?"

Greer beamed. "That's another complicated situation, but putting it briefly, Jericho and Cannon pulled a save there, too. I'm not sure what kind of connections they have, but," Greer held up a folder, "I received this the other day."

"Not sure I'm up to reading without it setting off a chain reaction."

"I'll summarize. Basically, it states that Admiral Jonathan Hastings approached you three years ago and offered you immunity if you agreed to be part of a joint JSOC unit dedicated to toppling Scythe and Rook Donovan. That intel Rook still had on him was more than enough to do that. Which means, you're free and clear."

Jordan stared at Greer, wondering if she'd faded out, again, and this was all a dream. "I'm what?"

Greer sighed. "I think that's enough for today. You look like you're ready to pass out, again. I just wanted to let you know that it's going to be okay. I've been told you'll be getting a number of visitors who'd like to woo you into joining their agency, but we'll go over that later. And I've told them, they'll have to go through me and my office, first. But for now, rest. Try not to kill anyone else for a while, okay?"

Jordan nodded, hating the way her head already felt heavier. "Bodie..."

Bodie stopped chatting to Chase and looked over at her. "Yeah?"

"Thanks. If you hadn't brought in Cannon and Jericho..."

"Pretty sure you would have come out on top regardless. But I'll accept if it means I'm no longer on your shit list."

"Would you settle for moving down in rank?"

He laughed. "It's a start. Oh, and Becca said she has one last surprise for you, but she'll be in touch once you're fully upright."

"That sounds... scary." She gazed up at Kash, blinking when his face got blurry. "Hey."

"You're fading on me, sweetheart."

"Still strong enough to go home."

He broke into a stunning smile that had butterflies fluttering in her stomach. "I love the sound of that almost as much as I love you. Rest until Chase can make the arrangements. Then, I'm gonna keep your ass on lockdown until you can toss me on mine. Deal?"

"Deal. And Kash..." She drew him closer with a nod of her head. "Love you more."

CHAPTER TWENTY

Three weeks later...

"Kash. Brother, I swear, if you keep pacing, you're gonna wear a groove in the hangar floor."

Kash looked over at Chase. His buddy was too calm when Kash felt as if his entire world was about to shoot off on some new tangent. "They're late."

Chase laughed. "Greer only called five minutes ago. Said something about grabbing us all coffee. Relax. They'll be here."

"This is the third time the CIA has asked Jordan for a meeting. It's hard to relax."

Zain wandered over. "Of course, the CIA's interested. Jordan's, hands down, one of the best operatives I've ever met. Every agency wants her to sign up. That doesn't mean she will."

Kash simply nodded. While she'd assured him she

wasn't interested in reviving Ember, a part of him wondered if she'd be happy staying outside the fray. He hadn't lasted more than a few weeks after moving to Raven's Cliff before the quiet had gotten to him and he'd signed up to become part of Raven's Watch. He couldn't fault her if she wasn't cut out for civilian life, either.

The fact that they were still unsure if their tumbles in the sheets had resulted in any longer-lasting outcomes only added to the stress. It had been too early in the hospital for the doctors to know if she was pregnant, and they'd been doing their best to let it be until she could find out for sure.

He wouldn't lie. The prospect excited him when he wasn't completely terrified by it. He barely felt as if he'd mastered taking care of himself, let alone a kid. His ability to keep Nyx alive and mostly well gave him a glimmer of hope. And there was the part where he wanted to spend the next fifty years with Jordan. Still…

Zain sighed and clapped him on the back. "Relax. Jordan's happy here."

"It's not about being happy. It's about having adrenaline wired into her DNA."

"There're other ways she can embrace that without being an assassin."

"Technically, I wasn't an assassin in the truest sense, but…"

Kash snapped his head around, breath stalling as Jordan stood in the doorway, looking sexier than ever in jeans and one of his hoodies — her hair up in some kind of messy bun.

Zain laughed beside him. "Breathe."

Kash batted his hand off his arm. "I…"

"We know."

"Jackass." He walked over to Jordan, nodding at Greer as she handed out coffee cups to everyone. "Where's your sling?"

She scoffed. "I tossed it."

"The doctor said you needed to wear it for a month."

"Well, the doctor hasn't done rehab with Zain. He's merciless and relentless. I already have seventy-five percent mobility back. Another two weeks, and I'll be good as new."

Zain moved over and bumped shoulders with her. "Don't put this back on me. You were the one who wanted to regain everything overnight. I merely helped."

"Which is why, I don't need the sling."

Kash shook his head. This wasn't a fight he'd win, and he had more pressing questions. "Well? What did they offer you this time? More money? A house on the hill?" He leaned in. "The heads of those who've wronged you?"

She smiled, and his heart flipped over. "I already have those. And it was more along the lines of my own unit. Something about heading up a task force."

Shit.

He forced a smile. "Sounds pretty hardcore."

She snorted. "Please. In all the time you've known me, do I seem like the type who plays well with others?"

"Maybe not with most people, but you've taken to our team pretty well."

"That's because your team's crazy matches mine."

"Pretty sure it's your team, too, now. And is that your subtle way of saying you turned them down?"

"It wasn't subtle. And of course, I turned them down." She sighed, looking unusually lost. "I've had enough missions to last a lifetime. Besides, I got a better offer."

He froze, staring at her, over to Greer, his buddies, then back. He tried to swallow, coughed, then inched closer. "A better offer?"

"God, you should see your face. I should have led with that."

"Jordan."

"Kash."

He huffed. "Are you trying to give me an aneurism so Chase has something to do?"

"Maybe, just a little." She laughed when he crossed his arms and stared at her. "Fine. Remember how Greer's been having a hard time finding anyone she trusts to give her a hand at the station?"

A dull roar sounded in his head, and he had to give himself a physical shake just to get everything working. "Wait. Are you saying that you're gonna be a deputy? Right here in Raven's Cliff?"

"Is that a problem?"

"Of course not. I just..." He stared at her, nothing quite forming on his tongue right. "I thought..."

She sighed and moved in close, tracing her finger along his chest. "I promised you I wouldn't run. I can't keep that promise and move to DC or spend most of my time overseas. I like it here." She paused, tilting her head to the side. "Actually, that's a lie."

She tiptoed up — got a breath away. "I love it here. Almost as much as I love you. If you're cool with me having absolutely no reason to ever leave?"

He kissed her. Right there in the middle of the hangar. His team and Greer standing there, watching. Nyx trying to squeeze between them. Jordan didn't seem to care, either, as she slid her fingers through his hair and tugged him closer. All but climbed him in an effort to get closer.

He rested his forehead on hers once they finally came up for air, drinking in the scent of her. A mix of roses and his cologne. An aroma that definitely smelled like home.

She smiled against his chin. "I assume that means you're good with my decision?"

"More than good. I... Wait." He eased back giving her a once-over. "Does this mean you're going to be legally armed? All the time?"

"Hell, yeah." She looked over at his buddies. "So, you boys better toe the line because I definitely have handcuffs. No fur included, purple or otherwise."

Kash glanced over at Greer. "Is that wise? Giving her a weapon."

Greer shrugged. "It's not like she'll be pulling it on me." She nodded. "Though, we did talk about restraint and curbing some of those ninja moves."

Jordan rolled her eyes. "Vault over counters and guys a few times, and you're labelled. I *am* capable of being discreet."

"Luckily, discreet isn't really necessary most of the time." Greer smiled. "Something tells me Raven's Cliff is gonna be a whole lot safer."

Chase ambled over. "No shit. Does this mean she'll have to go through some kind of police academy? Because I might need to stock up on supplies if she'll be hanging around a bunch of ambitious guys who are bound to piss her off."

Jordan gave Chase a swat as if she'd been part of their team forever. "Thankfully, no. Remember that surprise Bodie mentioned Becca had for me? Becca tweaked my backstop. Made it *her* level of secure. She also added some relevant data, including the fact I attended and passed a course in Spokane. Something about having an in there. Not exactly a lie, considering my training."

"And a thousand percent safer considering how likely you are to throat punch the first guy who tries to grab your ass. Now all you need to do is pass your firearm's certification once your shoulder's healed enough."

Jordan waved it off. "I already did that this morning."

"Didn't you have a sling on?"

"Like I said. I tossed it."

Chase looked at Greer. "And, how did she do?"

Greer scoffed. "Let's put it this way. I either need to shoot her in her other shoulder or make a much harder test. Which reminds me. We generally don't pull a KA-BAR and toss it at a suspect, even if it seems like the best option."

Jordan frowned. "Sister, give me a month, and you'll be tossing them, too."

"I think I might have gotten in over my head."

Kash chuckled and gathered Jordan in his arms. "Sounds like there's reason to celebrate, then."

Foster arched a brow. "Do we try another dinner at the house? As I recall, Jordan didn't kill anyone the last time."

"You should know better than to challenge me, Foster. And, you're on." Jordan smiled, and Kash knew he could spend the rest of his life staring at her. She gave him a nudge. "You're not going to attempt to cook, again, are you?"

"You're hilarious. I'll remember that when you want coffee in the morning."

"I'm gonna want more than just coffee."

Zain gagged, then stumbled his way over to Chase. "Brother, you need to help me. I think I'm gonna be sick."

Kash rolled his eyes. "Ignore him. He's just pissed because he's still treading water when he should be diving in. But that's another story. You ready to head home?"

Jordan leaned in — gave him a soft kiss. "I've been ready for thirty-two years. It'll be nice to finally have one."

Kash took her hand, enjoying the simple feel of her skin against his as they hopped in his truck, then headed home. They had just enough time for a quickie in the shower before they headed over to Foster's, waving off the ribbing when they sauntered in, hair wet, looking way too enthralled with each other.

Greer and Bodie joked with Chase and Zain, as everyone gathered at the table. They'd invited Saylor, but she'd gotten called off on another water rescue with Raven's Watch's other crew. Which wasn't sitting well with Zain. He'd been noticeably quiet all night, glancing at the clock on the wall as if it held the answers to whatever weighed him down.

Greer's phone rang just as they were clearing off the dishes, cutting through the easy atmosphere. She answered, nodding her head a few times. "I'll be there in ten."

Chase sighed. "Obviously, that was work related."

Greer shoved the cell in her pocket. "Seems that rescue call Saylor went on turned out to be drug smugglers."

Zain palmed the table as he pushed to his feet. "Is she okay?"

"Atticus said she's got them subdued but needs them picked up. Guess she forgot she's not still in the Coast Guard, too. That seems to be a recurring theme with anyone associated with your team." Greer shook her head when Jordan stood. "You're still recovering. You've got four more days before I want to see you back in the office. That should coincide with Kash's schedule. I figure you can work the same shifts since Bodie's agreed to continue on for a while longer. Not that you aren't always on-call, but we can try to set more reasonable hours."

Jordan hitched out a hip. "I assume that only applies to me and Bodie since you haven't had a day off since you were named sheriff."

"Have I told you that your observation skills are a giant pain in the ass?"

"A few times."

"I'll see you on Monday. Foster, thanks for dinner." Greer eyed Chase, then headed for the door, Bodie tagging behind.

The conversation lagged for a bit as they moved into the sitting room, Foster and Mackenzie glancing at each other, shifting on the couch as if they couldn't quite sit still.

Zain broke the silence, first. "For the love of God, Foster, just tell us the news before Mac's giving birth, already."

Mac swatted Foster's chest. "You told them?"

Foster glared at Zain. "Of course, not."

Mac eyed Zain. "Then, how the hell do you know I'm pregnant?"

"Please, we've been flying with you for months.

You never puke after a flight and yet, you've been chucking your cookies every day for the past week."

Chase nodded. "Not to mention, you're a lovely shade of green when you come back out. And don't think we missed how you've been avoiding coffee."

"And beer." Zain pointed to the kitchen. "Foster's supply of Smithwicks has barely been touched. I figure it's also the smell so, he's been avoiding it, too."

Mac sighed. "Then, I guess there's nothing to announce."

"Oh, no." Zain waved his finger. "We want to hear you say it."

Mackenzie looked at Foster, freaking glowed, then shrugged. "We're pregnant."

"Hell, yeah!"

Zain jumped up, clapped Foster on the back. Chase followed suit, leaving Kash to bring up the rear. Foster beamed, even if he did look a bit shell-shocked.

Mac held up her hand. "Just so you know, it's really early, but…" She smiled at them. "You don't keep secrets from family."

Jordan gave Kash's hand a squeeze then walked over and drew Mac in for a hug. "Congratulations. I…"

She pulled back as the color drained from her face, then took off, hitting the bathroom at a full sprint. The door slammed behind her, leaving an eerie silence in the room.

Kash sighed. "I've told her she's pushing her recovery too hard, but she's stubborn."

Chase frowned. "I don't know, Kash. I don't think this is from her previous injuries." He held up his hand. "Hold that thought."

He moved over to Mac, whispered something, then the two of them disappeared up the stairs.

Kash made his way to the bathroom door, leaning against the frame when Jordan finally opened it. Skin pale but with an odd glow about it. He brushed back her hair. "You okay?"

She swayed a bit, looking as if she might go back for another round of puking. "I might never eat pizza, again… In fact, let's not mention food at all for a while."

"Here."

Kash jumped when Chase's hand appeared between them, a box clenched in his fist. "Jesus, buddy, don't scare her into another round." He frowned. "What the hell is that?"

"Pregnancy test." Chase thumbed at Mac. "In true Foster and Mac fashion, they've got like a dozen up there. You know, so they can test several times just to be sure. I suggest you pee on it."

Kash glanced at Jordan, then back to Chase. "Why would you think—"

"Please. No way you knew what implant she was referring to in Bodie's office if you two hadn't discussed the situation. And since it wasn't for birth control, it's not a huge leap as to why she's puking a month later."

Kash scrubbed his hand down his face. "It's not like we weren't going to eventually test, it's just..."

"If you need some privacy, we get it."

Jordan tilted her head to the side, looking past Kash to his teammates before grabbing the corner of the box. "I think here's perfect."

Kash took her hand in his. "Sweetheart, you don't have—"

"It's like Mac said. We don't have secrets from family."

Kash snagged her hand. "You're not going to disarm the alarm and shimmy out the window, again, if it comes back positive, are you?"

She smiled, and damn, he already knew what the test would say. "I think you should be more concerned about having to console me if it's not. I just need a couple minutes."

Was his mouth hanging open?

Had he passed out and this was a dream?

Because he was pretty damn sure she'd just told him she wanted to be pregnant. Or at least, wasn't against it.

Chase clapped him on the back. "Breathe, brother."

"You and Zain really need to stop telling me to breathe."

"Then, stop holding your damn breath every time she walks in the room or smiles."

"Sorry. That's not gonna change as long as *she's* breathing."

"I'll keep the oxygen close, then."

"Jackass."

Chase chuckled then stepped back, hovering just far enough away Kash could suck in air without worrying he sounded as if he'd just run a marathon. The clock in the sitting room ticked, every second dragging on until he thought about running outside — double checking she hadn't taken off — when the door creaked open.

Jordan stood in the threshold, the test clasped between her fingers. She smiled, and he knew he'd been right. She held up the stick, the big plus sign staring back at him. "Looks like there's going to be another teammate."

"Damn straight, there is." He tugged her in close. Kissed her. "You sure you're okay with this?"

"Better than okay." She eased back then looked over at Chase. "But no one tells Greer or Bodie until I'm farther along. Clear?"

Chase balked. "Why are you looking at me? Zain can't keep his mouth shut, either."

"I can, and I'm not the one pining after Greer." Zain avoided Chase's slap. "Not that I think it'll stay hidden long. The lady's sharp."

"Agreed. It'd just be nice to legally shoot a few people before I'm sidelined." She laughed when his teammates sobered. "God, your faces."

Kash grinned. "And that's our cue to head home."

He shook hands, gave Mac a kiss on the cheek, then twined Jordan's fingers through his and headed home. Nyx obviously knew something had changed, staying super close to Jordan, constantly looking for any threat until the stepped inside. Even then, the dog curled up at Jordan's feet, calm but primed.

Jordan sighed. "It's going to be a long nine months if you're both going to be on edge the whole time."

"I'm perfectly calm, sweetheart. And Nyx is just showing you she's ready to protect you and the baby…"

Baby.

Christ.

'Breathe, Kash."

"God, don't you start, too. I'm fine. I just…" He leaned over, placed his hand on her belly and kissed her. "Why do I have the feeling you're still going to be vaulting over counters and taking down wet squads when you can barely see your toes?"

"I'll always be able to see my toes, and I'll always be Ember. At least, a part of me will."

"Good, because I love her, too. Now, how about we head into the bedroom, and I show you how much."

Jordan jumped up, walking toward their room before stopping and glancing at him over her shoulder. "You're on. And Kash… I love you more."

RAVEN'S NEST

RAVEN'S CLIFF BOOK #3

New York Times & USA Today
Bestselling Author

ELLE JAMES
&
KRIS NORRIS

RAVEN'S CLIFF

RAVEN'S NEST

NY TIMES BEST SELLING AUTHOR
ELLE JAMES
KRIS NORRIS

PROLOGUE

The Vigilant.
US Coast Guard contract research vessel.
Classified mission, somewhere off the Oregon Coast.

Screaming.

Rising above the pounding in her head. Mixing with the crash of the waves against the hull. The distant roll of thunder.

Lieutenant Commander Saylor O'Conner pushed onto her hands and knees, arms shaking, ears ringing. She moved one leg underneath her, nearly falling when everything shifted — the deck. The boat. Her damn memories.

She'd been inspecting the Zodiac. Double checking it could withstand the inbound storm — had enough supplies if any worst-case scenarios manifested out of the wind and the rain — when a deafening tone had pulsed through the air.

There'd been confusion and pain — faces fading in and out of focus — then her waking with her body plastered to the molded floorboards, nothing but empty memories filling the time between. Even now, as she fell back on her ass, everything seemed jumbled. Just disjointed voices amidst utter blackness.

She closed her eyes, trying to let the world stabilize before stumbling to her feet and tripping against the console, her head throbbing and her legs threatening to buckle. She waited, breath held, hands fisted around the panel until the dizziness eased.

Taking a chance, she gazed out at the horizon, praying the constant pitching didn't set her off. Only a hint of the sun sat above the water as a thick band of dark clouds quickly bore down on the ship. A few errant raindrops splattered across the windshield, the stinging cold lifting some of her lingering fogginess.

More screams cut through the numbing haze, followed by quick dull pops. What she swore was semi-automatic gunfire until that eerie tone lit the air, again. Stronger. Louder. Derailing her thoughts and dropping her to her knees as pain shot through her head, then into her chest. She covered her ears, but that barely diminished the ambient noise. Nothing dulled those vibrations rattling through her skull.

She blinked, and everything had shifted, again.

Any hint of daylight gone as the wind howled across the deck, blowing rain and spray against her face. The *Vigilant* listed aimlessly left and right with every swell, creaking and groaning against the strain.

Saylor grabbed the console, then dragged her butt onto the seat, bracing her elbows on her knees as she sucked in air, then pushed it out. She focused on the deck, waiting for the pain to ease before straightening. It took a few tries, but she finally managed to stand without immediately falling onto her ass. Her legs shook as she took a few stumbling steps, but at least she was upright.

Her boots scuffed the floor as she covered the short distance to the side. The ship's lights cast ghostly shadows across the deck, the lines swinging against the increasing winds.

Actually climbing out of the Zodiac and onto the deck took more effort than it should have, and she fell the last few feet, landing in a heap on the platform. Her stomach roiled, and she scrambled to the edge — puked off the side.

It took a few minutes to gather her strength before she pushed off the railing — took stock.

The deck was empty.

No crewman, no scientists. Just her and a few hours' worth of unanswered questions.

She needed to find Maddox. Ensure the rear admiral's safety. Then, they could make a plan. Figure out what had happened — get the ship back on course.

She headed for the bridge, bracing her weight on the railing as the *Vigilant* rose and fell with each violent wave. Water crashed across the deck, spreading the width of the ship before retreating over the edge. She got halfway to the stairwell when another pulse boomed beneath her. The force knocked her onto her backside as the ship's lights surged, glowing twice as bright before exploding in a shower of glass and filaments. Plunging the *Vigilant* into utter darkness.

Pain clouded her vision, every thought quickly crushed by the endless humming inside her head. She stood, legs shaking, her vision a mix of blurry gray bulkheads and black dots. But she managed to unclip her flashlight from her belt and grope her way along.

Were those lights flashing in the distance? Red and green? Slowly getting closer?

She blinked, nearly fell, then scanned the surface.

Nothing. No lights. No boats. Just endless white caps curling across the ocean.

She gave herself a mental shake, then tumbled through the hatch and into the stairwell. The ship tilted with the next wave, staying slightly off-kilter, this time, as lightning flashed beyond the windows. She staggered up the short flight, her stomach threatening to empty from the constant shifting of the small beam, before she reached the bridge. She took a breath, shoved open the door, then peered inside.

Shadows filled the room, the helm aimlessly

turning with the current. She stepped inside, falling against the rear bulkhead when the ship tipped up, cresting a huge wave before dropping off the other side. Water crashed over the bow, spraying across the glass as the vessel bobbed along the surface.

They should be moving. Making a run for the coast before the storm cracked the damn ship in two. The hull was already singing. An eerie tone she knew preceded a catastrophic failure. The kind legends were wrought from. Except where she couldn't quite remember how to get it all going. Which levers to push. How to activate the beacon.

She scanned the instruments, trying to get a single thought to take hold, when she spotted someone spread out across the floor. She tripped her way over, then stopped dead.

"Captain Baker?"

Saylor went to her knees, felt for a pulse.

Thready, but there.

She grabbed his arm and rolled him onto his back. Blood dripped from his ears, a grimace curving his mouth. He groaned, eyelids fluttering. He managed to open them for a moment, gasp, before drifting off.

Where the hell was the rest of the crew?

Where was Maddox?

She stood, then made her way to the radio. She didn't know if the damn thing had any power, but she'd make the call. Hope someone heard.

"Mayday, mayday, mayday. This is the *Vigilant*…"

Her voice trailed off, each word like a knife to her

skull. She stared at the handset, trying to piece together what to say — remember where she'd left off — when the floor creaked behind her. She spun, toppled against the bulkhead, then bounced the beam toward the door.

Rear Admiral Maddox stood in the hatchway, dried blood across his forehead. His eyes widened before he cursed and took a step inside. "Saylor? What the hell are you still doing onboard? I gave the evacuation order an hour ago."

She frowned. "Evacuation?"

He covered the short distance, taking the handset out of her hand. "Did you make a mayday call?"

Why was he yelling? Sending more dots dancing across her vision.

She groaned, palming her temples. "I tried, but.."

He simply nodded. "We need to get off the ship. I've got the research. Is the Zodiac seaworthy?"

"Yes, I…" She squinted. "Baker's hurt. We'll have to carry him out."

Maddox sighed. "There's not much time before this damn storm rips the *Vigilant* apart."

"I'm not leaving anyone behind."

He nodded, helped her lift Baker until the man was bridged between them, each shouldering half his weight. Baker roused enough to occasionally lift his feet as they stumbled down the stairs, then onto the deck. Saylor grabbed the railing with her other hand, then started moving. Slowly. Each step harder than the last. She passed where the starboard lifeboat should have been, noting the empty lines, then kept going, tripping her way back to the Zodiac, Maddox moving beside her. Steady. Oddly coherent considering she could barely string two thoughts together before everything went sideways.

They reached the stern, one side of the Zodiac dipping lower than the other, the broken line snapping in the wind. The harness console was dead, but she managed to access the manual override and lower the boat until it was level with the deck.

She waved Maddox on. "You and Baker get onboard. I'll lower you the rest of the way, then climb down."

"Not this time, Saylor. You take Baker and get everything ready. That's an order. I'll be right behind you."

She frowned, though, maybe this was more about him being the last person off the ship. The age-old tradition she suspected had been bred into him. And with Baker barely conscious, Maddox was technically the acting captain, even if he'd only been visiting the ship for an inspection.

Getting Baker over the side and onto a seat nearly drained her. Remaining on her feet after releasing him, an act of providence because she swore everything had shifted. Tilted off to the right, with more of those dots closing in from the sides. She glanced back at Maddox, a thought finally cracking through the haziness as she stopped just short of the helm. "Why didn't you go with the others?"

"I needed to secure the research, in case the ship falls into the wrong hands. Which won't matter if we don't get off her before she snaps in two."

She nodded. Not much, but enough he understood, then stepped behind the wheel. She'd need to get the engines going and the boat moving before the waves smashed the Zodiac against the hull. Or worse, capsized them on the spot.

The wind roared past, thunder and lightning dancing across the water, when those pops sounded again. Quick. Sharp. Pounding through her head until she wanted to scream. She glanced back when pain tore through her shoulder blade, smashing her against the console. She hit hard, knocking the controls, as the boat swung, pulling the line taut until it released, dropping the Zodiac the last several feet into the water.

The vessel bounced, nearly submerging as the *Vigilant* tipped, the resulting wave pushing the Zodiac away as the massive ship listed hard toward the port side. A horn sounded in the distance, the hollow tone lingering in the air until she bolted awake.

Rain stung her skin as she blinked away the last of the dots. Thunder clapped above her, each bolt of lightning giving a snapshot of the storm. Clouds circling. Waves looming above. Nothing on the horizon but endless swells. Like a movie advancing a frame at a time.

Saylor swallowed, nearly blacked out, then got the Zodiac moving as she took stock. Baker slouched off to the side, eyes closed. Chest barely rising with each labored breath. Realizing Maddox hadn't made it onboard cut deep. Had her scanning the horizon until she knew she either had to make a run for the coastline or concede they'd all die out there.

Assuming she could pilot the boat with her right arm hanging at an odd angle. Blood soaked through her clothes, tempered slightly by the cold. But she wouldn't survive long enough to get them anywhere if she didn't stem the worst of bleeding.

She grabbed the first aid kit from beneath the helm, then did what she could to plug the hole.

Had she been shot?

She couldn't remember. Couldn't get the memory to stick long enough to be sure.

A whispered pep talk, and she managed to crawl across the deck — grab them each a life vest. Not that it would do much if they ended up in the water. But it gave her a false sense of hope. That if she pushed past her limits — rose to the challenge — she just might get them to shore alive.

The Zodiac roared to life as she hit the throttle, riding the swells up, then down. She aimed the bow east, aware she'd likely capsize before she'd covered any significant distance, but she'd try. Go down fighting.

She worked the throttle, surfing the waves, using every trick she'd learned to keep the boat upright. Squeeze one more mile out of her before it all went sideways. More dots slid across her vision, the numbing cold slowly drawing her under.

The wind howled past, and the salt stung her eyes, but she kept pushing — clawing out a few more minutes of life. An ear-piercing pulse sounded in the distance, the deafening tone ringing through her head and into her chest. Rattling what was left of her thoughts and roiling her stomach, just like when she'd been back on the ship. Or maybe the noise was simply her imagination. Remnants of the *Vigilant* as it finally sank beneath the surface. Either way, hearing the reverberation echo as she slumped against the wheel, seemed fitting, that ominous tone following her into the darkness.

Light.

Brighter than it should be. Burning through her eyelids. Too white to be the sun. More like a spotlight. The same intensity she'd seen on the ship a moment before the bulbs had exploded.

Saylor inhaled, adrenaline spiking her heart rate as she pried open her eyelids. The harsh glare roiled her stomach, and she turned, — dry heaving over the edge — her cheek braced against a metal railing.

Gentle hands brushed back her hair, a soft, cool towel dabbing her forehead. "Easy. You're still too weak to be up and about. Sleep."

That voice. She recognized it. What was her name?

The thought drifted with her in a numbing haze, fading in and out of the images flashing in her head. The remnants of a memory trying to take shape. There had been screaming and chaos — people fading in and out of view — then some kind of pulse that had dropped her to her knees...

Saylor inhaled as she bolted upright, lines and stitches tugging against her skin. She held that breath, swaying as pain shot through her back, then into her chest, dimming the room until it was all she could do just to sit there and breathe.

Someone cursed, then bridged her weight, shoving a couple pillows behind her back as they grunted. "If you pull out your stitches or fall over that railing, the doctor's gonna put you back into an induced coma."

Saylor waited for the room to stabilize, then focused on the person's face. She blinked a few times, a name tumbling over in her head before she relaxed. "Mac?"

Mackenzie Parker, Coast Guard pilot and Saylor's best friend, smiled, though it didn't quite reach her eyes. "You remember, this time. That's good."

"This time?"

Two words — three including Mackenzie's name — and it had drained her. Had black streaks cutting in from the sides.

Mac sighed. "You opened your eyes a couple

times, but you weren't really awake. Not that you look like you're gonna last more than a few minutes, now. But at least, you seem more aware."

"What…"

Had talking always hurt this much? Pulsed pain through her temples? Had her chest constricting around each breath?

Mac frowned. "You don't remember?"

Saylor shook her head.

"What's the last thing you do remember?"

Saylor swallowed. "Boarding the *Vigilant* for an inspection, then…"

Mac pursed her lips. "That was three weeks ago."

"Three…" Saylor frowned. "Was there a storm?"

She palmed her head, crying out as pain shot through her temples, more images trying to claw free. Lights on the water. The missing lifeboat. Blood soaking her clothes.

Mac paled. "Easy. It's not important. The doctor said you might have memory issues for a while. But they'll likely return over time. Rest. We'll try again once you're stronger."

Saylor snagged Mac's hand, holding it tight until Mac leaned over her. She wet her lips, hoping she got out all the words before she faded. "What about Baker? Maddox? Where's everyone else?"

Mac pursed her lips, eyes glassy as she gave Saylor's hand a squeeze. "I'm sorry, Saylor, they're all dead."

Raven's Nest

ABOUT ELLE JAMES

ELLE JAMES also writing as MYLA JACKSON is a *New York Times* and *USA Today* Bestselling author of books including cowboys, intrigues and paranormal adventures that keep her readers on the edges of their seats. When she's not at her computer, she's traveling, snow skiing, boating, or riding her ATV, dreaming up new stories. Learn more about Elle James at www.ellejames.com

Website | Facebook | Twitter | GoodReads | Newsletter | BookBub | Amazon

Or visit her alter ego Myla Jackson at
mylajackson.com
Website | Facebook | Twitter | Newsletter

Follow Me!
www.ellejames.com
ellejamesauthor@gmail.com

ALSO BY ELLE JAMES

Raven's Cliff Series
with Kris Norris
Raven's Watch (#1)
Raven's Claw (#2)
Raven's Nest (#3)
Raven's Curse (#4)

A Killer Series
Chilled (#1)
Scorched (#2)
Erased (#3)
Swarmed (#4)

Brotherhood Protectors International
Athens Affair (#1)
Belgian Betrayal (#2)
Croatia Collateral (#3)
Dublin Debacle (#4)
Edinburgh Escape (#5)
France Face-Off (#6)

Brotherhood Protectors Hawaii
Kalea's Hero (#1)

Leilani's Hero (#2)

Kiana's Hero (#3)

Casey's Hero (#4)

Maliea's Hero (#5)

Emi's Hero (#6)

Sachie's Hero (#7)

Kimo's Hero (#8)

Alana's Hero (#9)

Bayou Brotherhood Protectors

Remy (#1)

Gerard (#2)

Lucas (#3)

Beau (#4)

Rafael (#5)

Valentin (#6)

Landry (#7)

Simon (#8)

Maurice (#9)

Jacques (#10)

Cajun Magic Mystery Series

Voodoo on the Bayou (#1)

Voodoo for Two (#2)

Deja Voodoo (#3)

Brotherhood Protectors Yellowstone

Saving Kyla (#1)

Saving Chelsea (#2)

Saving Amanda (#3)

Saving Liliana (#4)

Saving Breely (#5)

Saving Savvie (#6)

Saving Jenna (#7)

Saving Peyton (#8)

Saving Londyn (#9)

Brotherhood Protectors Colorado

SEAL Salvation (#1)

Rocky Mountain Rescue (#2)

Ranger Redemption (#3)

Tactical Takeover (#4)

Colorado Conspiracy (#5)

Rocky Mountain Madness (#6)

Free Fall (#7)

Colorado Cold Case (#8)

Fool's Folly (#9)

Colorado Free Rein (#10)

Rocky Mountain Venom (#11)

High Country Hero (#12)

Brotherhood Protectors

Montana SEAL (#1)

Bride Protector SEAL (#2)

Montana D-Force (#3)

Cowboy D-Force (#4)

Montana Ranger (#5)

Montana Dog Soldier (#6)

Montana SEAL Daddy (#7)

Montana Ranger's Wedding Vow (#8)

Montana SEAL Undercover Daddy (#9)

Cape Cod SEAL Rescue (#10)

Montana SEAL Friendly Fire (#11)

Montana SEAL's Mail-Order Bride (#12)

SEAL Justice (#13)

Ranger Creed (#14)

Delta Force Rescue (#15)

Dog Days of Christmas (#16)

Montana Rescue (#17)

Montana Ranger Returns (#18)

Brotherhood Protectors Boxed Set 1

Brotherhood Protectors Boxed Set 2

Brotherhood Protectors Boxed Set 3

Brotherhood Protectors Boxed Set 4

Brotherhood Protectors Boxed Set 5

Brotherhood Protectors Boxed Set 6

Iron Horse Legacy

Soldier's Duty (#1)

Ranger's Baby (#2)

Marine's Promise (#3)

SEAL's Vow (#4)

Warrior's Resolve (#5)

Drake (#6)

Grimm (#7)

Murdock (#8)

Utah (#9)

Judge (#10)

Delta Force Strong

Ivy's Delta (Delta Force 3 Crossover)

Breaking Silence (#1)

Breaking Rules (#2)

Breaking Away (#3)

Breaking Free (#4)

Breaking Hearts (#5)

Breaking Ties (#6)

Breaking Point (#7)

Breaking Dawn (#8)

Breaking Promises (#9)

Hearts & Heroes Series

Wyatt's War (#1)

Mack's Witness (#2)

Ronin's Return (#3)

Sam's Surrender (#4)

Hellfire Series

Hellfire, Texas (#1)

Justice Burning (#2)

Smoldering Desire (#3)

Hellfire in High Heels (#4)

Playing With Fire (#5)

Up in Flames (#6)

Total Meltdown (#7)

Take No Prisoners Series

SEAL's Honor (#1)

SEAL'S Desire (#2)

SEAL's Embrace (#3)

SEAL's Obsession (#4)

SEAL's Proposal (#5)

SEAL's Seduction (#6)

SEAL'S Defiance (#7)

SEAL's Deception (#8)

SEAL's Deliverance (#9)

SEAL's Ultimate Challenge (#10)

Texas Billionaire Club

Tarzan & Janine (#1)
Something To Talk About (#2)
Who's Your Daddy (#3)
Love & War (#4)

Billionaire Online Dating Service

The Billionaire Husband Test (#1)
The Billionaire Cinderella Test (#2)
The Billionaire Bride Test (#3)
The Billionaire Daddy Test (#4)
The Billionaire Matchmaker Test (#5)
The Billionaire Glitch Date (#6)
The Billionaire Perfect Date (#7)
The Billionaire Replacement Date (#8)
The Billionaire Wedding Date (#9)

The Outriders

Homicide at Whiskey Gulch (#1)
Hideout at Whiskey Gulch (#2)
Held Hostage at Whiskey Gulch (#3)
Setup at Whiskey Gulch (#4)
Missing Witness at Whiskey Gulch (#5)
Cowboy Justice at Whiskey Gulch (#6)

Boys Behaving Badly Anthologies

Rogues (#1)

Blue Collar (#2)

Pirates (#3)

Stranded (#4)

First Responder (#5)

Cowboys (#6)

Silver Soldiers (#7)

Secret Identities (#8)

Warrior's Conquest

Enslaved by the Viking Short Story

Conquests

Smokin' Hot Firemen

Protecting the Colton Bride

Protecting the Colton Bride & Colton's Cowboy Code

Heir to Murder

Secret Service Rescue

High Octane Heroes

Haunted

Engaged with the Boss

Cowboy Brigade

An Unexpected Clue

Under Suspicion, With Child

Texas-Size Secrets

ABOUT KRIS NORRIS

I'm just a small town girl, living in a lonely world. I took the midnight train…oops, sorry. Got off-track.

Author, hobbit, and crazy lady running in the woods, I'm either madly creating masterpieces in my dungeon, or out chasing Bigfoot with my dogs.

I see myself as unapologetically Canadian, and I love all things maple syrup.

I loves connecting with fellow book enthusiasts. You can find me on these social media platforms…

krisnorris.ca
contactme@krisnorris.ca

facebook.com/kris.norris.731
instagram.com/girlnovelist
amazon.com/author/krisnorris

ALSO BY KRIS NORRIS

SINGLES

Centerfold

Keeping Faith

Iron Will

My Soul to Keep

Ricochet

Rope's End

SERIES

RAVEN'S CLIFF with Elle James

1 - Raven's Watch

2 - Raven's Claw

3 - Raven's Nest

4 - Raven's Curse

'TIL DEATH

1 - Deadly Vision

2 - Deadly Obsession

3 - Deadly Deception

BROTHERHOOD PROTECTORS ~ Elle James

1 - Midnight Ranger

2 – Carved in Ice
3 - Going in Blind
4 - Delta Force: Colt
5 - Delta Force: Crow
6 - Delta Force: Phoenix

TEAM EAGLE

1 - Booker's Mission
2 - Walker's Mission

TEAM FALCO

Fighting for Fiona

TEAM KOA — ALPHA

Kian Unleashed

TEAM KOA — BRAVO

Flint's Battle

TEAM RAPTOR

Logan's Promise

TEAM WATCHDOG

Ryder's Watch

COLLATERAL DAMAGE

1 - Force of Nature

DARK PROPHECY

1 - Sacred Talisman
2 - Twice Bitten
3 - Blood of the Wolf

ENCHANTED LOVERS
1 - Healing Hands

FROM GRACE
1 - Gabriel
2 – Michael

THRESHOLD
1 - Grave Measures

TOMBSTONE
1 - Marshal Law
2 - Forgotten
3 - Last Stand

WAYWARD SOULS
1 - Delta Force: Cannon
2 - Delta Force: Colt
3 - Delta Force: Six
4 - Delta Force: Crow
5 - Delta Force: Phoenix
6 - Delta Force: Priest

COLLECTIONS

Blue Collar Collection
Dark Prophecy: Vol 1
Into the Spirit, Boxed Set

COMING SOON

Raven's Nest
Raven's Curse
Delta Force: Fetch
McGuire's Target

Made in United States
Cleveland, OH
29 July 2025